Beneath a Sky of Porphyry

Beneath a Sky of Porphyry

Aïcha Lemsine

Translated by Dorothy S. Blair

Quartet
London   New York

First published in English by Quartet Books Ltd 1990
A member of the Namara Group
27/29 Goodge Street
London W1P 1FD

Originally published in French by Jean-Claude Simoën 1978

British Library Cataloguing in Publication Data
Lemsine, Aïcha
Beneath a sky of porphyry.
I. Title   II. Ciel de porphyry
843 [F]

ISBN 0-7043-2695-7

Typeset by AKM Associates (UK) Ltd, Southall, London
Printed and bound by BPCC Hazell Books Ltd
Member of BPCC Ltd, Aylesbury

To my children
Adila, Akram, Ashraf

To those who have enriched my experiences, helping me
unwittingly,
and to those who, here or elsewhere, fight for true liberty and
peace, contributing by their actions to the rehabilitation of
man by man.

'When one day a people desires to live
Destiny must perforce reply . . .'

Aboulkacem Chabbi

'Bear, O my heart; thou hast borne
A yet harder thing, the day the Cyclops, mad with fury,
Devoured my brave companions: thou couldst contain thyself
Until the time when, by a ruse, thou hast found thyself
Outside the cave in which thou thoughtest to die.'

Homer, *Odyssey* XX

Note

This is a work of fiction.

The reader should not expect to find here the authenticity of an official chronicle.

Having said that, I have simply tried to throw out some bridges . . . so that others may cross them and build new ones, in tolerance, respect and friendship.

I sincerely pray that a meeting may take place somewhere half-way.

Glossary

Aïla   person of noble or highly respected family
baraka   blessing, favourable influence (of saint, etc.)
cachabia   peasant's cloak
Chaouïa   a member of a warlike Algerian tribe
djoundi, djounond (pl)   soldier
douar   hamlet, small settlement
Eïd el-Kebir   Feast of the Sheep, Muslim religious holiday, celebrating Abraham's sacrifice
fellaga   derogatory term used by the French to refer to the partisans
fellah, fellahin (pl)   peasant
fidaï   urban partisan
Francaoui   French nationals living in Algeria
gandoura   woman's loose tunic
goumier   Arab soldier who has enlisted with the French
haïk   woman's all-enveloping white veil
hammam   Turkish bath
harki   collaborator
kadi   a Muslim judge, interpreter of the law of Islam
macroud   small semolina cake stuffed with dates
méchoui   lamb roasted on the spit
mechta   hamlet
moujahid, moujahideen (pl)   partisan
pied-noir   person of European origin, who was born and lived in but left Algeria during or after the War of Independence, to settle in France or elsewhere
Roumi   derogatory term applied to French (or other Europeans)
smen   Arab butter
sura   verse of the Quran
wilaya   group or tribe
zendali   Algerian dance

Abbreviations

ALN   *Armée de libération nationale*, National Liberation Army

CAD   *Caisse algérienne de Développement*, Algerian Development Fund

CNRA   *Conseil national de la révolution algérienne*, National Council of the Algerian Revolution

CRS   *Compagnies républicaines de sécurité*, state security police, riot police

FLN   *Front de libération nationale*, National Liberation Front

GPRA   *Gouvernement provisoire de la République Algérienne*, Provisional Government of the Algerian Republic

OAS   *Organisation de l'Armée secrète*, Secret Army Organization (French terrorist organization opposed to the independence of Algeria)

SAS   *Section administrative spéciale*, Special Branch

SNP   *sans nom patronimique*, without family name, applied to an Algerian whose forebears are unknown

Ali gropes around in the dark searching frantically for Tahar. He is in the grip of a panic that turns his blood to water. He feels his way along the ground. He stumbles against some nameless object. His trembling fingers seize upon a piece of rag whose stench half chokes him. He is now paralysed with terror; there is a buzzing in his ears and a wave of icy sweat washes over him. Tahar's voice reaches him from a distance.

'Ali! Where are you? Answer me! . . .'

He is riveted to the spot, drenched in perspiration. He sees what seems to be the remnants of a vermin-eaten winding sheet. His fingers have closed on fragments of bone which dig into his flesh. His tongue seems to weigh a ton; he cannot let go of his grisly find; he feels himself in the depths of death's abyss. As in a nightmare, he calls his leader's name, but no sound emerges from his throat.

'Ali!' he hears Tahar shout again. 'Can you hear me?'

Tahar worms his way stealthily through the sinister labyrinth, sliding along the ground like a snake, all his senses alert for breathing or any sound to guide him to his young companion. The damp earth penetrates all his pores. At last he touches Ali's feet and reaching his hand up along the young man's soaking back, he shakes him.

'Good God! Ali, what's up with you?'

He jerks his friend towards him. They cling to each other in a cloud of blinding, choking dust which gets into their mouths, their noses, their eyes, intensifying the darkness of the pit. They start to cough. As they slowly get their breath back, Tahar becomes aware of the nameless terror which is paralysing his companion who mutters, 'It's . . . there's a skeleton . . . there . . . it's the shroud . . .'

Tahar realizes now what must have happened: when the soldiers came banging on the keeper's gate, calling on him to open up, they had both rushed for the trapdoor as their host had advised. Once they reached the bottom, instead of remaining where he had fallen, Ali had rolled over and over and, in his panic, had begun to crawl about in the dark. So he had moved some distance away from Tahar and from the pit, and had ended up in an actual tomb!

Tahar quickly pulls himself together. Bracing himself, he wrenches the piece of rag out of the youth's clenched hands, seizes him by the armpits and drags him along like a drowning man. When they hear the sound of boots crunching on the gravel overhead they know they have reached the right spot. Soon the voices and footsteps die away. The trapdoor opens, letting through the faint gleam from the cemetery-keeper's candle. The latter whispers, 'OK. They've gone, you can come up . . .'

Tahar takes hold of Ali's face and slaps him hard, first on one cheek and then on the other. The man up above crouches down to watch the strange scene taking place down below. Tahar murmurs in his young companion's ear, 'Ali! Pull yourself together! You're with me . . . Be a man! Pull yourself together . . . Be a man! . . .'

Ali once more feels this terrible admonition tear him apart: 'Be a man . . . Be a man . . .' There is an unending growl of thunder. Then gradually the tension relaxes.

'My God!' he exclaims under his breath.

He pushes Tahar's hands away, shakes his smarting face and bursts into tears. He begins to pray. From the depths of his tortured soul, words build up to form the prayer that he has so often heard his mother, Mà Chérifa, recite.

In those days, when they lived in the village of Dachra, he used to make fun of her . . . In retaliation for his mockery, she would drop her arms dejectedly and look up to heaven, murmuring, 'Allah! Strengthen my son's reason! Make him into a steady, thoughtful man.' The literal translation of the Arabic being, 'May your scales sink under a heavy weight', Ali thought his

2

mother was asking the heavens to drop a heavy weight on her son's head, like the weights at the grocer's corner shop, and he would retort with a laugh, 'Only rain falls from the sky, not weights!'

Yes, Ali has forgotten the mixed-up kid he used to be: part unruly brat, part anxious, sensitive dreamer. There is a poignant sweetness in his large, almond-shaped eyes, and the gravity of a man stricken in years, who knows the past and the future of every destiny.

What brought this strange look to the eyes of this generation? Was it the accumulation of outrages suffered by the preceding generation?

Under what sky did these children grow to manhood?

Dachra . . . August 1953

The first real present I've ever received! . . . A beautiful diary, bound in black leather. This lovely surprise was Alain's idea. The only present anyone's ever given me before has been clothes (people seem to think that's the most useful thing for kids!) Or for the Eïd and Mawlid feasts, I've had fireworks you can let off in the street for fun . . . But I've never had anything just to keep for myself, and that's not really useful! . . .

Everything's a jumble in my head, so I'll start at the beginning; that way I'll be better able to describe my happiness unfolding, like a long, multi-coloured ribbon.

Today, 23 August, is my thirteenth birthday. Alain was born on the same day of the same year as me, but I'm one hour older than him. That's why Madame Juliette, his mother, has always taken for granted that I share in her son's birthday celebrations.

This morning Alain came to our house shouting, 'Hurry up! Mother's sent me to fetch you. We're going to cut our birthday cake!'

After we'd stuffed ourselves with goodies, he gave me his present. Madame Juliette is a dressmaker, so in previous years she'd been in the habit of making me a shirt or a pair of trousers. Once she even presented me with a ridiculous outfit consisting of velvet breeches and waistcoat; my mother was so delighted with it that she insisted I wear it for our feastdays (making my pals tease me mercilessly) until I eventually grew out of it. But now, for once, it was Alain, not his mother who handed me my present, this book, with a mysterious expression. I didn't understand straight away.

'What's that for?' I exclaimed.

'It's for you!' he protested indignantly. 'It's a special sort of notebook . . . Go on, take it!'

I was so flabbergasted to see a notebook bound in leather, with a tiny key like a jewel, that I couldn't get a word out. I must have looked a real idiot, as Alain shook me, saying, 'I'm telling you it's yours, you clot! . . .'

Then he dug his hands into his pockets and explained, 'Actually, it was my mother's idea. She said it was time we had "serious" presents. And we should start by keeping a diary. She kept one when she was our age. Dad said that was just a craze girls had, and boys had better things to do than write a lot of rubbish! But she wouldn't listen to him and insisted that we both had one of these thingummies . . .'

Then my friend winked at me and whispered, 'I twigged what she was after! If I record everything I do, she'll soon know all my business. She's always declaring you must treat children gently, mustn't be too peda . . . peda . . . something, some complicated word she's always using, but I've outsmarted her. I've shoved mine out of sight, but I know you're fond of writing and drawing.'

He looked at me silently for a moment, then added with a smile, 'I knew you'd like something like this.'

I was running my hands ecstatically over this marvellous little object, when my friend's voice brought me down to earth.

'What about mine?'

'Your what?'

'It's your birthday, isn't it? So it's mine too . . . So, you owe me a present.'

I saw what he was getting at! I started to laugh. He was no fool, was my pal Alain! He wasn't going to be satisfied with the pastries my mother made for our birthday year after year.

I thought for a moment what I could give him. I beckoned to him to follow me. When we got to our house, we crossed the courtyard where my mother was sitting at the brazier, busy preparing the *galette* for our meal. She looked at us suspiciously, rightly fearing we were getting up to some mischief, and shouted, 'Where are you children off to?'

'I'm just going to show him something . . .' I replied.

She shook her head and resumed her cooking.

When we entered the living room, I looked on the sideboard for the brass dagger which my father had brought back from Oran, on one of his visits to his brother. It was purely ornamental, finely carved, with Arabic script in relief on the handle.

Without letting myself think about my father's anger, I picked it up and handed it to my friend. In my eyes, no object here, in our humble dwelling, could equal Alain's magnificent gift . . . And suddenly it was his turn to flush with delight, his eyes sparkling with wonder and surprise. He held the dagger in both hands, lifted it up to his face like a sacred object and stammered, 'I say, Ali! Is this really for me? You must be mad! . . . What'll your parents say? . . . Oh my! It's really beautiful! . . .'

I patted him on the shoulders, feeling very important and conscious of great generosity. 'Take it,' I said, 'and don't show it to anyone, least of all to the other kids!'

And now I'm alone at last, with my strange little book. I turn the key. I am dazzled by the blank pages. I have been thinking about all the things I shall to be able to write on them. For, contrary to Alain, I like the feel of books of every kind. I love their smell and the mysteries they reveal to me. At present I have a silent companion, who will never criticize me. I shall be able to write quite freely, nobody will spy on me behind my back as my parents can't read. I can also rely on the care my mother takes of all my possessions, especially my books.

Ah! You, my little diary, you'll be my friend . . . to share my craziest secret thoughts, my wildest dreams.

I am my parents' only son. It's true I have many cousins, not to mention my school-friends and street playmates. But I would never dare disclose, not even to Alain, the many worries and misgivings that trouble my youthful heart. With you, my dreams will take on all the colours of the rainbow, and like a magic carpet, your blank pages will carry me to the brightest stars, the most silvery moon will have velvet eyes and silken lashes to guide my first steps as a man, and her smiling mouth will allay my fears.

. . . 8 o'clock, the same evening

What a to-do! I'm still sore all over. My head and back have suffered the terrible repercussions of my present. When my father noticed that the dagger was missing he pointed an accusing finger at me and roared (I forgot to mention that he used to be a seaman) 'Who's taken the dagger?'

Mother had to rescue me from his stick. I know she guessed there was some association between Alain's visit this afternoon and the disappearance of the sole luxury article adorning our sideboard . . . What could I do? I bravely submitted to the volley of blows that rained down on my head, protecting myself as best I could with a cushion that I brandished like a shield. My mother wailed, 'Tell your father the truth . . . If you know where it is, son, speak!'

She was pretty sure that she knew where it was to be found! But in her infinite love for me, she left me to own up myself. And I finally confessed, not because of the blows, but because my father's face was getting redder and redder and the veins of his forehead were standing out like rope and throbbing so much I was afraid he was going to have an apoplectic fit.

And the strange thing is my father gradually calmed down. He considered my action to be a political gesture towards my friend . . . Even if it was a bit excessive for his taste, and cost him a valuable souvenir of his brother and his visit to Oran.

'Bah!' he sighed. 'The next time I go there I'll buy another one! But at least your friend won't think you a beggar. When anyone gives you a present, you must always give an even better one in return.'

So that's the story of my dear diary and my taste for confiding in solitude to its silent pages.

3

'I was twenty years old. No one can tell
me that's the happiest time of one's life.'
Paul Nizan, *Aden-Arabia*

Ali sighed and rubbed his eyes; the daylight was fading and he
could not see to read any more. He closed the diary and went over
to the open window. He gazed out for a moment at the town. The
streetlights were being lit, casting their soft glow into the room.
When it was completely dark, he went to lie down again on the
bed and turned to memories of his past. He was a man now; his
country was waging a war that held the promise of a new life; but
meanwhile there were many pitfalls ahead of him. He lay quite
still until he began to feel pins and needles in his legs. He got up
and switched on the light. The harsh glare from the naked bulb
revealed the narrow bed with its faded cover, the bare table,
frayed rug. The young man ran his fingers through his hair,
glanced round the room, picked up his diary and went out.

At the bottom of the narrow staircase he walked over to the
reception desk where a dark-haired young man sat, apparently
absorbed in a paperback. He looked up and smiled at Ali.

'What can I do for you?' he asked.

'I'm off now!'

'But you'll be back? Shall we keep your room for you?'

'No, I'm leaving for good. Can I have the bill, please?'

The receptionist handed him the bill, adding obligingly, 'If
your business brings you back to Baladia, come straight here, I'll
always be able to find you a room.'

'Thank you, I won't forget! I've left the key in the door.'

The young man watched Ali as far as the door, then went back to his novel.

At the corner of the road Ali asked a passer-by the time: 8 o'clock! He hurried through the maze of streets. In the Moorish cafés the waiters were busy clearing the empty tables, under the sullen gaze of a few belated customers, sipping their last drinks. There was nobody about except for an occasional military patrol, marching ceremoniously past, looking vaguely ridiculous in the bleak, deserted streets.

Here, in Baladia, the curfew did not come into force till 9 o'clock but as throughout Algeria it was heralded by a sudden hush, and the country more than ever resembled a vast graveyard.

The young man hurried on. He finally reached a street lined with low grey houses. He peered at the numbers, then plunged into a dark entrance. On the right was a staircase under which he groped his way to the far end of the corridor, where a glimmer of light could be seen beneath the only door. He lit a match and screwing up his eyes was able to make out the number five. He knocked twice, then gave a lighter tap. A sharp voice called out, 'Yes . . . Who is it?'

The young man put his mouth to the door and said softly, 'Let me in, Si Salah, it's Ali.'

A key could be heard turning in the lock and the door opened. Ali slipped in quickly. Si Salah shut the door behind him. Ali examined him curiously. He was young, slim, of medium height with a bony face whose severity was softened by big, startlingly blue eyes in which shone a mixture of intelligence and great kindness. Habitual tense contraction of his lips had carved deep furrows at the corners of his mouth, detracting from its fine formation. Although his face was youthful it was etched with lines, suggesting a strong will endlessly being put to the test . . . His hands were as mobile as his eyes and his arms were almost disproportionately large for such a thin body. He glanced from Ali to the table on which lay what seemed to be a road map.

Ali sat down on one of the chairs, saying, 'I was told to contact you here.'

The man held out his right hand. 'Welcome! We were

expecting you this evening.' Si Salah's voice had lost some of its brusqueness, though it seemed to cost him a certain effort to speak more gently. He pulled a thermos flask across the table then went to fetch two cups.

'Would you like some coffee?'

'Yes please.'

Ali relaxed. His discomfort, which reminded him of the feeling before an exam, left him, and he felt confident in the presence of this tough guy who was offering him coffee like an old friend . . . The two men sat watching each other as they drank, each apparently waiting for the other to speak first.

'Well now . . .' Si Salah began, 'let's get down to essentials: you were sacked from the railways in Dachra for beating up the European foreman . . . an "untouchable",' he added ironically, 'especially in these times when everyone's on edge. Then you let it be known that you wanted to join the maquis. The Brothers sent on your particulars to us and told you to turn up here . . . We know exactly what you've done since you got to Baladia. Not much, that is! You just waited in your hotel room, as you'd been told, till it was time to come here. Right?'

A smile flickered across his face at the sight of Ali's astonished expression. The latter simply nodded in acquiescence.

'The Brothers,' Si Salah went on, 'have examined this report and it's been decided, in view of your age and the level of your education, that you're more use to us here, in the town . . . As far as the maquis is concerned, we'll see later.'

He was silent for a moment, then suddenly looked Ali straight in the eyes and asked, 'Why are you so keen to join the maquis?'

Ali stirred his coffee. He screwed up his face with the effort of concentrating. He stared at his feet as if he'd find the answer to this complicated question there.

'I could give you a thousand minor reasons or one major consideration: the Fatherland! . . . But I'll be quite honest with you, I'm mainly motivated by my grief at the loss of my parents, and my deep sense of the injustice of their death which the barbarians' cruelty was responsible for . . .'

Ali realized that these words were tumbling in confusion out of

10

his mouth. He took a deep breath and then resumed more calmly, 'My whole family have been the victims of the colonial system. My father was so badly beaten up during paratroopers' raids that he began acting like a half-wit. He took it into his head that he had to kill the mayor of our village, the village where we all knew and respected each other in the old days. But before my father could carry out his absurd plan he was killed one evening by a band of drunk paratroopers, while on his way home a few minutes before the curfew.

'Your father was Si Abdelkader?'

'Yes. He was killed a year ago. I was seventeen and . . . all my illusions died with him . . .'

'He had the reputation for being very tough,' Si Salah said, 'and strong enough to take on ten soldiers!'

Ali smiled sadly.

'Unfortunately, he always had at least twelve against him! After the raids, when the soldiers had gone, my father would just sit by the fire, and you daren't say a word to him. He would just mutter, "The dogs bark, but the caravan moves on . . ." If we said anything he started to weep unashamedly, forgetting all his masculine pride after the humiliation of the beating. My mother bathed his cuts and bruises. Every time the soldiers burst in, he resisted the same way. Several times they nearly took him off to prison, but in the end they left him, perhaps because of his age . . . He would groan with fury and helplessness. He'd been a seaman. He'd sailed all over the world. He'd also worked here in Baladia as a stevedore. In our village, he lived quietly, dividing his time between his little grocery shop and his many friends who were all fond of him. The Europeans respected him as well. But when the revolution started, my father with his love of a fight, couldn't keep out of it for long. He was too old to take to the maquis, but he tried to help the Brothers by getting food to them, and he sheltered them sometimes. The local authorities had their suspicions of him. That's why the paras raided us without warning, looking for weapons or *fellagas*, as they called them . . . And one day, they did him in; they beat him to death . . . I was looking for an ideal and he taught me one: our people's liberty and

11

dignity. It was one evening, when the uncle he was hiding had just left to rejoin the maquis . . .'

Si Salah had been listening attentively. Then he interrupted to ask, 'Is your mother still alive?'

The young man half closed his eyes.

'She died last week . . . While I was in prison for the business with the overseer, I was told she wanted to see me. I realized she hadn't long to live. Madame Lavigne, an old European lady who was very fond of my family, managed to get me released . . . I remember how my mother stared at me without a word. When I pressed her to speak to me, she finally murmured, "Be a man, my son . . ." She passed away peacefully at daybreak; you'd never have thought she was dying. She was just tired of living. She was certainly never bothered by the thought she might go to hell . . .'

Si Salah winced. 'Drink your coffee, Ali, you don't need to blaspheme!'

While the youngster sipped his coffee, Si Salah asked him if he still had any other family living in the village.

'When my father died, the grocery shop was taken over by one of my mother's relatives; that's why I had to leave school to work on the railways so that I could look after my mother . . . I've nobody left now . . .'

As all these sad memories flooded over him, Ali nearly broke down. He stumbled over his words, as if there was a gap in his recollections. Si Salah observed, 'You sound as if you were tipsy. You mustn't lose heart so easily. You say you've no family left! But you've got one big family in the people of your country! You've got to fight for them, they must become your reason for living.'

'I don't want to look back . . . Only the future interests me.'

'Listen to me, Ali. I'm going to give you some idea of what belonging to our organization is all about. It's not a question of contributing five thousand francs a month and thinking you've done your duty. We lead a different life here, full of danger and upheaval, but you won't be joining the maquis . . . You'll remain here, in the town, where you'll have various missions to carry out.

But first you must be put to the test. Here is what you will have to do . . .'

Si Salah explained in detail the mission Ali would be entrusted with. He concluded, 'And remember we have to be quite ruthless in the fight we're waging, and even among the people we're fighting for there are some who have not yet understood and who hate us more than the others.'

After a pause he went on, 'How long were you at school?'

'Up to the end of the primary school, then my father sent me to the technical college here for three years to train as an electrician. Last year I was to have taken my qualifying exam, but when my father died I had to return to the village. I also studied Arabic when I was younger as my father was very keen on it. He used to say, "You must be able to speak and write your own language correctly for the future . . ." and he'd add, "If there hadn't been this revolution we Algerians would have been in a pretty mess with no language, no religion, no past! I'm old now, I've had such a struggle to survive, working just to earn our daily bread, that I just about know how to recite my prayers, and then I don't understand half of them!" '

'You talk like someone who's been to school for much longer!' Si Salah retorted.

Ali smiled for the first time, his face lighting up with delight and enthusiasm.

'I love reading! I love books! I was mad about reading. I was eager to know things, even if I didn't believe them, and my father was so happy to see my enthusiasm for books. I used to read to him about our Muslim civilization . . . He listened so attentively, and to look at us you'd think that I was the father and he the child, he was so delighted by what I told him! To tell you the truth, I learned more from books that I read by myself than from lessons at school.'

Si Salah remained thoughtful. 'This lad has two passions: his father . . . and books,' he mused. 'I don't know how many times he's mentioned them, and with such fervour!'

But he had to break the spell. He resumed in his normal curt

13

voice, 'You understand, we have to take precautions . . . We've only two sanctions: a warning and . . . death.'

Ali drew himself up and cried proudly, 'I am prepared for every sacrifice!'

Si Salah patted him kindly on the shoulder as if to restrain his excess of zeal.

'I'm sure you'll be able to contribute a great deal to our struggle. You've got nothing to lose, except . . . hatred. You'll be surprised to learn that you'll not be able to hate anyone any more. I don't know why, but that's the way it is mostly . . . You know, I'm not in the habit of talking so much, but with you it was necessary. You're so young!'

He seemed to reflect for a moment, then added, 'Well! Tonight you'll sleep here!'

Something moved behind Ali. He turned round, both surprised and anxious. He saw a thick dark brown curtain that he had not noticed when he came in. The dim light of the large room accentuated the atmosphere of mystery. Ali looked questioningly at Si Salah who continued to watch him with a slightly mocking smile. The curtain stirred. Ali started to his feet. He was now in the presence of three more men who had emerged as if by magic from the alcove hidden behind the curtain. Ali quickly regained his composure.

'What's the meaning of this?'

'*Essalam*! Greetings!' the three men interposed.

One of them came over to Ali, adding with a smile, 'We got tired of standing up, so we decided to come and join you!'

Si Salah glanced ironically at Ali and indicated to the newcomers that they should be seated.

'You've had the opportunity of admiring brother Ali's coolness. We don't need any further comments! I think you've understood, Ali; we always have to take precautions, even in our own family circle.'

A heavy silence ensued. The five men exchanged looks. Ali felt a lump in his throat. He could not get another word out. However, his eyes were drawn to one of them in particular, a tall athletic-looking fellow, with the appearance of a gentle giant. He

14

was very broad-shouldered. His wide brow and rather flat cheek-bones gave him a somewhat Asiatic appearance. His huge hands with their thick fingers could be those of a strangler. One felt that this man possessed an almost animal strength. Ali thought to himself that he must be a brute when roused. For the moment he felt irresistibly attracted to this fellow in spite of his disconcerting appearance. The other man smiled, and the hard lines of his mouth softened. His cracked, dry lips were those of a man who had been exposed to biting mountain winds. He returned Ali's stare.

'A pity we're not dogs! We'd either have made friends already, or been at each other's throats! Si Salah seems to trust you and he's a good enough judge. So, I'll introduce myself and the other brothers. My name's Tahar.'

He looked intently at Ali, adding, 'That's what I'm known as . . . My real name's been lost in the mists of time, or the night of the Nemenchas!' Then, turning towards the others, 'This one's Mounir. He's our propaganda expert, what's more he's a local fellow, really street-wise . . .'

The young man in question had a strikingly slender figure and wore a smart, well-fitting, dark suit. In spite of his imposing presence there was something that didn't ring true, possibly his over-ingenuous expression, his curiously receding chin and the slightly shifty look in his brown eyes. But it was his large, clumsy hands with their podgy fingers that were most at variance with his affectation of elegance. Mounir stood up, smiled and held out a hand to Ali.

'We call this flash, handsome fellow "The Dandy",' Tahar went on. 'He spends a lot of time at dance-halls with European girls who seem to fall for him . . .'

Tahar described Mounir as casually as if they were being introduced socially, Ali was frankly disconcerted. For his part, he considered his initiation into the secrets of the Front's cells and his contact with members of the resistance as something holy, and the slightest joke was well-nigh blasphemous . . . And here was this man shedding light on his first encounter with a new life, in which every step could mean death, and he seemed to be saying, 'Don't

15

be afraid, young man. The main thing is to know where you're going, and why. Nothing else matters . . . and it doesn't prevent you having a laugh.'

Mounir stiffened, and he pinched his lips. He probably didn't care for the rather offhand way Tahar spoke of him, Ali thought. Finally, he hid his discomfort behind a somewhat forced smile and remarked curtly, 'You're the only one, Tahar, who dares make fun of our militant actions!'

Tahar took Ali's arm and turned him to face the man sitting behind Si Salah.

It was impossible to guess at his age; he had a broken nose and dislocated jaw, giving his shrivelled, scarred face the look of a terrifying mask.

'This is Ramdane,' said Tahar. 'He's an old campaigner, aren't you, old thing?'

Tahar's expression had lost all trace of irony. He was now all gentleness tinged with great affection for the old man.

'Yes, indeed! Goodness me!' Ramdane replied.

A fleeting light lit up his eyes, to be as quickly dimmed. He opened his mouth as if to say more, but merely repeated solemnly, 'Yes, by God!' as if to convince himself of some truth. He rubbed his hands together. Ali noticed that they were deformed and covered with scars.

'Ramdane never shakes anyone's hand,' Tahar explained.

'And you want to know why?' the old man shrieked. 'Because the police have made a mess of me. They handcuffed me to an iron bar and beat me with chains and clubs. They stamped on my face . . . True or false, Tahar?'

'It's true, Ramdane.'

'And did I give in? Tell him, Tahar! I let them have it till I passed out . . .'

His voice became even shriller. He seemed to be addressing one person only, Tahar, the only one who counted in his eyes. This man, broken by torture, worn out by the misery of his lonely existence, seemed to have an almost fanatical admiration and a childlike affection for Tahar. He looked up, and his face became

16

strangely handsome, as if illuminated by some inner reverie that no one dared to interrupt.

'They beat me on the head, I can hardly use my hands any more . . . And like your father, Ali, I never gave in. I've no sons of my own, but all the street urchins are my children. And I know that eventually these children of mine . . . youngsters who are dragging out their lives in miserable hovels, will have clean houses, schools, sports grounds, and I shall be there to share their happiness . . . With you too . . . Meanwhile, I spit on anyone who tries to get me down!'

Tahar leaned forward and gently stroked Ramdane's back, as if he were massaging it, and murmured, 'We know that the man who can shut you up isn't born yet, Papa Ramdane.'

Ramdane sighed, 'Yes, I'll say!' And he closed his eyes, finally relaxed.

Si Salah had not said a word. He seemed far away, lost in thought, and yet he had not missed anything for a moment. His resolute, practical presence made itself felt. He now intervened. 'It's too late to leave now. It's after the curfew, so we'll have to spend the night here. We'll put a mattress on the floor and doss down together. Ramdane can have the couch which has a good blanket. Tahar and Ali, you take the mattress, and I'll be all right in the armchair. Mounir, you can sleep in the bed in the little room at the end, so as not to soil your smart suit . . . Tomorrow, Ali, you'll go to Tahar's place in the Béni-Ramassés district, you know, the slums of this town. The soldiers never venture there, unless they're heavily reinforced. When we need you, Tahar will let you know.'

Si Salah was silent for a moment. He caught Tahar's eye; the two men seemed to come to some mute understanding. Ali didn't miss anything of what was going on. Si Salah gave a little cough as if to clear his throat and the young man thought, 'My God! What's he going to come out with now?'

'I'd better tell you straight away that I teach Arabic at the boys' high school. A few months ago, a European colleague, who teaches music, and I set up a so-called "Cultural Committee" of students and teachers. There are naturally some Muslims among

17

us and some liberal Europeans. We meet on days when there's no school, every Sunday and Thursday that is, to discuss music, drama, etc. . . . At present, for example, we're working on a Molière play that we intend to put on in the municipal theatre. In fact, this is a cover to allow us to type and distribute leaflets and to pass on instructions . . . It's a sort of subsidiary to our local cell, which can hide behind the activities of the "Cultural Committee".'

With the ease of a master used to speaking to an audience of attentive pupils, Si Salah turned to Mounir. 'There are not very many of us, a dozen in all. Mounir is a primary schoolteacher and joins us from time to time . . . Tahar and Ramdane don't profess to be "intellectuals", but they've been co-opted, so to speak, as unofficial members of the group. So, that's all I had to tell you, Ali. Tomorrow evening Tahar will bring you to Monsieur Kimper's – he's the music teacher.'

Ali would never have thought Si Salah was a teacher, nor could he have imagined a cultural group with political activities. All these surprises and the thought of the experiences that lay in store for him with these new companions left his head in a whirl. But his recent experience of prison and losing his parents so young didn't encourage him to dwell too much on such problems. For the moment he felt particularly drawn to Tahar.

The five men pushed back the table and chairs to make room for the mattress. Mounir took off his jacket, hung it meticulously over the back of a chair, and lay down on the iron bed.

Before he switched off the light, Si Salah added, 'Tomorrow morning I shall be the first out at six o'clock; Mounir will leave at eight; Tahar and Ali, you'll be off at nine and Ramdane will rest here all day; there's enough food and I prefer him not to go out . . . He must give the cops time to forget about him.'

Ali admired Si Salah's commonsense. He mused over the different complex personalities of his new companions, all united by a common ideal.

Ramdane, looking like a tramp who'd been beaten up; Si Salah, the cold intellectual; Mounir, the smart, rather precious young man of good family; Tahar, tough, cynical, certainly

18

ruthless, but strangely attractive. And what about himself? Was he just a raw, hot-heated kid, full of his own grievances, imagining he was going to play Cowboys and Indians, firing his pistol – Bang! Bang! – at the Pale-faces? Or was he a romantic going to defend the revolution with words? What was he? As if by telepathy, Tahar murmured to him, 'You look as if you're a good kid, Ali! I'm glad to have you with us.'

'A good kid!' Ali smiled contentedly in the dark, relieved that no one could see his expression of delight.

But Ali could not fall asleep after all the excitement of the day. He tossed and turned on his mattress, afraid of waking Tahar, who however was snoring like a man without a care in the world. Dawn found him still open-eyed. He pretended to be asleep when Si Salah left, followed by Mounir. Ramdane was sleeping soundly.

It was hot in the room, which reeked of perspiration, cold coffee and the cigarette ends scattered over the floor, making him want to throw up. He went to the kitchen, drank a glass of water and lay down again on his mattress. He gazed at Tahar's huge figure lying there on its stomach, looking rather like the bloated body of a drowned man afloat. Ali turned his eyes away. He didn't like spying like this on someone sleeping. He felt embarrassed as if caught stealing.

From the street came the sound of children shrieking with laughter. He could hear the clatter of a tin can and realized they were playing hopscotch on the pavement outside the building. By the scraping of the can along the ground, he knew the child had missed the square, losing the game. The urchin's protests confirmed his impression. Ali smiled. Tahar would soon be awake.

Later that morning he accompanied Tahar on the first stage of his new life. He was introduced to the shantytown, known as the Béni-Ramassés, where his companion lived. Its inhabitants were a ragbag collection of fugitives from burnt-out *mechtas*, refugees from deserted *douars*, respectable families rubbing shoulders with young orphaned layabouts, beggars and women who had become prostitutes in order to feed their children or survive themselves . . .

19

A wretched red-light district! A veritable Court of Miracles, that Quasimodo himself would not have disavowed. But the miracle here was the solidarity reigning among these people who were united by poverty and fear, their sole horizon.

A few whitewashed houses stood cheek by jowl with squalid, corrugated-iron hovels. Veiled women bargained for vegetables piled up on a cart drawn by an adorable little donkey whose leather harness was painted in every colour of the rainbow.

The sky was overcast. There was a fresh wind. Urchins ran barefoot in the streets, others had lit a bonfire at which they warmed themselves amid shrieks of delight. From the radios in the cafés, with their volume turned full on, the voice of the popular singer, Farid el-Atrach, could be heard. In spite of their poverty these teeming hordes vibrated with life and hope.

Tahar walked without a word, leading Ali through the maze of streets. At last they reached a small house that had recently been whitewashed. Tahar opened the door and stood back to let the young man enter. The interior consisted of one large room. The walls were bare; an impressive-looking typewriter enjoyed pride of place on the table. An enamelled cooker stood on a wooden shelf fixed to the wall and crockery lay next to a pile of dusty books. Two mattresses covered with sheets and woollen blankets had been put down on a yellow mat on the floor.

'I'm hungry,' Tahar declared. 'Come and peel the onions, if you can stand the smell. I'll open the tins of sardines and make the coffee.'

Ali got busy preparing a salad of tomatoes, onions and olives, wondering meanwhile what the Brothers were going to do with him. Would he be joining the maquis? Suppose Si Salah had destroyed all his hopes? After all, he thought, they probably want to test me out! . . . But how?

He sat down on a mattress to eat. Everything was quiet. Footsteps could be heard on the pavement and the happy sound of children running accentuated the peace inside the house. Ali glanced at the alarm clock hanging on a nail near the door; it was one o'clock. He asked Tahar, who was concentrating on his food, 'What are we going to do till this evening?'

'Nothing! We don't stir from here,' he replied laconically.

Ali lowered his head and tried to swallow the last mouthful which now stuck in his throat. Seeing the youth's miserable expression, Tahar adopted a more conciliatory tone as he poured the coffee.

'But this evening I'll take you to meet the professor. And you'll get to see the district where he lives, the Orchards, with villas surrounded by magnificent gardens . . . There are never any raids or military patrols there! Naturally the slumbers of the lords and masters must not be disturbed by the clatter of jackboots on pavements . . .

Tahar rambled on for some time in this vein.

'Is Ramdane quite right in the head?' Ali suddenly asked, as he thought of the old man disfigured with scars.

'You mustn't take any notice of him . . . He's been beaten up so often that he's a few sticks short of the bundle now. But he's done a lot for us. For some time we've been keeping an eye on him to try to stop him getting his head cracked again by the cops. He can't keep his mouth shut. Now Mounir, mark you, he's never had any trouble, he's a right sharp one. Once, when there'd been a bomb attack and a whole district of the town had been cordoned off and Mounir was stopped and asked to show his identity papers, he was so polite, calling the soldier "Sir" that eventually they almost put a car at his disposal for him to get home!'

'Poor chap!' Ali went on, referring to Ramdane. 'I can understand his fury. One always has to have something to fight for . . . First of all my father was battling against hunger, then he fought for justice and his own self-respect. He was fighting desperately, against hopeless odds. You understand? And now it's my turn to feel desperate.'

Ali looked down at his empty cup.

'There's something else as well: anger; we all live with anger, like Ramdane, but some of us hide it or let it go up in smoke . . . which makes you cough, which chokes you.'

'Go on,' Tahar said. 'I don't know what you're getting at, but you must know.'

Ali banged his cup down on the ground.

21

'This is what I'm getting at! One evening, three men, maquisards, were hiding in our house. They were supposed to leave at dawn. I watched these men who'd grown up in the same situation as me. Their anger was different from mine. I had the impression it was the colonial system they hated, not the enemy . . . It was a quite different sort of anger, not rooted in despair. They kept quiet, how can I explain it . . . they were serene! They gave off an indescribable feeling of peace . . .'

'Are you trying to convince me, by any chance?' Tahar asked sarcastically. 'Have you forgotten what Si Salah said yesterday? You must rid your heart of all hatred, kid! It's sometimes difficult, I have to admit, but that's the way to become a true militant . . .'

Ali jumped when he heard these words which reminded him of others: 'You must become a man, my son.' And now he must learn to become a militant.

'No!' the youth resumed. 'I want to know how those men arrived at their serenity. I was eager for their peace, the hope that eluded me. I thought I knew more things than they did because I'd read a lot, but those men could guess at what I wanted. They'd found truth in the struggle, in the danger they confronted every day.'

Tahar lay back on the mattress with his hands behind his head.

'Good! If danger is all you need to make you happy, I can promise you happiness with us!'

'Are you the leader, Tahar?'

'There's no leader! I carry out orders like everybody else.'

'In any case you have a certain influence. I've noticed how Si Salah and the others listen to you as soon as you open your mouth . . .'

'You'll also learn,' Tahar interrupted, 'that we have good manners. We always listen to the person who's speaking. We don't all talk at the same time.'

Ali resumed more passionately, his face growing flushed and his eyes bright, whether with tears or the terrible need to convince his companion.

'Tahar! I want to join the maquis! Si Salah hasn't understood. Help me, please, I must leave, I must have action!'

'You want to get yourself killed, is that it? I agree with Salah that our organization needs a good typist and you're bright enough to be able to type leaflets. Look!' pointing to the typewriter, 'That'll be your weapon to fight for liberty.'

Finally he abandoned his mockery, his expression grew serious and his eyes took on a look of infinite sadness.

'Everything we do is important. Typing as much as living among the thorns of the maquis. No matter where we are, we are soldiers. You don't know when the enemy will bash down the door of your house, beat you to within an inch of your life and drag you off, God knows where! What is more, there are traitors everywhere!'

Then, with a smile and a tone of half reproach directed at Ali, 'You've noticed how I'm getting worked up now too? You've infected me with your damned enthusiasm! And since you're so curious, I'll tell you something that'll teach you a little about men . . .'

Ali drew closer to him and listened attentively. 'My fiancée was a nurse. We grew up together and joined the struggle at the same time. She brought medical supplies, went into the maquis to tend our wounded. She was twenty and wasn't afraid of danger. One day the soldiers burst into her house where she was hiding a wounded man. They went on the rampage, ransacked the place, butchered everyone, men, women and children . . . She was raped and beaten to death.'

'But Tahar! How did they know that there was a wounded partisan in the house?'

'Because someone had shopped them! A traitor who lived nearby . . .'

Tahar half closed his eyes and clenched his teeth.

'I finished that traitor off with my own hands!'

He got up and went to pour some more coffee.

'I'm sorry to have let myself sink into this bitterness, but when I think of her I go mad! When I first joined the struggle my feelings were like those of the maquisards who were hiding in your

23

house . . . I wasn't fighting with any hatred, but out of a sense of duty to our country. But then, you see, I'd never been hungry, my parents were well off. I could have studied or looked after the property we owned. But I threw all that up without any regrets . . . And now I'm haunted by the sight of her bloodsoaked belly, her breasts all black and blue and burnt with their cigarettes . . . I go quite mad, the desire for vengeance has got into my blood, and I have to keep on controlling my hatred . . . You're the only one I've ever told about this, kid. So, don't let yourself be filled with hatred; I'll never repeat this to you often enough.'

At last Ali understood the reason for the attraction he felt for this big fellow with the cold, cruel look. A similar profound sorrow united them. Tahar marked by the death of the girl he loved; Ali by the death of his father; both killed in atrocious circumstances.

Tahar suggested that they take a walk around the neighbourhood. It was gradually growing darker in the evening twilight. It would soon be night. They strolled about for a time. Then Tahar made his way to a garage near the outskirts of Béni-Ramassés.

'I didn't know you had a car,' remarked Ali. He couldn't understand how Tahar, who lived in a slum, could afford to own a car.

Tahar burst out laughing, that characteristic frank, hearty laugh that caused him to throw his head back and turn his face up to the sky as if he were about to swallow the whole universe.

'What a chatterbox you are! You never stop asking questions. This car belongs to the garage proprietor. He leaves it for us to use and keeps his eyes shut. And that's what he must be doing at the moment; everybody here's scared shitless, so they all turn in at seven o'clock, like the hens!'

'And what if the police take the number one day and come asking questions?' Ali asked.

'He's got his business and he keeps out of trouble, and he's an ex-soldier with a mass of gongs. He'll swear that his car's been stolen . . . And the trick works!'

Tahar seemed extremely amused by his companion's questions.

24

They both laughed as they drove out of the garage and reached the professor's house without any mishaps.

Tahar was quite right: what a peaceful corner! What fine houses! Some of them seemed like dolls' houses, white with wrought-iron balconies, surrounded by green lawns and trees. The contrast with the hovels of Béni-Ramassés was striking and for Ali these villas seemed like palaces. The one belonging to the professor was almost completely hidden by dense trees.

Tahar rang twice, the front door was opened immediately and the inscrutable face of Si Salah appeared. He closed the door behind them. They climbed a narrow stairway leading to a glass door through which light streamed. Then they took a corridor which opened on to a large drawing-room with white lacquered furniture arranged around a brightly coloured carpet. Ali had never seen houses so luxuriously furnished, except at the cinema. He was quite dazzled . . .

He envied the easy manners of his friends who were quite at home here. Deep easy chairs occupied the centre of the room. In one corner was a shiny piano, evidence of the master of the house's passion for music. A man was standing at the fireplace, busy cleaning his pipes. He turned round and walked over to the new arrivals. He held out a friendly hand. Ali thought, 'I'd have taken him for a shopkeeper . . . a notary perhaps, but a musician, never!' Indeed, Monsieur Kimper was small and rotund with a plump face, and a crown of fine white hair. He smiled reassuringly, dispensing infinite kindness towards his fellow creatures.

Si Salah's voice broke brusquely into Ali's thoughts.

'Monsieur Kimper, Ali, your new guest!'

The three men sat down. Si Salah whispered a few words to Tahar.

'What's your impression of Ali? I imagine you've had a chance of getting to know him a bit now . . .'

'He's all right! He's just rather too excitable . . . He wants action!'

Si Salah nodded without giving his thoughts away. He got up and with a friendly gruffness called to their host.

'Come on, Kimper, leave your pipes alone! You never stop fiddling with them. Come and sit with us!'

Later, Si Salah and Tahar resumed their whisperings while Monsieur Kimper went off to the kitchen. Ali seemed sunk in a daydream. His friends noted his calm expression, like that of someone half-asleep.

Tahar's voice broke into his reverie: 'Are you bored with us already?'

Ali started, embarrassed at being caught off his guard for a moment. In fact the warmth of the atmosphere had made him drowsy.

Monsieur Kimper came back with a tray of fruit juice and a plate of cakes, just in time to catch Tahar's words. 'Oh, these young people!' he exclaimed. 'They're always bored if they have to sit still for any time!'

'I'm eighteen, sir!'

Ali's ingenuous reply was greeted with a burst of hearty laughter. Even Si Salah had to join in the general hilarity. Ali looked down. He flushed with anger and muttered a few incomprehensible words through his teeth.

Monsieur Kimper had been in Algeria so long he could not remember the date of his arrival. He felt that this country was indeed his birthplace. He loved it as much as his native Brittany, that rugged, proud, generous land, turned in upon itself. He could have lived a quiet life, devoting himself solely to music and reading, and enjoying the sunshine. But no, this kindly, affable man had long ago chosen to struggle for an ideal which he had made his own: justice and the right of men to be free in their own land. Since the death of his wife, he had taken to his heart these men who aspired to a rebirth of liberty and dignity. As he had never had children of his own, he felt himself to be indeed their father.

'Don't be angry, Ali! On the contrary, it's wonderful to be your age! Everything is easy, you can defy danger and fear! But when you reach the twilight of your life, as the poets say, you realize that danger is lurking everywhere and we are the plaything of fear . . . Then we become cautious and this is the beginning of wisdom, for at that moment we know life has nothing more to give, but much to lose!'

Ali drew himself up. 'No! When you're braving danger for an authentic cause that you believe in profoundly, then that's the moment you no longer feel afraid. You refuse to accept fear, and that can happen at any age! My father was a worn-out old man, and yet he rejected fear to the end . . . You must banish all fear if you hope to succeed in your cause.'

Si Salah, astonished at the youngster's outspokenness, stared at him frowning slightly. He thought Ali's reasoning was wrong. He knew the professor's humanity, the invaluable help he had always given to the organization. He was about to intervene to upbraid Ali, but Monsieur Kimper got in first. 'Your theory is correct, but it doesn't apply to me, or to other people like me. Every struggle for liberty is mine. Long before the revolution began, I militated for the recognition of your people's identity. And for thirty years I have known that the time would come when All Saints' Day, would be the occasion for the children of Algeria to celebrate the memory of their dead martyrs. My love for mankind is as all-embracing as my love for music, devoid of any racial prejudice. And, believe me, this fear that lurks within me is not on account of my old carcass, but for the number of innocent young men like yourself that the country will lose tomorrow . . .'

The professor wiped his brow that was streaming with perspiration. His eyes shone with an inner light which irresistibly rejuvenated his whole face. The three men gazed at him with combined respect and affectionate attention.

Tahar introduced a lighter note into the somewhat solemn atmosphere: 'Well, Kimper, old fellow, you're not very encouraging about tomorrow's prospects! Ali will really have the wind up now!'

The young man didn't think of getting angry, he'd noticed that Tahar was fond of teasing him when the conversation got too serious.

As for Si Salah, with his practical common sense, he was the first to pull himself together.

'Tomorrow,' he said, 'there'll be the official celebrations for the 14 July; fairs are being organized in every part of the town. The curfew won't come into force till one in the morning. But we're particularly interested in the fête in the Rosiers district, as Colonel V— will be presiding. This district has been chosen as the population is mainly indigenous. There will be a Muslim band and also a European one.'

Monsieur Kimper had disappeared to make sure that the front door was shut and to give Khéïra, his servant, instructions for dinner.

'The Brothers have given the Algerian band permission to take part,' Si Salah went on, 'but all other Muslims will stay away from the celebrations.' He paused to take a sip of orange juice, then fixed his gaze on Tahar and added slowly, 'Tahar! You know what you have to do . . .'

Ali asked timidly, 'And what about me? What shall I do tomorrow?'

'You? . . . You've got work to do here,' Si Salah replied. 'You've got leaflets to type. You'll work here at Monsieur Kimper's, and you're not to move until one of us comes to fetch you. Even though your papers are in order, you can't be too sure.'

Ali felt a chill run down his spine. He thought, 'What can I do to prove I'm a man capable of carrying out delicate, dangerous missions? This fellow really gets me down!'

Suddenly Tahar's voice burst in on his reflections: 'I'd like to take Ali with me!'

Si Salah looked surprised. He stared at Tahar. They might have been two wild beasts sizing each other up before a fight to the death. But Si Salah realized there was a strange determination in Tahar's gaze that he alone understood. His features took on an expression of obscure melancholy.

Ali had understood nothing of this silent exchange. He waited for Si Salah's verdict, all his senses alert. Would he be allowed to accompany Tahar?

'All right! Just as you like!' Si Salah finally replied.

Ali's anxiety vanished; he jumped up and ran to Tahar who, by his trust in him, showed he was more than a 'Brother'; he was truly his friend!

'Thank you!' he murmured, so overcome he was hardly able to speak.

His eyes shone with delight. Ali knew nothing of the mission that Tahar was going to undertake, but the idea of being part of the expedition filled him with joy.

Tahar contemplated this shining, innocent young face. He, the tough guy, felt an unaccustomed pang in his heart, a terrible sadness for himself and for all mankind. He thought bitterly, 'Tomorrow, this face will have lost the glow of youth and will just be a mask expressing only the horror of blood . . .'

He concluded wearily, 'We must turn in now, Ali, if we want to be fresh for the party tomorrow!'

Monsieur Kimper came back at this moment, followed by Khëïra. 'Dinner's ready. Let's go into the dining-room.'

After dinner Tahar and Ali went off to sleep in one of the professor's spare rooms. Si Salah remained in the drawing-room to chat with his friend, as he was fond of doing.

'What are we going to do at this fair?' he wondered . . . 'Keep an eye on the Algerians who'll come to get drunk and have fun? . . . Pick up some information about the movements of the military? . . . Try to knock out a soldier to steal his rifle? . . .'

Baladia was all lit up on this 14 July 1958. Cars sounded their horns throughout the town. Except for the soldiers on the streets, no one could guess that a savage war was undermining the interests of the very people who'd claimed to have stopped the course of history with their military power.

The main square of the Rosiers district sparkled with multi-coloured lanterns. It was surrounded by white, Moorish-style, two-storey houses, inhabited by families of modest means who could live here comfortably at a reasonable rental; this was the period when subsidized housing was booming in Algeria. Muslims and Europeans lived side by side here in a climate of semi-trust. The latter were, for the most part, small artisans, hairdressers, bakers, etc. The better-off Europeans lived in the residential districts of Baladia.

A little further away from these houses, a road-block had been set up, sealing off the Rosiers as a protective measure. At the entrance to the area stood a CRS barracks, on the right a paratroop encampment, then the police station; at the back, towards the south a former school had been transformed into a barracks for *goumiers*. These were for the most part former members of the French rifle brigades or peasants who had fled from their villages and enlisted in the army of occupation, inspired mainly by greed. Actually they were dangerous and the population feared them more than the paratroopers. Nevertheless, the inhabitants of this heavily armed locality continued to go quietly about their daily business.

Life seemed serene enough on the surface. As soon as it was light, the main square teemed with children, playing football, screaming with joy. This square was the beating heart of the locality; but a hot, impotent anger lay simmering beneath the surface, waiting for the moment to explode.

This evening a reed fence had been erected round the square. Garlands of flowers decorated a large platform reserved for the band. Everywhere there were stalls selling lemonade, beer and hard liquor. The crowd was mostly composed of Europeans, soldiers on leave or on duty. They were scattered behind bars or sitting at tables set out in a circle around a vast dance floor.

The Muslims were watching the whole scene from their windows, thus refraining from active participation in the celebrations. The only sound this evening in streets which normally echoed with children's shouts, was the clatter of the soldiers' boots as they did their rounds. Behind the happy fairground atmosphere, every individual – whether civilian or military – was eaten up with fear of a bomb attack by the partisans. To dispel the shadows of anxiety, the popping of corks was soon heard. At last the band struck up a popular samba.

Tahar and Ali had left their car some way away from the fête in a dimly lit alley just off the main road. They walked along, laughing and joking like two carefree lads off to a Saturday night hop. They were both clean-shaven and smartly dressed in light summer suits. Ali was quite touched; as they set off, he'd noted Tahar's look of surprise and admiration at his appearance. He'd even exclaimed, 'You're a knock-out! All the girls will be falling over themselves to dance with you this evening!'

Ever since he'd stopped growing and started taking trouble over his dress, Ali noticed he tended to attract admiring looks wherever he went. Was he good-looking? It was difficult to say . . . It wasn't obvious at first glance. It was his casual appearance and a certain distinction in his whole personality which attracted attention. Ali could wear any shabby old pair of trousers and still look better than anyone. All his gestures betrayed a certain style and the way he carried his head high had caused him many a rebuff from his jealous school- and work-mates who thought him stuck up. Moreover his serenity added to his charm. His face was that of a youngster, scarcely more than an adolescent, yet it bore an expression of unshakable determination. His slightly aquiline nose was softened by the clarity of his golden-brown eyes and more especially by a funny little dimple in his chin . . . A light puckering of his lips when he smiled effaced all the solemnity of his serious look.

Tahar strode along breezily beside his friend. He waved to a group of paratroopers standing chatting on the pavement.

'Hi, fellers! Any nice bits of crumpet out this evening?'

'I'll say! Some real hot stuff!'

They apparently took the two young men for Europeans. Their light colouring and smart appearance left no room for doubt.

'I'm so happy, Tahar!' Ali exclaimed. 'My first "ball". I'll never forget it. Nothing I've ever done till now has had any meaning . . . How are we going to begin?' he asked naïvely.

Tahar stared at his young companion, then seeing his growing excitement could not help collapsing into a fit of laughter.

'Ali! Ali! Just how old are you really? I never know what you'll come out with next! I haven't got a plan . . . this is where theory's no use, you have to play it by ear. No two tactics are alike. And now just relax!'

They reached the entrance to the enclosure. Girls were laughing

31

and chatting with soldiers, who were probably telling them how lonely they were up in the mountains.

Tahar entered, followed by Ali. They made their way to one of the bars. Tahar's experienced eyes had picked out a few Algerians here and there among the dancers. He smiled inwardly as he recognized the 'Brothers' from the local cell. He patted Ali cordially on the shoulder.

'What'll you drink, sonny boy? Champagne? Beer? Wine?'

Ali flushed and stammered, 'Er . . . I'd prefer lemonade.'

Tahar laughed louder and this time his merriment was not put on. 'We're here to enjoy ourselves, sonny boy! Leave the fizzy drinks for weekdays!'

'I've never drunk alcohol in my life! And I never will!'

'Never! Always! Oh! These young people!'

Then he muttered between his teeth, still smiling, 'Watch me! You'll see how I drink!'

Tahar took his glass of champagne and sat down on a stool after ordering lemonade for his friend. As they talked, he lifted the glass to his lips, pretending to drink as he went on joking and ogling the girls. He told funny stories, gesticulating with one hand while the hand holding the glass slid casually down to his lap and spilled a few drops on to the ground. Then he lifted the glass to his lips again with perfect assurance, while the barmaid kept her eyes on him and listened to his stories with rapt attention; she herself seemed a bit tipsy. Tahar continued his manoeuvre until there were only a few golden dregs left in his glass. These he swilled down with obvious pleasure, winking at the smiling woman. Ali was quite overcome by Tahar's game.

'You're terrific!' he whispered. 'Nobody noticed . . . You're a magician! But why do we have to drink?'

'There are informers everywhere! You must drink and look as if you're having a good time. No one notices you if you're drinking and making jokes . . .'

They went over to a table not far from the band and sat smoking and chatting while they kept their eyes on the dance-floor. Tahar noted with satisfaction that there were very few Algerians except some *goumiers*, a few informers whom he knew

32

and members of the Rosiers cell. Girls were swaying on the dance floor to the rhythm of a cha-cha.

'Have you ever slept with a woman?'

Staggered by the directness of this question, Ali blurted out, 'Yes . . . No . . . But . . . That is . . .'

'So you've got no vices? You don't swear, you don't drink and you don't like women . . .' Tahar's eyes were mere slits. He seemed to be playing cat and mouse with Ali. He loved shocking and astonishing the youngster, as if he wanted to rid him of his cloak of innocence and good breeding that frightened him . . . Tahar seemed to be defending himself against everything that Ali represented for him. So, subconsciously he became aggressive, vicious even to protect himself against the admiring trust that the younger man felt for him. The latter lowered his eyes and murmured, 'Women, yes . . . I once went with some pals . . . to a "house". You won't believe me, Tahar, but I've always been afraid of them . . . afraid of being trapped.'

'Because they're too loving?' Tahar asked gently.

This time he didn't laugh. He was careful not to disrupt his young friend's moment of abandon.

'No, it's because I've seen fellows who let themselves be stupidly caught . . . They tried to make love anywhere they could . . . in a dark corner while their parents and neighbours were having their siestas. These fellows thought themselves clever. But sooner or later the girl got pregnant and they were hooked! They were only trying to spread their wings and they found themselves tied, fathers of families before they were proper adults . . . I'm afraid of that trap.'

'Really, my dear Ali, you are full of surprises! You're wiser than many a chap who thinks he's a man . . . I'm not interested in "houses" either! Since . . . I can't manage to think of those women simply as objects; to me, brothels are the mark of the most abject humiliation to which a human being can be subjected; they are cages set up to legalize rape! But when you've known fear and come close to death, you feel the irrational need to hold a woman in your arms . . .'

There was sudden silence. The band stopped playing. At the

33

entrance to the enclosure a drum roll sounded. A smiling man in a tight-fitting khaki uniform, with gold stripes on his epaulettes, entered slowly. He was followed by a group of officers, stiff and deferent. The colonel was short and his face was congested from the quantities of alcohol he had consumed during his fighting career. He was in the habit of constantly rubbing his plump little hands together, as if he were washing them. This gave him a wary, cunning look, with a falsely good-humoured expression on his face. But his blue eyes darted to and fro, showing a sort of permanent anxiety, like those of a watchful animal.

Tahar briefly told Ali what he knew about the colonel. It was whispered in every mess that the colonel had a particular weakness for big, strong, big-bosomed women, possibly because he was himself so short. He had had three wives, all of whom had been enormous. In addition to his pronounced taste for females who were bigger than himself, he had a holy horror of tall men. When he was walking or standing, he wouldn't allow anyone to be near him whose head came higher than his. And doubtless his constant state of exasperation was due to the fact that his company was composed of well-built fellows who appeared even bigger in their uniforms.

The colonel climbed on to the platform. He threw back his head and stiffened his shoulders while the band broke into the national anthem. Everyone rose to their feet and naturally Tahar and Ali stood rigidly to attention. Then the colonel, surrounded by officers and local civilian VIP's, took his seat at the head of a long table adorned with flowers.

A man leaned over and spoke to the colonel who nodded and looked up angrily at the windows crowded with people who preferred to watch the celebrations from a distance. He said something to the man. Tahar, sitting in his corner like a hunter stalking his prey, missed nothing of the colonel's movements.

The officer who had spoken to his superior, went over to the middle of the platform and stopped the band with a gesture. He read a short speech of welcome to the colonel. The assembled crowds applauded warmly. Then he introduced his superior officer. The latter unfolded a large sheet of paper and began to declaim:

'The gigantic work of pacification undertaken by our glorious army . . .'

He maundered on in these terms, then, hardening his tone, began to inveigh against 'the action of a handful of brigands, adventurers,' who were 'terrorizing the good and generous population of Muslims,' who had 'never ceased expressing their attachment to the Motherland! . . .'

Ali trembled with rage at these words. He clenched his fists till his knuckles were white. Tahar noticed and shook his friend's arm. The latter raised his eyes which shone with contained fury, but his face immediately relaxed as he met Tahar's amused expression at this fine speech.

'You're so calm, Tahar! As if you were watching an amusing farce!'

On the platform Colonel V— had finished his speech. He wiped his face with a large handkerchief. Then just when they all thought he had finished, and were getting ready to applaud, he cleared his throat, clasped his hands behind his back and spoke directly to the people who were watching at the windows all round.

'You, citizens, up at the windows, listen to me! If you don't want to come down and take part in these celebrations, I order you to close the shutters immediately! I don't want to see a single head at the windows . . . The police will see to it.'

The shutters were slammed shut, punctuating his words with a sound like gunfire. Others, more obstinate or curious did not budge, but their laughter could be heard like a challenge in the silence that had descended on the fête.

Immediately soldiers aimed their sub-machine-guns and ordered the recalcitrants to remove themselves. Soon there was not a single open window. Nevertheless, the presence of inhabitants could be surmised behind the dark shutters.

A different band was now invited to take up its position. Tahar watched most attentively; cradling his face in the palm of his hand, he looked as if he were deep in thought. As for Ali, he just

35

sat looking on. The Algerian dancer was announced. She wore a long, tight-fitting dress of red and gold, with a slit at the side that revealed a sinewy but slender leg. Her hennaed hair, with crimson highlights matching her dress, cascaded down her bare back in a shower of curls. In spite of her heavy make-up, her face with its childish laughing mouth was that of an adolescent. She launched into a dexterous performance of an Oriental dance, jerking her flat belly to the fast beat of the tambourines, then she twisted and twirled, swaying her hips languorously, lasciviously, heavy with a primitive sensuality. The men gazed at her, finding it difficult to swallow their saliva. A group of paratroopers who knew her well pressed close to the dance floor, shouting excitedly, 'Wow! Dalila! You're a devil! . . .'

She laughed and winked knowingly.

Tahar's expression, as he kept his eyes glued to the girl, was quite different. He was pale, thinking, 'You've betrayed your own people, probably just for a trashy necklace! You're happy, carefree, with no regrets . . . Last winter's over and done with for you, but your treachery, your greed resulted in a whole district being wiped out. You fled, we looked for you everywhere . . .'

Dalila was a mystery. No one knew where she came from. Her real name, it seemed, was Fatma. A star tatooed on her chin was the only indication of her rural origins. She was always on the move, appearing now in a city cabaret, now entertaining officers in their mess. She had recently turned up in Baladia. Aggressive and arrogant, she had taken a flat in a poor district. Her neighbours feared her, forbidding the children to speak to her when she was driven home in a military jeep after spending the evening in one or other of the town dives.

The Special Branch considered her a valuable mascot, and for months now the 'organization' had been trying to lay their hands on her; but it would have to be outside the neighbourhood she lived in. This evening was a unique opportunity to get near her and avenge the mutilation and death of hundreds of men which could be laid at her door.

Her final contortions were greeted by wild applause. She blew kisses to her enthusiastic admirers. The band did not move. They had played with bent heads to express their humiliation at having to perform for these people who would perhaps kill them the next day.

The star of the evening then disappeared behind the curtain and returned a few minutes later in high-heeled gold shoes and a black dress, which clung suggestively to her figure. She walked past Tahar's table to join the group of soldiers who had called out to her, and they all made their way laughing to the bar. Her deep-throated laugh struck Tahar's ears like a whip.

He saw her toss off two glasses of champagne, one after the other. The European band returned to strike up a rock and roll which galvanized the audience. The Colonel and some of his men took themselves off at this moment. Then there was a rush for the dance floor. Dalila dragged along a strapping, fair-haired fellow who was clearly sozzled. She planted herself in front of him and her whole body flickered like a flame to the beat of the music. Her partner had the greatest difficulty in following her. He clung comically to the girl's shoulders. She took no notice of him, abandoning herself whole-heartedly to the intoxication of the dance. She gripped his thighs, swayed backwards and forwards, lifted one foot after the other in a rapid rhythm, whirled around, then clung again to the soldier who lost his head and tried to smother her with kisses. The girl's suppleness made a fascinating sight. If her animosity or her obliviousness to evil was propor-tionate to her nervous energy or her extraordinary beauty, then she was indeed in danger. Especially at this time when the purification of morals was an essential stage in the fight for liberty . . . The organization forbade Muslims to drink alcohol and to smoke. Many recalcitrants had had their noses cut off . . . This was an infallible means of speeding up the political consciousness of those who had not heeded the injunctions . . .

Dalila soon grew tired and abandoned her partner. She stumbled through the crowd of dancers to return to one of the bars. She brushed past the table where the two men sat. Tahar, who had not taken his eyes off her for one single moment, slyly stretched out his long legs. She walked as if in her sleep, without looking where she was going, and tripped over him, but Tahar

37

quickly jumped up and caught her in his arms. She sank back against the young man's chest, murmuring, 'I'm thirsty!'

Tahar held her tightly.

'You're tired, rest here,' he said gently. 'I'll get you something to drink . . . My friend here will keep you company.'

She was surprised by the mixture of respect and affection in Tahar's expression. She gazed dreamily at him, thinking, 'What a lovely voice he's got . . . he speaks nicely . . .' She seemed to be falling into a doze, then she caught sight of Ali. He appeared only to have eyes for the dancers. She noted his youth, his distinguished appearance. She thought to herself that these men must be strangers here or they wouldn't have noticed her, or if they had, they'd have spoken to her much more roughly.

'Are you from these parts? . . . Are you Arabs?'

Ali searched quickly for an answer and said vaguely, 'We're students.'

The girl relaxed and burst out laughing. 'Your friend's a student! I never imagined students like that!'

She fell back in her chair, overcome with uncontrollable giggles. When she could get her breath, she gasped, 'He looks more like a boxer, or a pimp . . . Oh, my! Oh, my!'

Ali was very embarrassed. He thought he could have said Tahar was a primary schoolteacher . . . but a student! Tahar could be taken for anything but a callow youth still wet behind the ears . . . Taken all in all, Ali was more shocked by the expression 'pimp' than upset by his blunder. So he decided to hide his embarrassment under an air of amused surprise.

'Oh! You know, students aren't any different from other people . . . You've really never met any?'

'I don't know! It doesn't interest me! Men are all the same in bed, you know, whether they've studied or not.'

Ali was frankly at a loss, put off by the girl's behaviour and feeling as if he were walking through a maze or an unknown country. So he chose prudence and relapsed into silence. Dalila said thoughtfully, 'Your friend's all right . . . but I don't know, he scares you a bit, doesn't he?'

And she began to laugh again, throwing back her head and

repeating, 'Scared! scared! Everybody's scared. All these Arabs who're so proud of their manhood, their courage, they're all in a blue funk! They're all scared shitless, clinging to the walls whenever they go out, burying themselves like rats in a hole . . . My father beat me, my brothers beat me, my uncles and even my mother . . . men and women all beat me . . . And then, one day it was my turn to beat them on their own ground: their honour . . . so dear to Arabs! Now, they tremble at the sound of my name . . . And as for me, I've never been scared, I'm not afraid . . . of anyone!'

She was completely drunk.

'We're not wolves, going to eat you!' exclaimed Tahar who had crept up silently behind them.

Dalila started. She screwed up her eyes and watched Tahar setting down the champagne glasses on the table and struggling to open the bottle.

'A girl like you shouldn't use those terrible words,' he said suavely. 'Beauty is a woman's passport . . .'

She snatched greedily at the glass.

'Why do you drink like that? You'll spoil your pretty complexion,' Tahar went on, looking lovingly at Dalila's face. She seemed upset now, as she muttered, 'I like to drink!'

'What's your real name? Not your stage name.'

'The same: Dalila.'

'It suits you.'

She did not understand the irony behind these words. She took Tahar's comment for a compliment and snuggled up against him, giggling, 'You don't half have the gift of the gab!'

At a discreet signal from Tahar, Ali glanced at his watch and said, 'Eleven o'clock! We must be off!'

Dalila pouted with disappointment. 'So soon! The party's barely begun. We're going to have fun.'

'The curfew's at one o'clock,' said Tahar. 'We've just time to get back.'

She shrugged and grasped the man's hand. 'Is that all? With me you can stay till daybreak . . .' And she added proudly, 'Everybody knows me, I come and go wherever I like at any time!'

Tahar put his arm round her waist; she shivered and whispered, 'I like you . . . stay with me, get rid of your friend.'

At that moment a man stopped in front of their table. 'Well, lovely!' he said to Dalila. 'Are you abandoning us this evening? I've been looking for you everywhere! Can I sit down?'

As he spoke he pulled up a chair and sat down between Ali and Dalila, facing Tahar. The man was thin with dark eyes deep-set in a face like the blade of a knife giving him a wolf-like appearance. Ali shrank away, smiling awkwardly at the newcomer.

'Oh! It's Monsieur Cantini!' exclaimed Dalila.

She took the man's hand and throwing back her thick hair announced, 'I must introduce my friends! This is Monsieur Cantini, the Deputy District Police Superintendent. He's only been here three months and he's already got a reputation for cleaning up the area!'

She became animated, proud of being surrounded by such important folk. Just think, two students and an 'as-good-as-superintendent'! For once she was the centre of interest of educated people, not rough drunken soldiers who left her covered with bruises after they'd had their paws on her. Moreover, this Monsieur Cantini was 'chasing after' her, to use his expression. He'd caught sight of her one day in his chief's office, where she came and went like an old friend, and he'd immediately become besotted with her. This evening was the ideal opportunity to chat her up . . . All these uniformed 'dragons' were busy chasing after skirts.

Monsieur Cantini was resolved to get her for himself, in spite of the presence of these two suckers.

'You're not from these parts? I've never seen you before, at least not in the company of our lovely friend here!'

Ali answered quickly to give Tahar a hint of his lie. 'We're students . . . from Algiers . . .'

'Yes', Tahar added, smiling and using all his charm, 'and we decided to take advantage of the holidays to visit this beautiful town.'

Then he began to elaborate on their story: 'Some girls from the Law Faculty in Algiers invited us to a surprise party at their house

40

this evening and we should be there already! The party started at nine o'clock . . . We must show our faces at least.'

'Are your friends good-lookers!' asked Monsieur Cantini with a salacious smirk.

'I'll say! But you probably know them, Adrienne and Lucy, the daughters of Monsieur Dubois, the Sub-Prefect.'

This gave Cantini quite a jolt. His attitude changed suddenly. From being off-hand and condescending, he became deferential and all honey. 'Oh yes, I know them, but only by sight. They are studying in Algiers, it's true . . . They're all right, but a bit eccentric. Terrible snobs, aren't they, only going about with ex-pats.'

Ali was quite staggered at Tahar's powers of invention. He worried about where these lies would lead them. How were they going to get out of it all . . .? This Cantini didn't look as if he was keen to leave them. As for Dalila, she'd stopped playing the vamp and was eaten up with curiosity and respect for this man who was at home with the best society, who was studying with young ladies and was invited to the home of the Sub-Prefect . . . Even the pretentious Cantini was impressed.

'You know the way people talk! They are really very nice, simple girls. Is it really eccentric to choose your friends from so-called 'foreigners'? They were born in France. It's quite normal for them to go about with their friends from home. They also like to surround themselves with Algerian friends . . .'

'You're Arabs?' Cantini asked, suddenly suspicious.

'Well, more or less!' Tahar replied casually. 'My friend's father is the Bachaga Bou-tourni, whom I'm sure you've heard of . . . He's extremely rich!' Cantini nodded respectfully at the mention of this name.

'Yes . . . Yes . . . You're his son!' he said sympathetically to Ali.

'My mother's European,' Tahar went on, 'and my father's a Muslim lawyer. As you can see, we're not exactly steeped in the smell of the natives . . .' He put his arm around Dalila, who was burning with desire and gilded dreams. He smiled and added, 'And that smell has been dispelled long ago, thanks to the civilizing insecticide of our dear, common motherland . . . So,

41

there you have it,' he concluded forcibly. 'And if you want to come to this party with us, you'll be very welcome!'

Cantini had forgotten his lust for the lovely Dalila. He was trapped by Tahar's magnetism. He had only one thought in his head: 'This is the long-dreamed-of opportunity to get to know the VIPs in the administration . . .' Cantini, the son of a constable and a hairdresser, was ambitious. He had had to make innumerable sacrifices to reach his present rank. If he could have access to the Sub-Prefect's sanctum, his colleagues would respect him. And his Chief, this Superintendent from France, with his superior education and his stuck-up accent, would be careful whom he called a savage – just because he put his heart into torturing prisoners. For the moment his colleagues made fun of the relentlessness with which he tortured the unfortunate suspects who fell into his hands. He knew all the refinements of suffering: at which moment the pain began, how it developed, driving the human body to the brink of madness, till it is no more than a rag, a wretched object bereft of will-power. His morbid zeal had earned him a reputation for being a ruthless torturer.

He could already see himself seated at Monsieur Dubois' table . . . He said with a smile, 'That's very kind of you; this evening I'm free and feel like some fun.'

He had forgotten Dalila, who burst out in a fury, not giving Tahar time to speak, 'Not on your life! I'm not giving up my "treasure" . . . I'm taking him home with me.'

She clung to Tahar, cajoling, 'You're going to stay with me, darling, aren't you? You'll see, you won't be sorry. These stuck-up girls aren't any good. You do want to, don't you?'

Cantini was frankly irritated by Dalila's behaviour and exclaimed harshly, 'Nonsense, Dalila, you go and get your fun somewhere else! Our friends have got an invitation . . .'

Ali watched the scene with increasing anxiety. He decided to intervene, feeling as if he were jumping into deep water when he couldn't swim. He said firmly, 'Well, that doesn't matter! After all it's supposed to be a casual affair. Our friends said we were welcome to bring any of our pals along . . .'

'He's right!' declared Tahar. 'Come on, we must hurry!

42

Monsieur Cantini, you're a man after my own heart. And you, Dalila, my pet, I don't intend to let you go.'

He examined her critically. 'Too much make-up! It gives a bad impression . . . Anyway, let's go! You can do something about it in the car.'

The girl's face lit up with surprise and wonder. She clapped her hands excitedly, crowing with delight. Then, indicating the group of paratroopers crowding round the bar, she added, 'If they see me, they won't let me go. Let's slip out at the back by the stage door, there's no one there at the moment.'

She was very excited at the thought of getting to know another set, which she'd never imagined entering, even in her wildest dreams. She thought, 'These fellows are really all right! The big one had me worried a bit at first . . . I'm a fool to see danger everywhere, after all! . . . Anyway, I don't have to go with a stinking drunk soldier tonight . . . this chap's educated and he seems to fancy me . . .'

They slipped away unnoticed through the throng of dancers. Relieved though Tahar was that they were not accosted by another of Dalila's admirers, not a muscle of his face moved. He thought to himself that luck was on his side this evening. Ali wondered what Tahar was going to do with Cantini, as no provision had been made for him in the 'programme'. Nor did he know where they were going to take Dalila. He remembered Tahar's words, 'It's the dancer who interests us this evening . . . you'll see it's no use relying on theory, you have to improvise and play it by ear.'

So Cantini was one of the circumstances you had to count on. They walked a short way along the road. There was no one about at this hour. No doubt the lads of the patrol were having a drink inside. Tahar asked Cantini if he had a car. He replied that he lived in the locality and had come on foot.

'And is your car far?' asked Dalila.

Tahar and Dalila walked in front, their arms around each other like lovers. Ali and Cantini followed, chatting like two old acquaintances. When they got to the car Tahar casually suggested to Ali that he drive. The youngster obeyed mechanically. He hadn't a licence, but he had learned to drive when he was working for the railways. Cantini was invited to sit in front, next to Ali, which seemed quite natural, since Tahar appeared to be smitten with Dalila, and was keen to explore the amorous potential of the sexy dancer. This gave rise to some ribald comments: 'Hey, my friend! Leave some for our Dalila's other admirers! . . .'

He gave Ali a good-humoured nudge, adding, 'I'd say he's hot stuff, that fellow! Now you, I get the impression you don't care much for women . . . But you're still young. Even so, I was already wenching when I was twelve! Oh! We Latins, we get a taste for our greens pretty early.'

Tahar's voice reached them vibrant with irony and deliberate boasting: 'And when we're half Arab into the bargain, you can guess what we're like when we get going!'

Dalila giggled, hot with desire. She was already half naked as she pressed against Tahar. He tried to cool the girl's ardour by holding her firmly and keeping up the lively mood by joking with Cantini. He couldn't expect any help from Ali who had to keep his eyes on the road and maintained a sphinx-like expression.

'By the way, what are your first names?' asked Cantini. 'I mustn't look like a stranger in front of your friends.'

'Our young friend's name is Dahmane, but that sounds too much like a wog, so he's Didou to his pals . . .'

'Didou!' murmured Cantini. 'That really suits him. I must say, you students have got an answer for everything!'

Ali was nervous and Cantini's mockery didn't exactly put him at his ease.

'And my name's Jacky!' declared Tahar.

Noticing the policeman's surprise, he added savagely, 'Yes, it's my mother who wears the trousers in our house . . . My father considered his marriage to a European a heaven-sent opportunity to climb up the social ladder – not to mention overcoming racial prejudice . . . so unfortunately he just turned into a *terguez*,*

* A Berber word, literally meaning 'hermaphrodite', used for a weak, spineless man.

44

saying amen to everything she decided. He didn't call himself Mohand any more . . . but Momo!'

At these words a tense silence ensued. More than the actual words, the tone in which they were said changed the atmosphere in the car as if by magic. They had been driving for about twenty minutes. This tension was suddenly broken by a stifled cry from the back seat. Dalila had been knocked out by a blow from Tahar, reducing her to temporary silence. Tahar had a revolver pointed at the back of Cantini's head. Stupefied by the sudden change in the situation, he put up his trembling hands. 'What's got into you? What do you want?'

'Shut your jaw! And don't move unless you want me to blow your brains out . . .'

Tahar leaned over and rapidly removed the weapon that Cantini had in a holster under his left armpit. He sniggered, 'We're sex maniacs . . . We want to screw the girl.'

'Oh! is that all!' sighed Cantini with relief. 'You didn't have to worry about me. I'll even help you. She's only a tart after all!'

'Shut up!' ordered Tahar.

The long dark road, lined with dense tall trees, lit up by the car's headlights, looked threatening.

Tahar indicated the direction to Ali who silently carried out his orders. The youngster was suddenly afraid of the new Tahar: this cold, ruthless stranger curtly giving orders to the puppets in the car. He told Ali to turn off to the right into a narrow path in the forest. He slowed down, brought the car to a stop and switched off the engine.

He murmured, 'Is this it?'

Tahar nodded. The young man immediately opened the door and jumped out. Tahar then dragged Cantini out of the car – a Cantini livid with terror. He crawled along the ground, weeping and begging for mercy. But he sensed he was about to meet his end at the hands of this killer. He lost his head.

'Pity! Ask me anything, I can give you information . . . I'll work for you . . . Have mercy! Oh! Mother! Mother!'

His words tumbled out incoherently, he grovelled, he fell on his knees, clasping his hands together. Tahar handed a long rope to

Ali, telling him to tie Cantini up firmly. Meanwhile, he'd pulled Dalila out of the car and left her lying on the ground, still concussed. The cold air had shaken Ali out of his torpor, and he rapidly carried out Tahar's instructions.

Sobs attracted their attention. The girl had come round and quickly realized what was happening. She wept, frozen with terror, unable to make the slightest movement. Crouching like a wounded animal, she begged for mercy with a curious meekness. Then she began to sway backwards and forwards, not resisting, not crying out, simply murmuring like a litany, 'I don't want to die . . . I don't want to die . . .'

'Here, take this revolver, Ali,' Tahar said softly. 'Watch her while I finish him off.'

Ali took the weapon in a trembling hand. He soon regained control of himself and shoved the revolver into the girl's ribs, saying hoarsely, 'Don't move . . . and don't be afraid.'

Suddenly a nauseating stench arose from where Cantini was tied. The man over whom death had already spread her black mantle had been betrayed by his body, weakened by terror. His bowels had given way at the moment when Tahar, holding a large butcher's knife in one hand, and his pistol in the other, said softly, 'Cantini! We don't cut the throats of soldiers or policemen, as you're only doing what you suppose to be your duty . . . If you capture us, you kill us; if we catch you, we kill you. That's the rule . . . But we cut the throats of Muslims who betray their brothers! Men and women alike.'

Sickened by his victim's smell, Tahar pressed his gun against Cantini's temple. The shots rang out in the still night.

Ali moved as if in a dream, uncertain what was going to happen next. He felt uneasy, like a blind person venturing along an unfamiliar path . . . he looked at Tahar with an expression of mute interrogation. His distracted air was akin to the terror painted on Dalila's face. She and Ali were the same age. They suddenly resembled two poor children left in the forest, at the mercy of a wicked ogre. The moon shed its dim light through the trees. An anxious silence reigned, interrupted at times by the rustle

46

of leaves where the birds, like the rest of nature, paid no heed to the differences among men.

And suddenly the reality of the situation dawned upon him. The sky, the moon, the diamantine stars exploded around him in a bottomless crater of burning, bloody rocks . . .

Thunder roared in Ali's head. The girl's throat was going to be cut! . . . He looked at her and thought with horror: 'That young, smooth throat . . . cut? No, not that, by God! She's a traitor, it's true, she's done a great deal of harm . . . but she can't die like that!'

A wild look came into his eyes.

Dalila was the sheep being slaughtered on the morning of the Eïd el-Kebir feast . . . Tahar had become Monsieur Lavigne with the white beard and his cooking pot full of smoking blood.

Now his eyes filled with tenderness.

. . . This hair, this youthful face . . . it could be that of Meriem, his tomboy cousin.

Dalila realized the type of death that Tahar had in store for her. She saw the knife gleam in the moonlight and suddenly regained her strength. She lifted her head up to heaven and uttered a howl like that of a wild beast in the night. Ali held her tightly in his arms. Nevertheless, she went on struggling.

'Cut it out!' said Tahar. 'No one'll hear you here, we're deep in the forest.'

She fell silent, subdued by this calm voice. Then she began to moan again.

Tahar moved nearer to her: 'You know the Bou-H. cemetery . . . It's quite near here. You see that clump of trees? Behind them is a ditch; one jump and you're in the graveyard. I've brought you here so that the people who died because of your treachery can hear your terrified screams as they are avenged . . . The people you betrayed are buried there.'

He had spoken without anger. His level tone seemed simply to be stating a fact. Dalila was now the very picture of horror and loathing. Sweat had plastered her hair to her face and neck. Her tears mixed with her mascara coursed down her cheeks in black rivulets. Her lipstick had run, turning her mouth into a red gash. She fell back on the ground. Her black dress pulled up to her

47

thighs gave her the air of a tragedy queen. She writhed and spat. 'Filthy race!' she screamed. 'I'll be avenged. Your turn'll come! You won't win the war, you lousy lot! They're stronger than you! Stronger than you!'

She foamed at the mouth and shrieked her hatred even in the face of death. She was like a maniac. Even her voice had changed to that of a disease-ridden old woman. A hoarse, broken voice, interrupted by waves of sobs.

'Let's get done with it quickly!' said Tahar, still in the same calm tone.

'You . . . you're going to cut her throat?' whispered Ali, trembling.

Tahar frowned and stared at him for a moment, then went back to the car and returned with an electric torch which he handed to the youngster.

'That's right, that's my usual job and normally I do it alone . . . I brought you along so that you could see . . . Shine the torch, I want the job done cleanly tonight!'

Ali's mind was in a whirl. His temples throbbed, he felt he was going to vomit. He could no longer reason. He must act quickly!

The moment the girl saw the blade gleaming in Tahar's hand, she began to scream and Ali could feel her heart pounding under the arm which he held around her chest. It was this sensation which galvanized him to act, to put an end to this nightmare. He pressed the trigger. The shot went off in the back of the girl's neck. She crumpled up, jerked a few times spasmodically, then lay still. In her dilated eyes there was no trace of horror now, only surprise and grief.

Tahar leapt forward and grabbed the gun out of Ali's hand. His huge silhouette stood out in the beam of light from the torch, like a mountain threatening to roll down and crush all life. Tahar looked as if he were about to knock his companion down on the spot. He threw down the knife and holding the still-smoking revolver in one hand he seized Ali by the collar and shook him angrily.

'You fool! Why? Why did you do that? I ought to cut your throat, to teach you to make me fail in my job . . .'

He was like a man out of his mind. Ali felt he was being strangled in Tahar's powerful grip as the latter continued to shake him and point the gun dangerously under his nose.

He recovered his self-control at the sight of the boy's ashen face.

'Let's get out of here! We'll spend the night at the cemetery-keeper's . . . He's expecting us.'

'What about your car?' Ali stammered.

'That's not your business! Shut up and stop asking questions! I've had enough of your gab!'

Tahar was boiling with rage at the young man's behaviour. He'd have liked to beat him up, rid him once and for all of that guileless, vulnerable, fragile look. He recalled Ali's white face staring at him, wide-eyed with agonized astonishment. Now Ali stood beside him awkwardly, clenching his fists and breathing spasmodically, trembling like a young bird that has fallen from its nest . . . Tahar's anger abated as he realized that Ali no longer wore that look of innocence.

Tahar took the young man's hand and they ran together to the keeper's lodge.

When the lad felt his companion's rough hand against his own he knew that he was forgiven. But he also knew that no revolutionary struggle could be carried out merely with words. Whatever the period, whatever new weapons were available, the methods used were always cruel.

Ali closed his eyes. He imagined that, instead of this desperate race through the night to avoid the possibility of being caught at a road block, it was daytime, with the sun shining, and he was running to join his pals in the clearing . . . near the Roumières' field. He was going hunting sparrows with his catapult . . . he could hear the swish of the elastic and the laughter of Slimane, Abbas, Alain and Meriem . . . Ali shook his head, weeping softly inwardly.

'I am the catapult and I'm tracking down the young, sensitive lad in me, the little boy from Dachra with bright eyes and curly hair, the boy who kissed Meriem and was me, the youngster who rolled in the grass and was me . . . I won't let him live, I'll hunt him down. I'll destroy him, until my country, its grass, its landscape, its rivers and its shores are recreated, until fear and shame are strangled in the barbarians' dream . . . I shall pursue that sensitive, affectionate little boy in me until liberty is won!'

But the two men had already arrived at the keeper's house.

Then came the pit under the trap-door with its abomination . . .

'We were lucky!' Tahar said calmly.

Ali opened his eyes. Tahar was beside him, with his feet already on the ladder which the keeper had lowered for them. The latter leaned down. 'How do you feel, son?'

'OK,' he replied and then he too climbed up, without looking back at the gruesome pit.

It was four in the morning. The soldiers would not return.

'We'll leave soon,' Tahar decided. 'It's safer. Let's get a bit of rest now.'

But Ali could not relax. First the two executions, and now that decomposing corpse . . . He closed his eyes and then the memory of the kids playing hopscotch yesterday wafted over him like a salutary breeze. He smiled.

Hopscotch was really a game for girls, but he'd liked playing and had often had a try behind Alain's parents' house. Abbas laughed at them, saying they were just a bunch of silly females.

The scent of jasmin reached him from the surrounding houses, and with it the smell of fritters with honey or his mother's galette: 'Mà Chérifa'. . .

The sun dazzled these young urchins' eyes, as they ran and laughed excitedly.

4

> *'There is always a moment in our childhood when*
> *the door opens and lets in the future . . .'*
> Graham Greene

Dachra . . . end of August, 1953

This month of August seems endless; it's very hot in the village. The lucky devils who have an aunt or a grandmother in the city have left for the seaside. This morning, Alain came to say goodbye. He's going to stay with his grandmother. He won't be back till the next holidays. He's a boarder now at the *lycée* in town. He says that life is pretty boring except for lessons.

It's a year since he passed the entrance exam and left. We'd both been at the same school for as long as I can remember and I can say without boasting that I was a better pupil than him. His mother was always grumbling to him, 'How is it that Ali, an Arab, is better at school than you, a French boy! . . .' Of course, she didn't mean anything personal against me. But she couldn't understand this curious 'unfair' distribution of intelligence or whatever! . . . Anyway, as I was saying, we both had one more year to go at the village school and what did our classteacher and the headmaster decide? To enter all the European children for the entrance exam to the *lycée*. As far as the Muslims were concerned, the youngest ones would have to repeat the year, in spite of getting good marks; the ones who were over fourteen would go up into the last class of the primary school.

I was so keen to go on to high school and learn new and exciting

51

subjects and I realized how unfair the system was . . . Alain himself was aware of the teachers' favouritism.

'I don't understand, old thing,' he said. 'You always come top and they make you stay down, when they let me and the others, especially that clot Pierre, go on to the *lycée* . . . There's some hanky-panky business going on that I can't make head nor tail of. Can you?'

I did have a pretty good idea what was going on, and I spoke to my father about it. He put on his new trousers and the white shirt he kept for best and went off to the school. No one ever knew exactly what happened, but I saw my father storming out, settling his beret angrily on his head. That evening, at suppertime, he grumbled into his moustache, 'The dogs! They think the high school is too good for my son! They don't even give him the chance of taking the exam like the others! But he'll be a man, a real man, for all that!'

So, at thirteen I found myself repeating the same class while Alain started high school. He showed me his text books and talked about his new pals, assuring me, really kindly, that I was still his best friend. 'The bastards!' I fumed. 'They won't give me a chance because I'm a native!'

I realized my outburst had been preying on his mind, when one day as we were playing dominoes, he suddenly said, 'You know, Ali, there's quite a few Arabs there!' He was doing his best to console me.

'Oh, yeah!' I replied, 'And are their fathers the same kind of Arab as mine?'

Alain screwed up his eyes in bewilderment, but I went on, 'I mean they must be the sons of naturalized Arabs, you dolt! Oh! I know all about these things, my father explains them to me . . . And also, when you're poor they don't want you in certain schools.'

Alain was upset; he replied, 'But my father's not rich, he's just a barman!'

'Yes, but he's a European, if you don't mind!'

I didn't like talking like that as we'd never had any arguments up till then. But it had needed the unfairness of grown-ups to cause this difference between us.

52

Alain gave this wonderful reply that I'll never forget: 'Well, OK, it's not important. But as you're so fond of books, I'll pass mine on to you and when I come back for the holidays I'll teach you everything I've learned at high school.'

He lowered his eyes miserably and from that day we've never mentioned the subject again. But he'd just given me the most touching proof of friendship from one thirteen-year-old to another.

I'd also like to talk about our village. It's not perched on a hill as a small market town might be. No, it's quite flat, situated between two commercial centres. The one, about sixty miles away, is Baladia: a port that seems a land of plenty to us village folk. The other, to the south, is an important village, twice as big as ours, famous for its souks where cattle, sheep and race-horses are sold.

We are not near the sea, but surrounded by plains and dense forests. Our little village seems to have been thrown up at random for weary travellers. A main street runs through the middle. On one side are some old dilapidated houses, interspersed with a few shops selling sundry goods, and on the corner, the biggest native grocery shop, owned by the Mozabite, Si Saïd. On the other side is the European section: at the very bottom the school, then the clinic, next the high class grocery where Monsieur Tagliota sells fruit, vegetables, cheese, wine and even toilet preparations and cleaning materials for the administrative élite of the village and finally the police station with the mayor's offices next to it . . . What a fine building that is, with its curious pointed roof and red tiles, just like a castle! It's got an immense, curved balcony, with little carved cherubs on the rails, carrying the national flag.

I never tire of admiring this building every time I pass it on my way to school, nourishing crazy dreams of one day building myself a house like it.

If my parents or schoolfellows suspected what I was thinking, how they'd laugh at me! . . . But, let's go on. I've forgotten what I was writing . . . I must re-read. When I think about our municipal building I forget everything. Oh, yes, next comes the post office and further on is old Monsieur Lavigne's shop where he repairs radios and other electric appliances. It's full of boxes of all shapes and sizes. He's a do-it-yourself enthusiast, mad about anything to do with electricity. He's very kind to children, never missing an opportunity of trying to interest us in his work, probably hoping to inspire us with a vocation.

In the middle of the little square, forming a pyramid joining the two sides, is the church, with an imposing flight of steps in front. Whenever there's a wedding we take the opportunity of slipping among the crowd of Europeans in their Sunday best waiting for the bridal couple to emerge. We watch out for the moment when they throw sugared almonds at the smiling pair. Then we make a dash for the sweets. So weddings are lucky days for us, when we can satisfy our greed. Afterwards we remain clinging to the rails, silently watching the bride depart in her rustling gown. And the priest, seeing us lost in admiration and moved by our shining eyes, never chases us away. We always come home with our pockets filled with sweets, as if returning from a cloak and dagger adventure.

Alain's father, Monsieur Marcel, has his bar next to the native houses, on the other side of the road from the other Europeans. No one knows by what irony of fate it came to be there. But it isn't far from the church, so when the excitement of a funeral or any other celebration gives people a thirst, they can quench it conveniently. Alain's family lives over the bar. Our little house with its crooked roof looking as if the slightest breeze would blow it away, is tucked modestly in next door. My father's shop, on the ground floor, doesn't look more impressive. How can I describe it? A shop? . . . It's more of a lumber-room in which my father sells tins of sardines, semolina and pots of *smen*. Together with all these heterogeneous articles, for some unknown reason, he also stocks an assortment of berets and caps: some plain or with a plastic peak, some with pompoms like the ones French sailors wear. Why he should stock these unexpected objects in his shop is a mystery to me.

The caps are set out on a separate shelf, clearly displayed near the door. Where does he get them from? Another mystery! . . .

It's quite funny to see the number of people sporting these

54

berets over the hood of their burnouses. The young men come from the neighbouring *douars* to buy the smartest caps and depart proud of their acquisitions. My father sells bits of everything, but puts all his heart into this headgear.

And who could describe the stars of my village sky? They are beautiful beyond belief! How constant they are, never failing to appear in our sky! I am as much in love with them as with our municipal building. I don't know what they are like in other places, but I can say that in our village they seem so enormous that you'd think they'd fall on your face like a hail of diamonds . . .

I'm not making up stories about our village stars, even Alain, when he went to Europe once, assured me that he didn't find them the same. Over there, he told me, the stars are scarcely visible, as if they were sad and people didn't love them enough. It's stupid to talk like this, but you must believe me, they really can grow dim if you don't look at them lovingly.

Dachra . . . 9 September 1953

I am sitting in my bedroom-cum-dining-room-cum-lounge, with the paraffin lamp placed in front of me on the low table, and I open my diary to pick up my memory's multicoloured thread. After dinner my father went into the courtyard to chat with one or other of the uncles who live nearby. My mother has settled herself down at my side with her needlework. Always the same: a white sheet on which she's carefully embroidering a host of little butterflies flitting round flowers. Since Madame Juliette taught her to do cross-stitch and stem-stitch, my mother has found a haven, as it were, in the eye of her needle, and her nimble fingers, under the spell of the silken threads, trace her dreams on the spotless stuff. Her face lights up as the colours come alive in her embroidery. She must surely imagine herself a golden butterfly fluttering in the calix of the flowers. While I write, I hear her ask from time to time, 'Haven't you finished your homework yet?'

Seeing me bent over my pages, my parents naturally think that

I'm busy with some school exercise. But I'm happily setting down my memories in the reassuring certitude that they will not fly away in the dust of sleep or oblivion.

These reflections bring me to observe more closely the life of our village, to make it live on the pages of my little black book. I love to preserve things or events, prevent them from crumbling away with time . . . I am afraid of forgetting. To forget is to be impoverished, it is a slow death. At least, that's how it is for me. This fear comes, no doubt, from the fact that I don't know my family's history, at least, that of my father.

My mother comes from Dachra. Her ancestors have always lived here. My father never knew his parents. He was brought up in an orphanage. He was born in Ouargla, a peaceful town lulled by the murmur of palm-trees. I've never managed to find out how and why he landed up here. I often ask him, but he can't remember. He was brought up by an old couple, together with his younger brother, and when he was five years old they died and both children were sent to the orphanage.

Later, my father joined the navy and his brother went into the army. So they never really tried to get to know their own family.

They are what is known as 'SNP', *sans nom patronymique* (no family name). That goes for me too: SNP. Abdelkader, Ali. This lack of a name is my ball and chain. I drag it after me in a silent fury.

Before my father, there is a void. Who was my grandfather? Where did he come from? Sometimes I get the impression that my father was born from the desert sands, or took shape like an angel from one of the foam-crested waves of the sea which he loves so much. So, in the face of this man with no past, no memories, my desire to set down all the events of my life is like the sun lighting up a grey day.

We know my mother's family. Her father was a grocer, her brother is a shoemaker and her cousins simple peasants. So they are unsophisticated folk, the sons of a modest family, but one that can boast of an ancient and illustrious name. To be the son of an *Aïla*, means that one has had a good education, and has acquired a moral standard and a sense of tradition in the bosom of the family. My father has become a part of this family and is respected by his neighbours. The types of rich households, the only ones entitled to bear the title of *Aïla*, are usually to be found in big cities where people distort everything, confusing honesty with worldly wealth. None of that in our village! The poultry merchant is a person of standing because his ancestors are as familiar to everyone as the ancient stones of our walls.

I particularly remember last year when Alain was still here . . .

Alain is the only one of the European children to join in our games. There is also Abbas, whose father is a sort of manager, working for Si Hafid who owns a bakery, the village café and other property in the town of Baladia. Abbas is the same age as me. His father has two wives and no one knows how he manages to keep up two households as his boss Si Hafid is reputed to be extremely stingy. His wives live in the same house and get on quite well. Abbas is the eldest of the five children. His mother, Khalti Kaltoum is very resourceful. She's prettier than her co-wife and she's the one who rules the roost. When she goes to the *hammam*, or to any women's party, she joins in the gossip and gives them all the benefit of her advice, as if she were the hostess. She's said to be conceited as she claims to know everything and tries to talk and act like a city lady, because she's sometimes been to town with her husband.

Naturally, all that is just the tittle-tattle that never failed to reach our ears when we were youngsters of ten to twelve, since we lived amongst the women, mingling with them even at the *hammam*.

Khalti Kaltoum's son, Abbas, is just the opposite of his mother. Where she's stuck up and cocksure, he's very reserved and rather shifty. He plays with us and joins in our pranks, but there's something funny about him, something a bit crazy, unreliable in his character, that grates on us. To tell the truth, he hasn't any friends; he just trails after us, for want of better!

He's well-known for his underhand tricks. For example, he never says no, outright, when anyone asks him a favour, but he contrives not to do it . . . He's full of complexes, I think. He takes everything seriously and he's so quick to take offence that he becomes a pain in the neck, and we often tell him to go to hell! Still I do feel quite friendly towards him, in spite of him being such a hypocrite. For some reason or other, I'm rather sorry for him, because he's always on his guard, like a wild cat. He's not quite at ease with us, always feeling the need to challenge us. Perhaps it's because his father is known to be partial to alcohol. In our village the men are very observant in the practice of their religion, just the opposite of the Europeans. As my father says, we natives may lack power, but our secret weapon is God and his many Saints . . . It's true! I've always noticed that for every church set up in a village, there's a mosque not far away . . . not to mention the many little domed shrines of the marabouts scattered about the countryside. It's a fact, the weak are wiser than the strong! . . .

To come back to our village, on Fridays most of the Muslims gather at the mosque, giving Marcel's bar a wide berth. As for Abbas's father, he couldn't give a damn! When the café is closed, he settles down in the back room with a few other old campaigners, and they indulge in their little vice: beer or rosé around endless games of cards.

So Abbas is perpetually on edge, aggressive, expecting people to think the worst of him . . . Even though I don't treat him as roughly as the other kids, I don't know if he's noticed my friendliness. He seems more at home with boys from outside our village. I see him laughing, running about and even scrapping with them. Apparently he only opens up with people who don't know him. With us, his neighbours, he's a blank wall. Besides which, he's got a funny way of staring at us, as if he wanted to fix our image permanently in his mind. Some of the boys make fun of him because he always looks so injured, particularly Fatty Slimane. He loves making a fool of people and Abbas is his favourite target.

Rachid is another boy that I like; he plays the flute. He's rather a queer customer, a tall, gaunt fellow who likes to sit in a corner of the clearing behind his father's little field, playing for hours and never tiring of his sweet, rather sad music. From always blowing into this instrument, his big mouth with the fleshy lips has taken on a sulky twist, and we've nicknamed him 'M'chanef, the Silent'. Still, he manages to join in our fun. When he plays, we listen to him in silence, lulled by the sound of his wonderful flute; at that magic moment, we cease to be noisy urchins and become multicoloured water-lilies, floating on sheets of whispering water. Rachid means all that to me . . .

He doesn't say much, but his little black eyes shine with an almost mystical fervour, bringing light-heartedness to our company. He's older than us all so we respect him. Besides, he's the best Quran reader in all Dachra.

Rachid attends the *medresa*, the Quranic school; his father works for the only rich French settler in our area, Monsieur Roumière. In between lessons, Rachid runs errands for Madame Roumière, Elise: the most important lady in the village, together with the mayor's wife.

We also attend classes at the *medresa*, after school is over. We learn to recite the verses of the Quran. Rachid is obviously the best. He crouches down on the mat in the classroom, totally absorbed, never taking his eyes off the Sheikh Mokhtar.

The rest of us are easily distracted and ready for a lark. As we arrive, we jostle each other, like a swarm of flies buzzing round a market stall. Then we recite the verses with mock enthusiasm, mumbling through our teeth and swaying convincingly backwards and forwards, as we've seen the Quranic teachers do. But the Sheikh isn't taken in; he cuts short our play-acting with the *falaka*, a punishment that consists of a beating on the soles of our feet. Then Rachid has the honour of immobilizing the feet of the unfortunate miscreant, while another pupil holds the culprit firmly at his back. The Sheikh conscientiously inflicts the ten or twenty blows for insolence, going up to fifty for blasphemy or a badly learnt *sura* . . .

It's really a scream to see one of us hobbling home on his bruised feet, but not daring to complain for fear of getting another hiding from his parents. We don't really have it in for

Rachid, the 'torturer's assistant', as at heart he quite likes us. He loves taking pot shots at sparrows with his catapult. We sincerely admire his uncanny aim, and the almost diabolical precision of his movements.

But I'm the only one to have guessed his secret. Rachid-the-Silent, becomes handsome, his sulky lips stretch into a slight enigmatic smile when Madame Elise appears. This woman really has a regal bearing. She's fairly tall with a velvety skin and beautiful brown hair, done up in a bun; her face with its regular features would be pleasant if it were not for her mouth, which is too thin, with sharp lines at the corners, destroying the impression she tries to convey of an affable lady. Her way of carrying her head upright shows how highly she thinks of herself. Yes, Rachid is quite bowled over by her. I now understand better the almost doleful tones of his music.

When Madame Elise sits on her veranda, facing her husband's fields, sipping her aperitif, Rachid watches her pensively from the other side of the enclosure, playing a sad tune on his flute. Sometimes he breaks off his playing, to stare at the distant point where the beautiful lady sits: then the forest is silenced, the birds cease their twittering and time itself stands still. I've tried to guess what brings this light into his eyes: is it scorn for these impudent *Roumis*? Or the desire one day to possess a similar woman?

Yes, Rachid is indeed different from us, secret, illusive, he seems to have come from outer space.

The other scallywag is Slimane, the shoemaker's son. He's a big, fat, jolly fellow, who seems to gulp down his life in big mouthfuls – quite literally, as he never stops eating. He's so fat that his breasts are like a girl's. We often tease him but he takes it all in good part. He's in the same class as me, a good pupil who's very popular. He's always ready to do anyone a good turn. But the best thing about him is his extraordinary sense of humour! He's always making puns and telling funny stories that are sometimes a bit *risqué*. He's the only one to have had amorous adventures so young. We're quite stunned when he tells us how he had his first woman when he was only twelve; it's true he was big for his age and could have been taken for seventeen or more. According to him, he's now got as much experience as a man. We find it hard to believe him, but he's given us rather disconcerting details. So we consider him emancipated on this score.

He disappears into the mountains for whole afternoons on end, with girls from the neighbouring *douars*, and comes back bright-eyed to recount his exploits. What's more, he takes it on himself to explain the secrets of our bodies to us. He often asks one of us, 'So, have you seen your map yet?'

Anyone who has done so, makes a proud declaration, explaining to the boys who are still children what it's all about, and the latter wait impatiently for the fantastic day when they can boast like the big boys. Slimane has let us into the secret. He says that when one morning we see a yellowish stain on the sheets, the shape of a map, it's the beginning of our adult life . . . And so we've each had our turn to give ourself airs as we announce, 'That's it! I've got my map!' . . .

The boys who are not in the secret think we're swotting up our geography!

Sometimes Smartypants Slimane doesn't take us seriously and gets a kick out of our indignation. 'Show me!' he plagues the wretched boy.

Some of us just shrug our shoulders and give him a fairly accurate description of the phenomenon. Slimane boasts of having the biggest cock . . . Once he even gave a demonstration behind a bush.

'Who's got the biggest one, eh?'

Each of us showed off his assets but we had grudgingly to admit that Slimane's was the best developed. Seeing our disappointed looks, he reassured us kindly, advising us that the secret was to eat lots of nuts.

But for all the almonds and peanuts we stuffed ourselves with, most of us simply made ourselves violently sick! Rachid, in his great wisdom, put our minds at rest, while making fun of Fatty Slimane. 'You idiots!' he said. 'Can't you see how big and fat he is? And he's older than you, so naturally he's more developed . . .

Stop worrying your heads about it, God provides for every man according to his size . . .'

That's how we lost our complexes about Slimane, but he still impresses us with his countless exploits. Sometimes he gets it into his head to tease Alain and falls about laughing as he shouts, 'I say, you've got to have your willy snipped before you can be a man! So when are you going to have it done? Tell your mother it's soon going to be the feast of the slaughtered willies, like when they slaughter the sheep . . .' And Slimane races off, hiding behind trees with Alain furiously at his heels . . .

In this way, each of us puts the stamp of his personality on our little group and turns our lives into a perpetual holiday.

Alain is naturally a part of our world, like another brother. And his parents, like him, are appreciated by the whole community. They had settled in our village long before I was born. My mother told me that when Madame Juliette arrived she seemed like a sheep lost in the steppes. She was used to big towns and being surrounded by an affectionate family, the sort of noisy, warm-hearted Jewish family that is common here, accustomed to sharing everything. Suddenly cut off from her world, she felt isolated, as she was the only Jewess in this village. And the snobbish wives of the European élite looked down on her. Her husband is older than her, but he's always been very considerate to his pretty young wife, so she's gradually adapted herself to life in our 'back-of-beyond' as she often calls our village.

Juliette has never really mixed with the ladies on the other side of the street; they are quite nice to her, but never very intimate. On the other hand, she comes and goes freely in the Arab houses. So she's got into the habit of coming to buy eggs from my mother, or popping in to have lessons in weaving wool. She regularly attends the *hammam*. Of course Juliette speaks Arabic as well as my mother. At home she always wears a *gandoura*. When her mother or sisters visit her, you should see what a fine old time they have, with tambourines beating out the frenzied rhythm of the *zendali* dances for hours on end. Monsieur Marcel, her husband, is a Catholic, a typical Frenchman, a *Francaoui*, as we say here! He

62

comes from a town called Toulouse. Since he got to know Juliette he's no longer keen to leave this country. It seems his family in France has fallen out with him because of his marriage, since for some families there marrying a Jew is as bad as marrying an Arab or a Black. That's why Alain's father can't stand anything from his own country. And he gets furious when he hears anyone running the natives down. It's his way of defending his love for Juliette.

She really is a beauty. When she goes out shopping, all the men turn round to stare after her. She's tall, plump, with magnificent dark red hair. But her best feature is her eyes. They are green like emeralds and with her perpetual gaiety, she personifies the joy of living! You should just see her dancing at a wedding. She wears her finest *gandoura* and lets out a long ululation when she arrives; then, at the other women's insistence, she rises, slowly, almost voluptuously, adjusts her sash, and dances. She becomes a goddess of beauty and sensuality as certain poems that I've recently discovered express it . . . Yes, you have to have seen this woman dance for the other women's pleasure, gently undulating her belly to the beat of the tambourines. Her shoulders sway like rose petals in the breeze and her arms dazzle the spectators with their whiteness. She is the finest ornament of every celebration. When my mother, Chérifa, and Juliette dance opposite each other, their feet keeping time to the same rhythm, their hands clasped and their waists keeping up a dialogue with the oriental music, I can't tell you how happy I am. It's as if the whole world belonged to me . . . And I'm going to admit to a terrible thing, that the Sheikh would punish me for, with a thousand *falakas*, if he knew: at that moment I no longer doubt that paradise exists, or that there will be a better life after death . . .

Monsieur Marcel, alas! has not got his wife's carefree grace! He's grumpy and bad-tempered, always grousing. Juliette says he wasn't like that before; he's changed since his family ostracized them. His parents still refuse to recognize his marriage, even after Alain's birth. And that's how Monsieur Marcel has got embittered over the years. His life seems to be measured out by the number of glasses of beer or anisette that he serves in the course of the day.

63

And Juliette, just like any Muslim woman, busies herself with her domestic duties and bringing up her son. She's a good needle-woman and her machine is always humming as she makes dresses for the European wives in the village.

She and my mother are great friends, linked especially by a strange coincidence: as I've said, Alain and I were born on the same day and our first names both begin with the same letter. You might think that we'd have similar characters. But no, Alain is a dreamer, he always seems to be in the clouds. He puts on grown-up airs as if he was always keen to be taken seriously. His black curly hair forms a sort of crown for his delicate features, but his green eyes can flash thunder and lightning when he's angry.

I, on the other hand, am more determined and quicker off the mark, because my parents are always dinning into me, 'A man doesn't cry!. . . A man gives as good as he gets! . . . A man doesn't hang about the house all day! . . .' I've become impatient, always on the go, while my parents look on proudly, mistaking my restlessness for energy! I very early realized I had to show my teeth when I really dreamed of solitary walks in the country with a book under my arm, lying late in bed, enjoying the cool sheets, starting the day when the whim took me. My parents always say fortune awaits the early riser. . . Then I'm sorry for people who get rich this way! And I'm probably not intended to make a fortune as I delight in the afternoons when the sun is at its height, and later, when it begins to sink and night falls. The night is my favourite time, for then, if I keep my eyes open while all are sleeping, I live twice over . . .

Basically I hate arguments and dream of living happily and peacefully amongst those I love. But that isn't very manly!

Dachra . . . 20 September 1953

The village is dull at the moment; when the school closes and the children go back to town or to their *douars*, there's no more life here. Of course you're free to play anywhere and anyhow. But it's boring when you can't get a change of scene. Oh! if only I could go

64

and swim in the sea! It's true we have the *wadi* here, and my pals and I make the most of it, but it's not the same as the warm sand, the blue sea bordered with foam-capped waves . . . I day-dream and I miss school. It's funny perhaps, but when I'm sitting in my desk, with the teacher standing at the blackboard, I'm like a bird soaring above the earth. There's no more gravity, just this key to the world elsewhere, by which I can get to know or imagine it even if I can't actually see it. Every hour spent at school is one more step towards the conquest of future freedom. I know that so many unknown things lie hidden in the world and I certainly couldn't discover all of them, so I learn as much as I can.

At school, during break, when we all play together, there's not much difference between us. It goes without saying that afterwards, except for Alain, the European boys don't mix with us; they are barely allowed out of their enclosed gardens. We others run wild in the hills, taking pot-shots at birds with our catapults, while Rachid, that lanky chap who's shot up too fast, peers among the eucalyptus trees, keeping a sharp look-out for the local policeman and watching us pick up the birds as they fall out of the trees.

Alain never misses an opportunity of following me. We often hear Juliette calling him from her balcony. In desperation, she sends Salim, the boy who helps in the bar, to go and tell Alain it's teatime!

She mixes up Arabic and French, just like everybody else. For the most part we're not far away, just hidden in the shed in our courtyard. Alain pulls a face when he hears the word 'teatime', as he knows 'tea' will consist of the eternal dry bun with chocolate or bread and jam. He prefers a slice of our *galette*, with olive-oil, salt and pimentos, sometimes with the addition of fragrant, juicy black olives that have a delicious tang. For a change, we add fresh butter and honey to the slice of *galette*, while it's still hot.

Oh! the pleasure of those moments, squatting on our heels near my mother, waiting patiently while she kneads the dough for the *galette*. With her loose muslin sleeves rolled up and tied at her back, and the tattoos on her face glistening in the heat, she seems to us like a powerful, kindly genie, created for our happiness. . .

65

With a knowing wink at us, she takes the *galette* on to her lap, gives it a sharp tap in the middle with the edge of her hand and breaks off a piece for each of us. Alain shuts his eyes and chews every mouthful ecstatically.

Then, when Juliette doesn't see her son arrive, she knows where to find him. She hurries over to our house and apologizes to my mother for her son's bad manners.

'My God! I'm ashamed of this child! Sister Chérifa, do forgive him!'

And, quite naturally, she pulls up the sheepskin and squats down facing my mother and continues, 'This kid eats up all your *galettes*, but you ask for it! You've accustomed him to them yourself!'

My mother smiles and pushes the steaming coffee-pot towards her friend. Both women share a taste for good Turkish coffee, which to be just right must be made in a special metal pot which just holds enough for two, and served in tiny cups to which a bed of coffee-grounds clings. They consume it with the same concentrated enjoyment as we youngsters do our *galette*. Then my mother gives her a slice to take away for herself and Juliette thanks her and goes on gossiping.

I must add that Marcel doesn't look too kindly on this friendship between the two women and his only offspring and myself. He would have preferred his son to mix more with the schoolteacher's and the mayor's children. . . Needless to say, the relationship between him and my father is confined to the barest courtesies between neighbours. Basically, it's like with wars: they are decided and declared by governments, over the heads of the people who only want to understand and like each other.

One day Marcel came on Alain, barefoot, playing marbles with us. He fell into an almighty rage, seized his son by the ear and let fly against all us kids, heaping every insult in French and Arabic on us especially on me. 'Tykes! Riff-raff! *Shmaïts!* . . . ' We scurried off like rats, leaving our wretched pal red-faced and wincing under the torture inflicted by his father's fingers.

'And you, Ali! Just wait till I catch you!' he yelled. 'It's you who're leading him astray and trying to make him into a lout like yourself!' And there followed a repertoire of insults, of which Monsieur Marcel has an inimitable mastery.

In fact, Alain has always gone barefoot. When he's not with his parents he gives free rein to his delight in leaping around us in the dry grass. When he grazes his feet on sharp pebbles, he lets the blood dry in the sun without complaining.

At first I couldn't distinguish between a Jew and a French person. With Alain, the question never arises. Juliette behaves just like our women. She puts henna on her hair at the Turkish bath and removes the superfluous hair from her face, armpits, legs and arms with a sort of caramel preparation that she makes with my mother.

We've watched them mixing the sugar and lemon juice in a saucepan and stirring it continuously as it simmers. Then they take the golden-brown paste, draw it out and apply it to their skin. They often give us a bit to taste. It's delicious. They go through this performance before going to the *hammam*. And when Juliette's angry with her husband, she calls him 'the *Roumi*'. I wanted to get to the bottom of this problem and asked my mother, 'Why do Juliette and her family live like us and the others don't?'

My mother thought for a moment and then explained: 'The "others" as you call them, are stuck-up because they're Europeans. Juliette is Jewish. She was born here, she's like my sister, you understand? There are plenty of Jews who put on airs and think themselves superior because they're rich, but basically they know the others despise them. The ones, like Juliette, who aren't obsessed with making money, are more at home with us! That's all! Now, don't bother me any more! Alain is just like a brother, don't you ever forget, and don't go poisoning your mind with thoughts like that.'

The feast of Eïd el-Kebir is a great occasion. Sheep are sacrificed and everyone competes to provide the finest, the strongest ram. We kids couldn't care less if the animal is fat or not; it's the horns that interest us: the bigger and longer and more curly they are, the greater is our pride. We yell, 'I've got the *ragadin*!. . .' a word we'd invented, meaning the most dangerous.

When the sheep is slaughtered, every youngster grabs the horns and rushes into the street to show them off to the others, and compare them. The one who has the *ragadin* of the season becomes the local king and has certain rights.

For the feast, Monsieur Lavigne, the electrician, comes in the morning to collect the fresh blood from the slaughtered sheep, saying it's full of vitamins.

For a long time I was afraid of this old man. I imagined him drinking the blood in the evening, licking out the last drops from the bottom of the saucepan. I avoided passing his shop. So, when my father realized my fears, he began to threaten to take me to Monsieur Lavigne's if I didn't behave.

Then, once I did pass his shop window and in spite of myself I was attracted by the sight of a wireless set. It was magnificent! It seemed like a treasure chest to me and the little gilded knobs were like the eyes of a real person. I was fascinated by this wonderful box from which emerged music, words and laughter. Suddenly I heard a voice behind me saying, 'You look on top of the world, young man!' It was Madame Lavigne. She isn't often seen about, because of her rheumatism, so they say. She stays in a wheelchair in the garden behind the shop and only goes out for church on Sundays. She's not as old as all that, her hair hasn't turned grey and her face is scarcely wrinkled, but every step is an effort if she tries to walk.

'What is it that so attracts you in our window, son?

She approached me and stroked my hair, murmuring, 'Come now, you're not ashamed to tell me, are you?'

I stammered out, 'It's that set there . . .' pointing to the object of my admiration.

'Oh, I see! Haven't you got one at home?'

Then I thought she was going to make me a present of it, just like that, she seemed to be so affectionate towards me. But she went on, with a sort of surprised look in her eyes, 'Whose son are you? Oh, I know! You're the son of Abdelkader, the sailor, aren't you? How quickly you've grown!'

She smiled at me and lifted my chin to examine me more closely.

68

'What a dear little boy, you are! You don't look a bit like your strapping great father! You're not so crude. . . Do you work hard at school? How old are you?'

The lady was so kind that I fell for her little game. She asked me all sorts of questions, and though I was in a hurry to get away as I was going to be late for school, she seized my hand and drew me into the shop. I was afraid I'd meet her husband. Fortunately there was no one there except the apprentice, Hassan, buried in a tangle of wires coming from an apparatus similar to the one in the window. He didn't pay any attention to us. Madame Lavigne reached for a tin and offered it to me, smiling affectionately.

'Here are some biscuits for you to eat during recreation. But you haven't told me your name.'

'Ali,' I replied, not knowing what she was getting at. Everyone knows she adores children, because she's never had any of her own. She spends her time knitting clothes for the babies of her family or friends. She puts all her love into her knitting, probably to delude herself that the babies are really hers.

She smiled at me and I stood there clutching my tin of biscuits, not knowing what to say, worried at the thought that Monsieur Lavigne might appear at any moment.

'Wouldn't you like to become a radio-electrician later on, Ali? You could learn the trade from my husband . . . You would be paid. I know your father, he'd be pleased to know you were with us.'

Really, she was bent on keeping me there. I said, 'But I'm still at school!'

She shrugged her shoulders casually. 'I know you're at school! But after your Primary School Certificate, you'll want to learn a trade, won't you? You're not going to look after your uncle's sheep or become a grocer? You'll be better off with us! Think about it, son. And then you'll be able to come here every day after school and listen to the radio as much as you like!'

She touched on a tender spot, the sly woman, by mentioning the radio! She was surely thinking that I wouldn't be able to resist the prospect of finally getting my hands on the object of my dreams . . . But if the gentle Madame Lavigne had only known the horror I had of her husband, drinking sheep's blood, and my fear that he might perhaps drink mine!

So these are the people who interest most of us.

Dachra . . . 22 September 1953 . . . It is 2 o'clock . . .

Yesterday there was a wedding in the family. We youngsters raided the goodies in the kitchen. The women were chattering away like magpies, surrounded by their cooking pots, and didn't pay any attention to us. We guzzled so many sweets and cakes and so much couscous and meat that we made ourselves sick. I am now in bed with a scarf tied round my head in which my mother has placed slices of lemon that she changes every hour. It's cool and does me good. But she forces me to drink a horrible infusion of thyme which is supposed to cure this sort of bilious attack. My parents think I'm sleeping. They are having a siesta themselves, as it's not only very hot outside, but they are tired after their late night at the wedding.

I'd like to talk about Abdi, the 'big booby', who's the leader of our village gang. He organizes all sorts of pranks, and particularly the worst one, for which I got the biggest hiding of my life, although my father hates to beat me, usually being content to shout and threaten me with this sandal. The game is to see how much in the way of sweets and lemonade we can wangle out of the Mozabite and stuff ourselves with.

This is how we go about it: Abdi chooses boys with nice innocent faces, like Abbas and me (according to Abdi I look the well-bred sort). Then Slimane, Abbas and I all go to the Mozabite's shop which has a huge counter with rows of sacks filled with toffees, chewing-gum, lollipops, sugared-almonds, etc. Behind this display there's a table on which the bottles of lemonade stand, then against the walls are shelves where the different footstuffs are arranged. At the back of the shop, behind a dirty curtain, or perhaps the dirty grey is its natural colour!

70

anyway, there are sacks of semolina, flour, barrels of oil and butter. This is just to show that we know the place and where everything is kept.

So we turn up with a shopping list for the errands we are supposed to be doing for our parents. It's agreed that Abdi will drop in later. I don't do the talking as Saïd, the shopkeeper, knows that my dad stocks these provisions himself. Slimane begins: 'Good morning, Si Saïd! I need five kilos of granulated sugar.' The man weighs out the heap of sugar, while Slimane, looking as if butter wouldn't melt in his mouth, dips his hand in the sack of sweets.

'Put a couple of dozen sweets on the bill, as well . . . Then, I want five kilos of coffee . . .'

The shopkeeper and his brother, who acts as his assistant – everyone knows the Mozabites always work as a family – are both busy with the orders. At that very moment Abdi comes in to buy a candle, for example, and chats to us while waiting to be served.

Slimane orders three bottles of lemonade. Si Saïd takes the tops off. While we drink them and chew the sugared almonds, the poor man busies himself with the numerous items which Slimane orders, adding anything that comes into his head: 'Oh! and two kilos of chick-peas . . . ' He dips his hand into the sack of peanuts and adds for our benefit, 'Eat up, they're good for your health . . .' He winks at us, knowingly. We get the message.

'Give us four hundred grammes of shelled nuts . . .' And this time he murmurs audibly, 'They'll make your willy grow!'

We stuff ourselves with all these goodies while Si Saïd heaps up the packets as fast as he can weigh out the orders. Slimane doesn't give him a minute's respite until the propitious moment when he sends him to the back of the shop. When he's sure that we've stuffed our pockets and had enough to drink, he gives his final order: 'And lastly, I want three litres of oil and ten kilos of semolina . . .'

'You must be having quite a party, son!' the good man exclaims in astonishment, and the wily Slimane replies, 'It'll soon be Eïd, and my mother wants to get her supplies in well in time to make her cake.'

'She's very sensible; later on it's difficult to get your cakes baked properly at the baker's as so many people want to use his oven!'

It takes a long time to weigh out ten kilos of semolina and Si Saïd calls his brother into the storeroom to help him.

Once we are alone, we help ourselves to the chocolates and make off as fast as we can to the clearing behind Monsieur Roumière's field, which is an ideal place for our feast and where we're out of Si Saïd's sight. You can imagine what ensued, dear diary, Si Saïd rushing out of his door, tearing off his tarboosh and yelling, 'Dogs! Thieves! I'll let their fathers know! . . .'

Naturally, the parents are appalled, but each one accuses the others' sons. As for paying, it's difficult to assess the individual responsibilities, so they promise to make amends by administering a colossal thrashing to each of their layabout offsprings.

The hiding is carried out on our return to the fold! The next day we each compare our weals. But Abdi, the so-called big booby, is miraculously unaffected, as there is no evidence against him. He's the smart one, is Abdi, and we are the morons . . . When we point out that he's got off scot-free, he laughs and says, 'You're the ones Si Saïd saw, not me! He noticed I wasn't with you. And anyway, you had a good blow-out, thanks to my idea, so what are you complaining about!'

After punishing me, my father began to lecture me on the dangers behind the intrigues of depraved boys, as he calls them.

'Let this be a lesson to you in future, my boy! You tell me it was Abdi's idea, you saw that he's cleverer than the rest of you . . . In life there will always be folk like him, wolves that want to corrupt you, they will lead you into evil by flattery, by offering you an easy way into temporary pleasures, in order to get a better hold on you, the better to drag you into the mire, with the ulterior motive of taking what belongs to you . . . Always beware and be on your guard against people who amuse you and make you laugh!'

I didn't understand everything he was saying, as my father philosophizes a great deal on people's behaviour. But I've made a note of this sentence and perhaps it will be clear to me when I'm older.

And you, dear diary, please don't think we're a lot of bandits! It was only meant for a joke!

In class, Abdi the dunce sucks up to the teacher. He sits right in front, ready to dance attendance on him. If the teacher runs out of cigarettes, Abdi offers to go and buy some for him. He collects the exercise books, cleans the blackboard, brushes the chalk off the master's overcoat at the end of every lesson. When the latter's wife needs some domestic jobs done, like getting wood for the fire, she always asks Abdi. For this reason, he's unpopular with the other pupils who are a bit afraid of him.

Someone quite different is Yussef, mother's great-nephew, whom I've not yet mentioned. He's a loner, and very uncouth. He can't open his mouth without uttering some obscenity. He's like that, and neither beating by his parents or punishment by the Sheikh has managed to correct him. He's older than me but is in my class, as he had to repeat a year. He sits at the back and tries his best not to be noticed, which suits the teacher, Monsieur Durand. Yussef has the same gangling figure as Abdi, but has a very different character. He's an average pupil, quite intelligent, but bone idle and extremely proud.

Yussef and the teacher can't stand each other. When the latter does happen to address him, you can sense the angry tension in his voice.

A few days before the holidays we had to hand in an exercise on the conjugation of irregular verbs, as the conscientious M. Durand permitted no slacking off at the end of term . . .

Abdi goes round to collect the homework from all the boys, but when he gets to Yussef he sees nothing on his desk.

'Where's your exercise?' he asks, adopting a peremptory tone that puts Yussef's back up and to which he replies, 'Up your arse!'

Abdi flushes and hisses, 'You'll have to reckon with Monsieur Durand, you idiot! You're going to cop it!'

They continue to exchange insults and Yussef clenches his fists and spits right on Abdi's chin.

At this stage they attract the master's attention. 'What's going on there at the back?' he shouts.

The whole class falls totally silent. Abdi howls, 'Sir! It's

Yussef! He hasn't got his homework. And he's insulted me,' he whines. 'Look! he spat at me!'

'Oh! it's you again, trying to be clever!' Monsieur Durand, who has a very quick temper, is crimson with fury. 'Come here!' he thunders, his voice not auguring much good for Yussef. Our classmate gets up and ambles up to the front desk as if he had all eternity in front of him. At fourteen he's as tall as the teacher, who is no midget! Yussef stoops a bit from having shot up too fast, according to his mother. Compared with us, he's a giant.

So our Yussef shambles along to the teacher who's getting more and more worked up.

'Get a move on, you blockhead!'

Abdi gives a nasty smile.

'Where's your homework?'

Monsieur Durand stands on his platform, a stony-hearted judge, looking Yussef angrily up and down.

'Haven't got it . . .' Yussef gulps and lowers his head like a bull about to charge.

'What d'you mean, you haven't got it? Are you trying to make a fool of me? And where's your book of exercises?'

Yussef has clearly had enough. He sighs, shrugs his shoulders and says softly, 'Sir, I forgot to do the homework, that's all.'

'That's all?' sneers the master. 'You think it's as simple as that! The gentleman has forgotten, that's all . . .' he mimics. So what do you come to school for? To waste our time, and to insult your friend into the bargain!'

Yussef's patience is now exhausted. He shouts, 'That sneak is no friend of mine!'

Monsieur Durand has never known such scandalous defiance. He roars, 'You'll apologize to Abdi immediately!'

For a moment a stunned silence falls on the class. None of us will ever forget this moment.

'No, Sir!'

'What? You refuse? . . . You will apologize, I say!'

Yussef maintains his obstinate silence; he does not look up but the sweat can be seen trickling down his forehead. Suddenly, out of the blue, an arm swings out and lands a clout across the boy's face. Instinctively, he catches hold of the master's hand and, looking him full in the eye, exclaims, audibly, '*Attaï*!'

This is the worst insult you can offer a man. It's a word we use when we're angry, as other people might call each other idiots! But said in this way by Yussef, the term is one of the utmost contempt. He has called the master a pederast.

Monsieur Durand chokes. 'What? *Attaï*? You think I don't know what that means . . . Me . . . Me! *Attaï*? You'll see . . .'

Yussef is already at the door, he turns round and calmly and derisively retorts, 'Go and piss in the street for all I care!'

That's the traditional expression to denote the contempt with which one consider's an enemy's threats. The teacher is on the verge of an apoplectic fit. He threatens, 'You'll be expelled, you lout! If I have anything to do with it, you won't go around acting the tough guy here much longer . . . You'll be packed off to a borstal . . .'

So Yussef helped us get our own back for all the injustices we suffer at the hands of this bad-tempered brute who puts the fear of God into us, a man with a permanent chip on his shoulder who makes the classroom into a torture chamber. The head was summoned. There were long discussions. The school was in a state of revolt for several days.

We subsequently heard that our classmate had in fact been expelled. For all that his father, Uncle Driss, spent hours cooling his heels outside the headmaster's office, nobody would see him, Monsieur Durand carried out his threat. He moved heaven and earth until he managed to get Yussef sent to a reformatory.

One morning the police turned up at his father's house, asking for the boy. Yussef was in the yard, buried as usual in his comics – Butch Cassidy, Kit Carson, Mickey Mouse – which he bought half-price from the European boys. He was mad about adventure stories. The police explained to the parents that they had to take the boy to the borstal situated to the north-east of the town of Baladia. They aren't rich, and a boy who's struck a European, as the schoolmaster claimed, is considered a delinquent. However, the police allowed the father to accompany him.

And Abdi wasn't very proud of himself! For a long time none of the gang would speak to him.

Yussef was the second kid in the village to be shut up like this. A couple of years ago it happened to Francis, the Tagliotas' son, who's been in that place ever since, only allowed home for a few days sometimes during the holidays. Then he stays indoors the whole time, never coming into the village. In fact I saw him yesterday morning.

He watches us enviously when a group of us pass his father's shop. He looks a likeable kid, with his blue eyes and mop of corn-coloured hair.

His is a sad story, which I'll tell to complete my memories and prevent them from fading. After all he belongs to the village of Dachra, where he saw the light of day like any one of us . . .

Francis's mother died when he was quite small. She was an Alsacian, hard-working and a good soul. His father remarries. Angèle, his second wife, is a fat, hairy woman and a boozer into the bargain. She used to spend her time drinking and complaining about Francis. Monsieur Tagliota is rather a spineless character. It was his first wife's idea to open the grocery shop. After that, old man Tagliota and Angèle just managed to eke out a living on what the business brought in, and Francis grew up in the flat above the shop, continually beaten by Angèle and scolded by his father. The lad was always on the balcony, looking like a prisoner behind the iron railings, while his father worked downstairs and his stepmother slept off her hangovers.

At school he had no friends. Neither did Angèle, who's very unsociable, speaking to no one except Madame Lavigne, who between ourselves is rather eccentric and loves interfering in other people's lives. Soon Francis distinguished himself by a talent for thieving, according to his stepmother, at least . . . I never knew him personally, but his story is still told in both European and Muslim homes.

When he was ten, Francis acted as a choirboy; he was so good-looking and his face was so innocent that the scarlet cassock and pretty white ruffled cape suited him better than any other European child. The priest was very proud of him and possibly hoped that Francis would in this way get over his bad habits.

Suddenly, one day, the little church community was in an uproar! The pair of silver candlesticks from the sacristy had disappeared. The priest questioned all his flock, in vain! No one knew of their whereabouts. It was the sacrilege that scandalized the pious folk more than the value of the stolen objects.

A month later they turned up. The doctor's wife had gone into town to look for copper articles in the market and lighted on an old antiques merchant on whose stall she immediately recognized the candlesticks from the Dachra church. Naurally she bought them and asked the man where they'd come from. He told her that he'd got them from a little fair-haired boy.

That's how Francis's theft was discovered. My opinion is that he acted not so much for the money, but as a gesture of revolt and to get his own back on all the people who comfortably pray to their God, without any thought for the drama of a lonely little boy living in their midst.

The priest lamented, 'Francis! Good heaven! Such a pious little boy! The best behaved of all my choirboys! He even said he wanted to take holy orders!'

Naturally there was a general outcry in the Tagliota home. Angèle won the day and had him sent to a borstal.

We were very upset when we heard this story. So, when he's here and we see him in the distance in the shop, we wave to him to show our friendly feelings, and he replies with a timid smile.

We take every opportunity of making Angèle's life a misery. If she goes out to get a breath of fresh air in the square behind the church, we manage to be a nuisance, either throwing stones at her or letting loose a cat with a pin in its tail which gets mad and runs between her legs, while she chases us with her umbrella that she always carries to support her unsteady gait.

Perhaps Yussef will meet Francis now in that reform-school.

Dear diary, I have recounted to you the lives of the principal inhabitants of our village. You know them all, now. For me they form an enormous multicoloured mosaic, making Dachra a village dear to me, where its children will always share common memories, come what may.

October is upon us, bringing the beginning of the school year. I shall be going into the final class. My only consolation is that we shall no longer have the irascible Monsieur Durand. The headmaster will be teaching us himself. He's the one who prepares pupils for the Primary School Certificate. He's not as irritable as our previous mentor. He can control the class without shouting, although, according to pals who've been in his class, he's cold and sarcastic, with the habit of pinching a misbehaving boy's ears till they bleed. Every teacher's got his own particular form of punishment. Some of them hit us across the hands with a ruler, others rely on a few kicks on our backside, while the ones who are too lazy to exert themselves, make boys kneel down with their hands up until the end of the lesson. This is the punishment we dread the most, as it's very painful to remain kneeling on the ice-cold floor with your arms in the air.

Some teachers prefer mental torture: they punish a pupil by making him wear a pair of ass's ears made out of paper, tied behind his head with string. He has to wear this badge of disgrace the whole day, right through recreation and then at lunchtime go home and back through the village with it.

We particularly dread this punishment, and the class of the ingenious teacher who devised it has the best discipline in the whole school. As for the head, he has the knack of twisting the lobe of an ear until the boy goes purple in the face! The pain is terrible as he calmly digs his nails into one's flesh, smiling his sarcastic smile all the time. The wretched boys who have experienced this torture say that everything begins to swim in front of their eyes, the pain drills into their head like red-hot needles. I know what to expect, and from now on I shall do everything possible not to have to endure that torment. . .

Alain is back from the city to collect his things. He came last Sunday to say goodbye. He asked me if I'd started keeping my diary. I replied, 'Not yet.' If he only knew how many pages I've blackened! You see, dear diary, I didn't dare tell him what bliss it is to me to confide in you, and I'm not keen to betray the secret that links me to your pages. But it was hard, all the same, to resist the pleasure of showing Alain the nice drawings which adorn them.

My mother sent me to the Turkish bath in preparation for the new term and my father has bought me a new satchel, as my old one, which I've had for three years, was falling to pieces. My cousin Meriem has been creeping around me like an inquisitive mouse.

She cooed with admiration over my school things, and got on my nerves with her exclamations of 'Oh! How I'd like to go to school! How I'd love to learn to read! You're so lucky to be a boy . . . We poor women have no luck!'

I lost my temper and shouted at her that it wasn't my fault if her father wanted to keep her at home.

To come back to the matter of the school, I must explain that we are all boys. The few European girls are in a separate class and their playground is divided from ours by an iron railing. As you may imagine, we're not interested in these girls. However, there is one we quite like, Lydia, Pierre's sister. They are the children of the cantankerous Monsieur Durand. Pierre is a stupid, pretentious oaf, but his sister, who's younger than him, is sensitive, gentle and very nice. She's always so neat, she looks as if she's come out of a band-box. She's like a flower with her short skirt, gathered in at the waist. Her chestnut hair is tied up with pink or red ribbons, in petal-like bows. During recreation she breaks away from the other girls and comes to glue her face to the railing, pensively watching us race about our playground, shouting. Once Alain went over to her and I saw them chatting. Suddenly Pierre tore over to them like a wild beast, yelling, 'I forbid you to speak to my sister! . . .'

Alain retorted roughly and a fight broke out with Lydia looking on horrified. In spite of her brother's tough airs Lydia still finds an opportunity of talking to us. She often brings us toffees and swops comics with us. The other girls, who are more stuck-up, tease her about her wish to be friends with boys – and what boys! A noisy, ill-bred, good-for-nothing lot! . . .

And another curious character! My cousin . . . Meriem, She told me one day, with a mixture of pride and defiance, that she is

79

Lydia's friend. How on earth did they get to know each other, since my cousin doesn't go to school? Then one day Meriem confided in me that once, when she was doing errands, she saw the girls in the playground, and as she is deeply attracted, fascinated even, by the school, she stopped to gaze at these privileged creatures. She clung to the railings separating the playground from the yard, forgetting the basket at her feet, lost in a mixture of resentment, regrets and rebellion . . . and her eyes and Lydia's met. The latter came over quite spontaneously to talk to her.

And so they got into the habit of chatting until my cousin was veiled and kept at home and Lydia left to go to high school in the city. At the age of eleven, the one girl was to prepare herself to fulfil her destined role as a wife, the other to organize and strengthen her own freedom . . .

Meriem has retained an affectionate memory of this friendship, filled with nostalgia. From time to time she jibs at the injustice which makes her live as a prisoner in her parents' home. She often says, 'Their courtyard is a prison, domestic work is forced labour!'

So, she relies on me to know what happens in the outside world.

But she irritates me, and frightens me a little. I find her disconcerting, and I don't like things I can't understand. My schoolfriends who've got sisters avoid talking to them in the street, as if they were ashamed of them. If one of the girls passes on the way to do some shopping, her brother or her cousin calls to her roughly, to show he's the master: 'What are you doing out in the street? Get back home immediately or I'll bash your head in!'

But sometimes the girl answers back without mincing her words: 'Who d'you think you are, you little shit? At least I help with the shopping, I don't spend my time loafing about like you, scratching my fleas! Just get your numbskull over here and we'll see who'll bash whose head in!'

The Dachra girls are terrible! Their brothers may well act the tough guy, but they don't talk so big when the girls show their claws.

Our lives are adapted to every season of the year. During

80

Ramadan or the Eïd festivities, girls and boys gather together in the evening to dance and sing and listen to the wonderful tales told by the grandmothers. The astonishing thing is that I can't remember the names of my girl-cousins. I can't distinguish one from another, except for Meriem, who, I have to say, is different from the rest. And she's always barging into our house, ostensibly to help my mother, bothering me with her endless chatter.

With her laughing black eyes, her funny little snub nose, and her way of looking at me ironically out of the corner of her eyes, she always disconcerts me. To tell the truth, Meriem is quite unpredictable . . . She looks fragile, delicate and as highly-strung as a gazelle, as her parents say, but in fact she can get quite violent and do something stupid when she's angry; for example I've seen her get into a rage and smash a cooking-pot. She's a mixture of deliberation and recklessness; one day she lowers her eyes respectfully before older people, the next she doesn't hesitate to answer her father back cheekily. She's as fickle as a firefly, but full of charm and everyone loves her and easily forgives her lack of discipline. One day she announced to me, as seriously as anything, 'When we're grown up, you and I will get married . . . You'll have a good trade and you'll take me to live in the town.' I was flabbergasted at this outspokenness, so unusual in girls of our family, but she continued calmly, 'We shan't live here, shall we Ali?'

I was dumb-struck. She'd decided! . . . She'd chosen . . . What was the world coming to? I stared at her as if I was seeing her for the first time. I felt I was suffocating, she frightened me as if she was going to shut me up in a cage. Her words inspired me with a terrible desire to run away. Meriem represents a danger, an obscure inexplicable threat. She was going to steal my dreams of freedom . . . My diary . . . My friends . . . My games . . . I recoiled instinctively: 'Go away! Don't ever say that again, you're mad and impertinent!'

She burst out laughing. 'Are you ashamed? All cousins intermarry, and I've chosen to marry you, that's all!'

I ran out of the room into the yard, under my mother's bewildered gaze.

5

The two men left the keeper's house very early the next morning. Once back safely in the Béni-Ramassés district they went straight to bed without exchanging a word. Ali woke up about four in the afternoon, with a dry mouth and stiffness in his limbs. He had no idea of the time or place. He sat up and saw that Tahar was not there. The door of the shanty was ajar. He glanced at the alarm-clock. Had he slept so long?

Then he remembered the execution in the forest . . . The sinister hole . . . His terror. The memory of all the events of the previous night filled him with mortification. He told himself he had not been equal to the task: his nerve had given way and now Tahar would never trust him again. He wondered what penalty he must expect for showing himself unworthy of a *fidaï*, for not acting like a man . . . Wide awake now, he got up and went to wash.

'So, up at last!' Tahar called to him cheerily.

Ali turned round and saw his companion standing calmly in the doorway, his solid form silhouetted against the light. He shuddered inwardly, remembering how Tahar's smile could harbour a lethal threat.

For the moment, Tahar was gazing at him quizzically. He put down a basket of provisions on the table.

'How do you always manage to appear so silently?'

Tahar laughed softly, 'I fly, the better to catch little boys napping!'

Ali was once more under the spell of Tahar's charm. He tried not to dwell on the image of the man ruthlessly administering summary justice whom he had discovered the previous night, and only recall his friend's kindly, humorous smile. He shivered again at the macabre memory. Would he never forget this?

He seized the towel and scrubbed his face as if to wipe away his agitation. Tahar noticed the fleeting shadow pass over his young friend's features and said gaily, 'I've brought some food. This evening we're to meet at the Prof's house. We're invited to a little party to celebrate his birthday.'

'Isn't this Monsieur Kimper ever bothered by the police? It seems strange to me that he entertains so many people, especially Muslims, without his neighbours gossiping . . .'

Tahar teased him about his habit of asking endless questions. He explained that the professor was engaged in the struggle and the Brothers trusted him. At first his friends had thought his interest in the 'natives' to be one of the eccentricities of a lonely and charitable old man. But in recent years his activities had aroused the suspicions of the authorities. They kept a discreet eye on him, without collecting sufficient evidence to arrest him. On the other hand they were afraid of the professor's many Parisian contacts: journalists, deputies and even friends in the present government. Besides, everyone knew that the young people who gathered at his house were either his pupils needing advice, or colleagues with a passion for music and literature. This information left Ali a little sceptical. He couldn't understand a man risking his safety for a cause which was not his own. Ali was too young and still suffering from the shock of discovering his own relatives' greed when his parents died. Suddenly, out of the blue, he asked, 'What do you live on, Tahar? . . . Was your mother really a European?'

'My boy, if you go on like this,' Tahar said, wagging his finger at him, 'I'll be forced to think you're grassing for the Military Intelligence! But I'll satisfy your curiosity. My mother is still alive; she's a tough village warrior woman, a typical *Chaouïa*. She was born among the Nememcha, those intrepid horsemen caring as much about the preservation of their folklore as they do about their mounts. One day perhaps, the story of this extraordinary tribe will be told at length . . . But you must realize that they form part of the real strength of Algeria. Imagine three thousand

83

armed, trained, disciplined *Chaouïas,* and you can be sure Algeria is in good hands.'

Ali interrupted him with a laugh, 'You exaggerate! Three thousand . . . they're not the only ones, surely . . .'

Tahar grew serious and screwed up his eyes as he was wont to do when he was about to reveal his deepest feelings.

'Yes, there are others . . . But it is important to realize that such people offer a potential that we must learn to use to enhance the human resources of the country . . . Later, when this torment is behind us and we think of nothing but programming, restructuring, profit-making, etc., I'm afraid the tribes will be scattered and these people will lose their individual personalities as they are swallowed up by the unfeeling society of the cities. They have incomparable gifts for improvising poems, inspired by love or hatred . . . I can see myself as a small boy, back there, sitting round the fire at night, listening to the fantastic legends of our ancestors and songs both sad and merry . . . The women are free back there, they don't hide from the men, they live like them, shouldering the same responsibilities, beside them in peace and war . . . My work ? I'm employed at the abattoir. I help slaughter animals! My bosses think a lot of me; they appreciate my strength and the fact that I keep my mouth shut. I do my job correctly, I don't argue and never ask for a rise. So I've got access to certain houses, including Monsieur Kimper's, where I deliver meat. My bosses who come from Brittany like him send him the best cuts. I've also frequently had the opportunity of delivering sheep for the *méchoui* to Monsieur Dubois, the Deputy Prefect . . . That's how I know so many people! . . . Are you satisfied now, nosy parker?' he concluded with a flourish, like an actor finishing his big speech.

The professor's dozen or so guests could barely fit into his drawing-room. They had already eaten the birthday cake and were now busily discussing the play they had put on the previous evening, the 14 July, at the municipal theatre, to celebrate the national holiday and the end of the school year. They were clearly still excited about it. It had been a great success with the audience, mainly composed of pupils and their parents, teachers and local

VIPs. Gradually the drawing-room emptied. The guests said goodbye to the professor, without noticing the two new arrivals. One girl remained behind. She came over to Si Salah and said a few words to him looking up at him rather sadly. Her face wore a prematurely bitter expression. Ali watched her from the back of the room. She seemed tall, then he realized that he got this impression because she was standing next to Si Salah who was of average height only and very slim. Ali thought he had seldom seen such a lovely girl. She looked like the photographs of fashion models he had seen in magazines. Her ease of movement, her slender figure, her natural elegance, as if to the manner born, also reminded him of someone . . . He racked his brain: who did she resemble? . . .

The young man got up and moved over to their group. He heard the girl say, 'I can't get over my stupidity yesterday, during the show. When I saw all my friends, my family and teachers in front of me in the theatre, I lost my head. I dried up . . . And here am I hoping to become an actress later on . . .'

'Rubbish! That's nothing!' Si Salah replied. 'It's too soon to get disheartened. First do as your parents want and pass your *bachot*; then when you're more mature you'll have more self-control and I can see you becoming our greatest actress!'

The girl smiled. She turned round and noticed Tahar just behind her. He had his hands in his pockets and was watching her with rapt attention. She exclaimed happily, 'Oh hello, Tahar! I didn't see you come in.'

As she held out her hand her face had lost all trace of sadness. She was clearly delighted to see him.

'Really! This is the second time today I've been taken for a ghost! Come, Fella, I must introduce you to my cousin Ali who's recently arrived from up country.'

'Hello, Ali,' the girl said softly.

'Ali, this is Fella, Mounir's sister.'

The young man realized why he thought he recognized the girl. Her resemblance to her brother was striking.

Tahar continued, 'She's still at high school but she's mad about the theatre! One day she'll be the star of the Algerian stage!'

85

Ali gazed at the girl's face as Tahar spoke. He glimpsed a new horizon full of promise . . . He realized that everyone involved in the struggle was already training for the future, according to their vocation. Tahar, in his present existence, had chosen to kill, so that he could contribute, as he said, to the purification of the society of tomorrow . . . Si Salah will perhaps fight for the elimination of illiteracy among our children; Mounir is confident of wresting a place for himself, by tooth and claw, like the ambitious Young Turk he is; Monsieur Kimper is helping to attack injustice by proclaiming all peoples' sacred right to independence; if poor old Ramdane survived this war he would bring a brain damaged and clouded by torture . . . but he would find his reincarnation in the dignity of the children of a country finally emerging from shame. If Fella's dream was realized, she would make her début on the stage as a woman with a thousand faces, immortal, full of love for her country and for all those who fight for the ideal of liberty . . And Ali himself? What would he contribute? 'Tomorrow? Shall I see tomorrow?' he wondered. 'For the moment I am only a raw recruit who rejects doubt and believes only in victory!'

Fella noticed Ali's youthful face and his absent-minded look as he gazed into the distance, looking right through her as if she were a cloud lost in the immensity of the sky. Disturbed by this vacant look, the girl shivered and was eager to leave.

'I have to go now,' she said softly as if afraid to disturb Ali in his mysterious daydream.

She said goodbye to the two men and hurried out without looking back. Ali did not notice her departure till the door slammed behind her. 'Has she gone?' he asked Tahar.

'Yes, while you were asleep!'

'What a pity! She'll think me churlish,' the young man murmured, clearly upset.

Si Salah sat down with a sigh. He lit a cigarette and seemed to be lost in contemplation of the smoke rings. As usual, the professor was busying himself with his pipe.

'Everything go off all right?' Si Salah asked.

'OK,' Tahar replied. 'Chance took a hand once more,'

'You didn't follow the normal procedure, so what happened? And what was the other one doing there?'

Ali instinctively looked down to hide his discomfort. He heard Tahar reply casually, lying to cover up his blunder, 'Chance intervened, as I told you, and then we were short of time.'

Ali knew that if Tahar had mentioned his sentimental, confused behaviour, Si Salah or the heads of the organization would not have forgiven him . . . What would the penalty have been? They would never have trusted him again to take part in a large-scale mission . . . Ali was filled with affectionate gratitude to Tahar.

Tahar went on. 'As for Cantini, heaven dropped him into our laps. I spun him a yarn and he insisted on tagging on to us and Dalila. It was a heaven-sent opportunity . . . We killed two birds with one stone . . .'

Si Salah made no further comment on the circumstances of the double execution, but continued, 'I've just come from the Rosiers district . . . The bodies were discovered by a patrol of *goumiers* on their way for their usual exercises. What a panic! A deputy-superintendant and, what's worse, that woman! . . . Naturally they cordoned off the whole district immediately and began their endless interrogations, whereas it goes without saying that the ones responsible for the attack couldn't be locals. Nevertheless, they're making a big show of strength with street patrols, jeeps and sentinels stationed in front of houses, Moorish cafés and at street corners. That's the news I got this morning . . .'

Si Salah kept silent for a moment, then, noticing that Monsieur Kimper was no longer in the room, said, 'He wants us to stay for dinner. I think he's busy warming up Khéïra's couscous. Ali, you can go and help him!' Then he added with a smile, 'Since you'll be living here from now on!'

'Here?' Ali was intrigued, not understanding what was going on.

'Go along! We'll explain to you later!'

When they'd finished dinner, they cleared the table, one collecting the plates, the second one doing the washing-up, while the third one made the coffee and the professor tidied up the drawing-room.

'Well, Ali! Are you pleased to be staying with me?' he asked.

The young man nodded rather doubtfully. He preferred to let them do the explaining.

'Tomorrow I'll introduce you to our local police super-intendant . . .'

'At the police station?' Ali was startled.

'Take it easy, Ali!' the professor interrupted. 'Let me finish. The superintendant in question is a decent chap. I phoned him to tell him I'd engaged a gardener who'd also be my watchman. He knows I live alone in this big house . . . I also told him that you were my daily woman Khéïra's cousin; he knows her as she used to work for him. Naturally I told him you'd had a bit of trouble in your village and had come to look for work in town. As you probably know, since the recent events one has to declare to the local police station every person living in one's house, so I have to register you as my employee, that's all!'

Si Salah asked, 'What did the super reply?'

'Oh! You'll be amused! "My dear fellow, aren't you afraid he'll cut your throat?" . . . I burst out laughing, and so did he eventually, thinking it a good joke, and he made me promise to call in at his office with "my protégé". We are on very good terms. He considers me an eccentric old man and I'm in his good books, so to speak. In spite of your little incident with the foreman, your papers will be in order and you'll be ready to face all the inevitable checks . . .'

Ali was lost in admiration at the way they had organized everything without even consulting him. Nevertheless, he enquired anxiously, 'So I'm to spend my time gardening? Looking after the house? But that's not what I wanted . . .'

The three men silently exchanged glances, Si Salah intervened, in a kindly voice, to reassure the youngster whom he sensed to be suddenly antagonized, suspicious and about to fly off the handle. 'Come, Ali! Everything in good time. For the time being, it's better you lie low and you must have a job and a fixed address.

You can be picked up at any moment for vagrancy. To be able to do anything concrete, you must be part of the crowd.'

The evening passed in an atmosphere of warm friendship. They chatted about everything, especially about the newspapers . . .

La Depêche de L'Est reported that twenty rebels had been killed in the course of a skirmish in Bélia . . . Ammunition had been abandoned on the spot . . . Five of the rebel leaders had been taken prisoner . . . Then, according to the journalist, a policeman had been shot near the port and the author of the attack had been captured. All these figures reported by the newspapers almost made one believe that, with the rapid increase in those killed and arrested, there would soon be no resisters left; no more armed revolt, no more threats to the goose with the golden eggs . . . But the people had learned to read between the lines, drawing their own conclusions from these falsely optimistic reports, knowing in general that the 'rebels' in question were in fact innocent people who had nothing to do with the action, and that the 'author' of the attack was more often than not a passer-by who had lost his head and made off like everyone else at the sound of shots. The soldiers would catch him and he would be labelled the culprit, even the 'big chief'. In this way many people became involuntary 'heroes'. There were often poor fellows among the prisoners filling the camps, who had landed there by a tragic mistake. The genuine ones were executed on the spot, at the beginning of the events.

After the initial outbreaks of resistance in the rural areas, there was a succession of partisan attacks in towns.

Life was calm on the surface. Europeans and Muslims rubbed shoulders with expressions of incredulous astonishment, as if to say, 'After all, that rumour from the hills was a false alarm. The order of things could not change . . .' But when towns were affected by the attacks, then the Europeans' confidence began to be shaken. Suspicion and fear were born, transforming neighbours and even passers-by into possible murderers.

The Muslims, for their part, were caught between the devil and the deep: they had to comply with all the orders of the army of occupation while vying with each other in a show of militancy for the benefit of the patriots . . . Some of the men went off into the hills, others risked their lives in the cities, and the shrewd ones intrigued. Mothers stayed at home looking after their families and praying; and girls were no longer carefree but dreamed of joining in the fight for freedom.

There were signs that the armed struggle was meeting little resistance and increasing its effectiveness. Ambushes were methodically laid. Powerful men, previously considered to be 'sacrosanct', were assassinated in the very centre of the cities, traitors were tracked down and ruthlessly executed. This daring inspired pride in the people who no longer doubted the final victory.

An insidious fear sneaked through the cities . . . There was danger everywhere: in the rustle of leaves, a dog barking, a window rattling, the sound of whispering. Was it the paratroopers? The moujahidine? . . .

About the same time a strange exodus began. The Muslims who could afford it started to leave the country, to protect their families and, above all, their interests. They settled in Tunisia or in Morocco, or on the salubrious banks of Lake Geneva or in the peaceful Parisian suburbs . . . Of course, from there they were transformed overnight into militant supporters of the cause . . .

The others, the mass of impoverished Muslims, faced arrest, torture and a variety of humiliations. Even those on both sides who did not yet understand what this tragedy was about, paid their tribute to fear . . .

The entire population, fenced in by war, learned to tread the hard, blood-stained path of heroism. Even the humble passer-by, captured by mistake, was in fact a martyr writing a new chapter in the bloody pages of history.

For the Europeans – since the 'French' of Algeria were for the most part people who had come from every corner of Europe – the same tragedy was being enacted, from their point of view. Some of them departed for 'home', where in fact they had no roots. The others held on pathetically. Even in their blindness, their deadly hatred of 'the Arab' was not without some reminder of a hopeless love. They would vie with each other in sacrificing their lives for this land which is as passionate as a woman.

6

Dachra . . . 2 March 1954 . . . 11.00 p.m.

It's a funny thing to admit, but I've felt more sure of myself since I've had this diary. I'm no longer afraid of the dark; on the contrary, the night has become my friend and accomplice, whereas previously, when it was time to go to bed, I felt I was about to take up arms against a sea of perils waiting to ambush me in the dark.

This all began at the age of three, when my father decided that I was big enough to sleep by myself. The sitting-room-dining-room, furnished with a sideboard, mattresses piled up around the walls, and a large, low table in the middle of the room, became my bedroom, and the scene of my nightmares. What is more, it is separated from my parents' room by the courtyard, so that I was left quite alone from far too young an age!

The first few nights my mother was allowed to stay with me and tell me stories until I fell asleep. Then I had to get into the habit of going off to bed by myself.

One night, when I was about five, I woke up suddenly in the dark to find I was lying under the table unable to move. I was terrified, thinking that some evil spirit had cast me into a pit. When I tried to get up I banged my head against the edge of the thick wood. Sweating from fear and shivering with cold I wept silently. Believing myself far from home in some terrifying spot, my sole thought was not to give expression to my panic so that I wouldn't upset the genie who wished to harm me (as I'd heard my mother say that the more you showed your fear the worse the evil spirits would treat you . . .) On the basis of this information, I trembled, and moaned under my breath. Numb with terror, I groped around in the dark for some familiar object until my hand came up against a cushion . . . I slowly pulled it towards me, and clutching it in my arms, I felt reassured and finally sobbed myself to sleep. In the morning I was discovered hugging the soft cushion which had kept my terror at bay.

Adults don't know the anguish of growing up. You'd think they'd never been young.

Everyone thinks my eyes are very big and bright . . . Mother says it's because I read so much, but I think it's from straining desperately to keep them open, on the look-out for dangers that can attack me in the dark.

I've never told anyone about this fear, as a man is not supposed ever to be afraid, is he?

At present, I'm lying with my diary on my lap, the flame of the paraffin lamp lighting me as I write, and it is as if I were talking to a friend. I also draw pictures. I talk aloud, just like that, to give myself courage when I hear the door creaking in the wind or the scary cry of some animal.

With my pals, I feel much stronger – as if I had the key to some magic secret. For I'm no longer alone.

Dachra . . . 30 August 1954

I'm crazy about history. One day we had to write a composition for homework on 'What would you like to be when you grow up? Give your reasons.'

I spent the whole night writing. For the first time, I felt I was expressing something close to my own heart.

I wrote that I wanted to be a journalist, devoting my life to telling the truth, combating falsehood and every form of falsification. I would travel the whole world writing about my country so that other people could get to know and love it, its customs etc. . . . I mixed up what my father had told me and my love of writing. I said that journalism was the finest profession as it allows just men to put their talents at the service of the welfare

92

of humanity by hunting down injustice, blind greed and evil. I concluded by saying that I wished to be a beacon of truth for a better world . . .

I handed in my homework the next morning, with the rest of the class. Two days later the master approached me wearing his most sarcastic expression. He pinched my ear and murmured, 'You're going to read your masterpiece aloud to the whole class.'

Cowering under the relentless grip on my burning ear, I was delivered up to the unbridled ridicule of my classmates. They fell about laughing, jeering and mocking spitefully, realizing it pleased the master to see them make a fool of me. He derided my literary pretentions. He sniggered just like the pupils. 'Just look at him! This little snotty-nose wants to be a journalist and write the truth . . . The only truth you'll ever write will be about your own lice!'

When lessons were over, all the other kids, who'd been my friends the day before, set on me; they surrounded me and grabbed my satchel. I fought like a tiger. They were maddened, like wolves who've tasted blood. Abbas looked on surreptitiously without intervening. When he saw the boys get threatening he turned and sloped off. Slimane was absent; he'd had to stay in bed with a bilious attack. First the kids dragged me by the feet, then one of them got hold of a bucket of water from somewhere and poured it over my head. Drenched to the skin, trembling with rage, I tried to run away on my thin legs, as there were really too many for me to tackle by myself. Abdi, the big booby, egged them on viciously. They yelled, 'You'll write about your grandfather's goats, you big show-off!' Another smartypants shouted, 'You'll tell about your father's rusty tin-cans and his crazy caps.' From then on, with the master's malicious encouragement, I became 'the lousy village clever-dick'. Abdi's spiteful wit transformed *'Qarraï'* (swot) into *'Kharraï'* (snot).

I can't bring myself to hate them as they themselves are prisoners. It's their way of ingratiating themselves with the head by ganging up on me. And probably their way of getting their own back on any boy who wants to stand out from the crowd.

As for the head, he wants to humiliate me, destroy my ambitions. He didn't understand my dreams. But he failed in his attitude as my pride is intact.

The following days they tried to call me 'snotty', encouraged by my silence which they took for fear. They jostled me spitefully. Then . . . it's the end of recreation; we're getting into our lines to return to our classrooms. The masters are still chatting in the playground. Then Abdi trips me up with a sneer, 'Hey, snotty, did you do a lot of reading yesterday in your pigsty?'

I felt my blood turn to ice. I dropped my satchel and went and picked up a stone. I put it on my shoulder and glared at him, saying 'If your mother's virtuous, come and get it!'

That's our challenge to a fight. If the fellow challenged has got the courage, he must come and take the stone and fight begins. Either way, he must react to wipe out the insult, as it's sacrilege to invoke anyone's mother.

Everyone fell silent. Abdi went rather white as he's not accustomed to being challenged like that. He walked up to me rather casually, reached out his hand towards my shoulder and I suddenly charged him like a maddened bull. He fell backwards under the weight and surprise of my attack. Without giving him time to collect himself, I went for him; sitting astride his body, I hammered my fists into his face, yelling, 'Yes, I will write, I will become a journalist, I will write, I will write! And don't anyone call me snotty again! . . .'

I scratched his face, tore out his hair by the handful, banged his head on the ground, repeating over and over again, like a litany, 'Say I'm the strongest! Say I'm a man . . . Go on, say it!'

The blood throbbed in my veins, I was a solid block of hatred, with eyes only for my motionless prey, gripped between my legs. I vaguely heard Slimane shout, 'If anyone goes near them, I'll bash his head in! Let Ali settle his own score!'

Then they did try to pull me off Abdi. But I held on to him with superhuman strength.

Finally I heard his voice implore me, 'For pity's sake, let me go! I agree you are a man! Yes, you are the strongest'

Suddenly a shower of water on my face brought me down to

earth. I felt myself choking. I looked up and saw we were hemmed in by all the pupils and masters crowding round us. It was the headmaster who had the idea of throwing water over me to calm me down. I stood up, shouting, 'If any of you ever calls me snotty again, I'll kill him!'

At the sight of my white face and shaking shoulders they drew away from me. My determination had got the better of them. Abdi struggled to his feet, blood streaming from his nose. One of the masters took him to the dispensary, murmuring, 'That youngster's a savage!' As for me, the head sent me home, forbidding me to return to school unless I was accompanied by my father.

For the first time in my life, I had won through violence, I who only aspire to peace. I was distressed to find myself capable of destructive anger. If Abdi had not shouted and begged, I'd have gone on hitting him and if I'd had a weapon I'd have killed him . . . It's a terrible thing to discover a wild beast slumbering inside yourself, waiting for an opportunity to show itself . . .

At least my lack of assurance melted away in the blows I planted on the dunce's face, he himself the unconscious victim of the headmaster's unscrupulous machinations.

Baladia . . . 25 October 1954

At college: we're supposed to be doing our homework. Some of the boys are revising, others are reading magazines hidden in their text books, but the young assistant master in charge takes no notice; he's a decent chap who doesn't bother us as long as we don't lark about.

I'm bringing my diary up to date as so many things have happened since that last evening when I described my fight with Abdi. I passed my Primary School Certificate and father decided to send me to technical college on the advice of the headmaster who told me, 'You'll write about "the truth" with your electrician's diploma, young journalist!'

Rachid-the-Silent was the first one to leave the village. One

September morning, when we'd arranged to meet in the clearing, Rachid didn't turn up. His father told us he'd sent him to study at the Zitouna, the famous University of Tunis. It appeared that a cousin living there would pay for his training to become a *kadi* or a teacher at the Quranic school in the capital!

So Rachid left the village without saying goodbye to us, taking his flute with him. We continued our games as before but we missed our friend's sad, inscrutable gaze. Our meetings in the clearing would be the poorer without the subtle magic of Rachid's music and his enigmatic expression, now kindly, now mocking, a mixture of cynical amusement and curiosity, reminding one of a mischievous monkey . . .

When father heard he'd left, he said, 'Rachid will go far, but alone; he will have no friends . . . Of all of you boys, he's the most disconcerting; he'll creep and crawl if necessary to reach his goal. And that's worth more than a whole olive-grove . . .'

This is true, up to a point; although Rachid was born in our village and grew up among us, no one really knows him.

The village is changing now, the boys are leaving one by one. A curious feeling is in the air, the sky seems to be in suspense as if awaiting new events. No doubt because we are rapidly becoming adults in our turn.

The bell's ringing, it's time for the next lesson.

Baladia. . .13 March 1955

I have a recurring dream. I am a green fish with golden fins and red eyes, disporting myself in an azure sea. It's a curious sensation, I seem to be able to see myself from the outside, but I am not afraid. There is no horizon, the whole ocean is mine . . . A green fish in the blue water, I fly, I leap over the waves which open up to enclose me, but I swim on and up, almost touching the sky . . . I wake up, surprised to find myself lying on a stupid mattress, with the rigid walls of my room as sole horizon.

I had this dream again the night before I left for college. I was excited at the idea of starting a new school. My father was as moved as I was. He went with me to say goodbye to all our friends. The family heaped presents on me as if I was off to distant shores.

I met up with Slimane again here, in the commercial section of the college where he started last year, because he'd been a year ahead of me at the village school. I noticed he's already popular, surrounded by boys who laugh at his jokes. The majority of the boarders are Muslims, but most of the day-boys are Europeans.

I see Slimane at meals or in the dormitory, the rest of the time we're in different classes. I admire the easy way he gets on with the masters. And one day, thanks to football, I too became the good guy all the other fellows want to be friends with.

The football captain, a senior in the third year of book-keeping, asked me, 'You there, have you ever played?'

'A bit,' I replied modestly.

'All right, you can take this position next to me.'

He was the centre-forward and I was inside right. I didn't want to mention I'd been playing football since I was six, when we kids made a ball out of rags to satisfy our passion for the game.

Before school, after school, on Thursdays and Sundays, we indulged in epic matches, in which the biggest boys usually won as they were the referees . . . The law of the jungle! I learned fast by watching the others and I was soon better than them all. Dodging, dribbling, shooting had no secrets for me.

Fernand, the captain, didn't have to be told all that. He realized straight away I was a dab hand, and so did all the rest of the team. We won 6–2 and I scored three goals.

Baladia . . . 19 January 1956

I haven't written for a very long time as life has taken on the job of writing for me. Our country is shaken by war. I try to understand, but when I question father at home he just murmurs, 'Don't worry about politics! Study, work hard, and become a credit to those who are shedding their blood for you.'

As usual, he falls back upon his own thoughts. At college no one mentions the war.

And then, there are my new friends, the new things I learn every day. And . . . even women! But I'll tell it all in order . . .

First, my two years at college have been unforgettable. An atmosphere of genuine good-fellowship reigns, with warm friendships reinforced by football. Being part of any sports team is a way of discovering the real meaning of solidarity and fraternity . . .

What better than a sportsfield, uniting men in the exhilaration of a common aim? And that rapturous feeling when I score a goal and the whole team throw their arms round me in gratitude! Then I really feel they love me unreservedly and I'm ready to give my life for such happiness.

Slimane isn't jealous of my popularity at college as he's a keen supporter of our team, betting on who'll score and never missing an opportunity of making a few pence.

But, I have to admit he's very generous and always shares his winnings with us. He's much thinner now, what with boarding-school diet and sport, but he's as greedy and full of fun as ever. On our free days I go to a friend of my father's who's supposed to act *in loco parentis*. . . In fact, I just dump my things there, have my meals and spend my time with my pals. Slimane never stops teasing me about my virginity. He continues to go on the spree and still loves to recount all the details of his amorous escapades. He and the older boys are regular visitors to establishments catering for men's pleasure.

Yesterday, after a memorable match in which Slimane bet on our team and won, the whole college was in a frenzy of excitement. The students organized a party and in the midst of the mutual congratulations Slimane said. 'Ali, I've decided to give you a treat! But you must swear you won't refuse it.'

'First tell me what it is before making me swear,' I said suspiciously, as I knew my pal's love of teasing.

The other boys agreed with me. We're a fairly united group and I'm the youngest. Slimane whispered something in Mahmoud's ear – he's a great practical joker. They both burst out laughing, then Slimane said solemnly, 'Well, I've decided to treat you to a woman, I'll take you with us to the cathouse and I'll pay for everything.'

I wasn't surprised as the idea had been in his head for a long time. What's more he adores this kind of treat. Initiating others into life's pleasures is his speciality. Whether money, food or love, he has to share everything: a real good Samaritan.

And so I went with Slimane, Mahmoud and Fernand to the White Horse, a house specializing in Arab women. A single-storey establishment with several rooms opening on to a large courtyard. I'd imagined the women would be extravagantly made up but they aren't; they're dressed normally, in long *gandouras* with frills at the bottom and round the neck. With their scarves tied coquettishly round their heads and their eyes outlined with kohl, they could be mothers or girls from good families. The madame welcomed my pals delightedly, repeatedly calling them, 'My boys!' and fussing round them like a mother-hen. Slimane put his arm round her waist like an old friend and whispered something in her ear. She glanced at me and said softly, 'I've got just the thing for him, but she's busy at the moment. Go and wait in the lounge.'

The lounge was large and simply furnished with several men and women listening to a group of singers, some chatting while clearly waiting for their 'turn'. Slimane leaned over towards me, 'They're not all here for the "naughties", some of these people come for the pleasure of a chat and a drink.'

I gazed around this place with curiosity; I thought it would be the gateway to hell. If it were not for the number of men and all the glasses of alcohol on the tables, it could be any respectable Arab home. And these women in their brightly coloured *gandouras*, dressed up as if for a party, suddenly reminded me of my mother . . .

My immediate reaction was to leave. No! I can't do it, I can't go with any of them. It's frightful . . . But how can I explain these feelings to Slimane and the others? My friend saw my tense expression.

'What's the matter? Don't you like it here?'

'I want to go!'

'You're afraid, or what? They're clean, you know! They have to be examined medically every week . . .'

I felt wretched. I looked him straight in the face. I declared flat out that I wouldn't go with any of them.

Slimane was dismayed. 'Don't you like women?' he murmured with a worried look, as if I was stricken by some shameful disease. At the sight of his frightened expression I burst out laughing.

'Let's go! I don't feel like it, that's all.'

I made my way firmly towards the exit. Slimane called the others, they discussed my 'case' at length, and finally I heard him grumbling, 'I've paid to come here! That's what you get from trying to do a spoil-sport a good turn!' Then he called me, 'All right, we'll go on condition that you wait till we've had our turn . . . We're not going to miss our fun because of you!'

Shortly afterwards they joined me, in high spirits and looking very pleased with themselves. They teased me. But I thought to myself they'd been helluva quick over their 'visit'. I've still got no experience of instantaneous pleasures . . .

Slimane won't give up so easily. He's pig-headed. As we have plenty of time still, after we've walked a little way, he announces 'Let's go somewhere else! We know just the place for chaps with complexes like you.'

And so I find myself at the Black Bird . . . There's no doubt about it, this is my day for doing the rounds of the Lovelies! Here it's different! It reminds me of scenes from films. A large lounge with an impressive bar at one end. The walls are decorated with suggestive pictures of naked women. Girls in different stages of undress lie about on divans in titillating poses, while the heavy perfume and the buzz of laughter increases the erotic atmosphere. As for me, I am torn between the desire to stay and to flee . . . A vague feeling of guilt assails me, but at the same time it all seems a dream.

The madam, a fat woman known as Madame Nini, jokes with my pals. She looks at me kindly, asking, 'You've never been here before, have you?'

100

I shake my head and Fernand anawers for me, 'It's his first time, that's why he's rather shy . . .'

Slimane began the same game, taking the madame by the arm and whispering something in her ear. She nodded her head in understanding and sent for a girl with whom she exchanged a brief stage whisper.

The girl's name is Rosy. She seems pleasant. There's nothing suggestive in her smile as she tells me to follow her. When we reach her room she asks, 'Is it the first time?'

'Er . . . no . . . yes . . .'

She murmurs, 'I see . . . Just relax, we've plenty of time, I can stay with you as long as you like . . .'

She took me gently in her arms . Her tongue is sweet and agile. She began by covering my whole body with kisses.

It's all so new and unexpected; she made me so happy that I took her face in my hands. Then I ventured into completely unknown territory. Instantly the heavens opened and swallowed me up. I felt myself become the green fish in my dream . . . When I came to myself, I saw her caressing me gently. I was exhausted but she seemed fresh and serene.

With a smile she began to caress me anew, gradually teaching me how to control myself, how to become a man. And, from an innocent adolescent, she made me into a man who is master of his own body.

Baladia . . . 12 March 1956

It's the humdrum, daily routine: classes, prep, lessons, tests, sports. We have Saturday afternoons and Sundays off and then I sometimes go to Dachra to see my parents. Abbas passed his Primary School Certificate, but instead of sending him to learn a trade in technical college his father decided to keep him at home to do Si Hafid's accounts. Abbas has changed. He is more mature, less tense than before. He's particularly interested in politics. Always glued to his transistor, he follows everything that happens in our country and the rest of the world. The last time I saw him he told me, with shining eyes, that he was going to leave . . . When I asked him where to, he simply answered vaguely, 'I know a scheme for getting into France . . .'

But I'm sure he was lying. As for Abdi, he's found his level working as a waiter in the village café, serving tea or coffee to the customers and catching up on all the gossip . . . he knows everything that happens in Dachra.

I sometimes go alone to the Black Bird, without waiting for my pals. Now I'm more confident I even change partners. Rosy is pleased to see me. She gives me a friendly wave and goes off with her clients.

To tell the truth, I'll never forget my friend Slimane's 'present'. The revelation of my sexual potential made me at first deliriously proud and happy. I was like King Midas discovering that everything he touched turned to gold.

After each of these short-lived encounters, I have added to my knowledge of life. I feel like Christopher Columbus sailing off to discover new lands, mysterious continents in the form of unknown women's bodies. For, in addition to giving me physical pleasure, my temporary partner enriches me with fragments of her hidden personality. We are, in my view, two subjects who for a fleeting moment have revealed something of themselves, if only through their bodies.

Dachra . . . 29 September 1957

Tonight I am at the crossroads. I advance between the mist and the darkness. The evil spirits of my childhood nightmares no longer haunt my nights, for they beset me now by daylight. Yes, indeed, for the last few months they have singled out my home and my life.

First came my father's death, forcing me to leave college immediately and get a job in the village; then there was my imprisonment and release to return home to look after my sick mother. All the members of my family are here buzzing like flies

102

round our house. And my aunt nags me to marry her daughter Meriem!

I think of what she was like . . . With her bright eyes and pretty little face, so sure of herself and not a bit shy. I remember how, during the long summer afternoons, when everyone was having their siestas, I liked to lie on a mat under the fig-tree in the courtyard and read. Meriem would pass at that moment on her way to the tap. She would lift up her skirts and let the cool water run over her legs. I was fascinated by this sight which filled me with admiration while making my heart beat faster and my mouth feel dry. I greeted this reaction with a mixture of anxiety and joy as, according to our friend Slimane, it was an indication that I was about to become a man. Meriem continued her game, watching me out of the corners of her eyes. She was the same age as me, but already knowledgeable about matters of love. She told me proudly that she was old enough to have a child. That's how I learned about women's menstruation. When she hung around me I looked at her with increased interest. She took on a certain importance simply because she was a girl and, to be honest, she intimidated me a bit. One day I ventured to put my hand on her budding breasts; she blushed and slipped away.

Today my dear cousin returns to stir my senses. She can be simultaneously tender and violent; I am both fascinated by her charm and awkward as a little boy under her mocking eyes that shine with a sharp and often cynical intelligence. She has such a magnetic personality that even when she remains silent in her corner, you can feel her presence, palpable, real and seeming to weave a magic spell around her.

There were very soon requests for her hand in marriage, but she's the only girl in her family to say no, calmly, categorically. And no one dares insist. I am the one she wants to marry. Her parents have told me so, but I have given no reply . . . Now that we are no longer children, marriage means freedom for Meriem, but offers a threat to me.

She drifted towards me in the curious way she has of seeming scarcely to touch the ground; she was more like a panther than ever . . . She looked at me with a smile. I am moved to see the passion blazing in her eyes that reminds me of our childhood games. Meriem has not forgotten. She whispered, 'Tonight I'll meet you in the shed, like we used to . . .'

I wondered how she would be able to slip out of the house with so many people around. But she managed to join me late at night. She sat down beside me without a word. We did not move until a rustle outside the door made us start. Meriem jumped to her feet saying 'Someone's coming!'

I put my arms round her and we remained like that, listening to the sound. It suddenly dawned on us what it was and we both burst out laughing . . . The hens in our little farm-yard had been disturbed by the wind.

'Ali! Tell me honestly, you don't want to marry me, do you?' I did not know what to reply to this point-blank question.

'No,' I said. 'I've always thought of you like a sister . . . And besides, I'm still too young . . .'

She sobbed, 'I'm not your sister! And, Ali, you remember, you seemed to love me before . . .'

I did not know how to react to Meriem's despair, her tears – I'd never seen her weep before – the heartbreak in her voice, which I'd only known carefree, vibrant with gaiety. Yes, I could accept her proposal . . . Marry her, work in the village, giving her a child every year while she looks after the house and the children . . . and then? But I don't love her enough to accept such a future. Before I could make any move, Meriem had fled with a rustle of her dress, like a frightened swallow.

A week later . . .

This October I'm not getting ready to go back to college . . . That period is all over for me. But it has not been unproductive. In spite of my frustration at being prevented from going to high school as I wished, I've been able to persevere with my reading. At college, I never did very well in things we had to learn out of text-books, but I was full of enthusiasm for French, history and most of all geography . . . I felt I was surreptitiously pocketing bits of information I needed to realize my ambitions. For two and a half years I cheated by working for a diploma that doesn't interest me. And now that my mother is dead, I have my answer. Tomorrow I am leaving the village. I am filled with a curious feeling of euphoria; I know where I am going, but how am I to find the way there? I am going in search of freedom and to defend a certain idea of honour . . .

But perhaps I shall be thought reckless! To lose the last person one loves: one's mother! And to talk of freedom! . . . Yet I have a sense of deliverance, reinforced by all the pseudo-grief that surrounds my isolation.

For my mother's family, with the exception of Uncle Driss, Yussef's father, turned out to be a bunch of predators. He has been a real support to me. What is more, as a survivor of 8 May 1945,* he's been responsible for my underground activity by introducing me to the cell in our village.

When my father died six months before my mother, countless maternal cousins descended on us, each one helping himself from our modest grocery store. I sold the business for a song to one of the brothers-in-law. I did not realize at the time how shabbily I'd been treated; he swindled me quite unashamedly, taking advantage of my haste to get rid of the shop which reminded me too much of my father's presence.

My mother sat speechless with sorrow as the vultures swooped on the feast. After the brother-in-law had commandeered the shop, he wanted to make me marry his daughter. Just imagine what a prize! A young man who's about to finish training for his electrician's diploma, and a little house, even if it is falling to pieces! But the only thing I could think about was my mother left all alone.

That was why, a few months before I was due to take my exam, I left college and came back to work in the village. At the same time I joined the underground, hoping to be able to get to the maquis. From that moment, I had only one aim, to devote my life to a worthwhile struggle.

* On that day, the French army killed hundreds of demonstrators calling for the independence of Algeria.

105

Oh, Mother! How often have I wished you were younger, stronger, so that you could accompany me in my dreams and flee with me into the mountains where honour and liberty are being won! With you, the thorns, the burning sun, the cold snow, and even death would have been sweet, with one truth alone to guide our steps: the acquisition of our dignity and identity. But you had already departed for another dream. Without my father's noisy, energetic presence in the house, you were like a poor sparrow fallen from its nest, Mà Chérifa. I was not enough for you. My orphan's world no longer rang with your laughter and your clothes, little mother, lost their sparkle; you were now nothing but a thin pathetic silhouette constantly dressed in sombre colours. The fine tatooing on you cheeks lost its emerald sheen, becoming grey, sunk into your wrinkles.

You, so prompt to laugh at people's stupidity, you who despised the hypocrisy of certain members of the family, you withdrew behind a wall of grief and passivity. You, the proud wife of Si Abdelkader, the sailor, you submitted to the condescending goodwill of your sister-in-law when she offered you a daily meal, as you no longer even bothered with your household tasks. When that fat busybody Rim borrowed your copper tray when she had guests, and then 'forgot' to return it, you said nothing. And gradually, your utensils and your rugs disappeared. When I questioned you about them, you shook your head with an embittered look and murmured, 'Your father, my most precious possession, has gone . . . So, what do things matter, son? Nothing matters any more!'

Can you die from a broken heart? I think so now, after seeing my mother wither away, like a plant deprived of water and sun. Shortly afterwards, Madame Lavigne, realizing that I'd never agree to work for her husband, helped me find a job as an electrician with the railways. This good soul has been a great help to us, as she had a lot of respect for my father whose strength of character and honesty she appreciated. Juliette and her family left the village at the outbreak of the troubles. But she came to visit us on my father's death and wept sincerely with us.

Two months later, the fury that I had pent up in my heart

suddenly erupted, and I struck the foreman when he called me a 'filthy wog' and I landed up in prison . . . Once more, you were alone, little mother. I thought of you from my cell and thought I would go mad . . . You were my fragile, vulnerable child, and I had not succeeded in being a strong man, sufficiently in control of myself so that I could remain near you. I was responsible for you, and I failed in my duty to surround you with love like my father.

When I was released from prison I found our three rooms practically denuded . . . You looked so small, lying on your bed, surrounded by all those termagents weeping crocodile tears and leering covetously at our few remaining possessions. And when I asked Rim where all our copper utensils had gone and our mattresses, and all our woollen rugs which used to be piled up on both sides of our living-room, brightening it with their warm colours, she replied with a sniffle, 'All sold! Your mother had to sell everything to buy medicines for herself!'

. . . Liar! . . . Oh, little mother! How could you have sold everything which stood for so many memories for us, and in just three months! But I was too sickened to confront these shameless people.

And eventually you opened your eyes to smile at me; your lovely eyes were bright with fever as you stared at me for a moment and whispered, 'Leave it, son, don't worry about things any more, I've lost your father . . . Nothing else counts!' You pulled me to you and added softly, 'Look under my mattress. I've kept back a little money for you, no one can take it. Go! leave the village! Just like your father used to say, "Be a man! The dogs bark, but the caravan moves on!" . . . Your father and I will always be at your side to protect you . . . May Allah bless you, Ali!'

When she breathed her last, I could not move. I was lost, broken, as if I were floating not in an azure sea but in waters black as ink . . . under a threatening sky . . . Mà Chérifa, you look as if you have fallen asleep, and suddenly you have become a stranger to me, you are now detached and at peace in a world I do not know.

Someone said, *'Allahu Akbar!* God is great.' A voice murmured, 'It's all over, there's nothing more to be done now, come!'

Yes, there's nothing more to be done . . . What will become of my life? I thought. Where will the tunnel lead? The reply came so naturally that I was reminded of my time at the village school. However difficult a problem was, I had to find the solution. Afterwards, it was a weight off my mind. When the bell rang for break, it rang for freedom. When the master nodded his head to show he was pleased with my homework, that was a bell ringing for my freedom. Every daily success signified one thing, all the rest was simple, clear. And yet, that day, I was in a predicament. Everything was a jumble in my mind: my childhood vanished away, my parents, my friends become dust scattered in the wind. Man is born from nothing, so I have read. And now I truly believe it. It's as if God had created the world by mistake. The only positive element is my youth. But that only makes me feel all the more the precarious nature of my future.

And so, without a glance behind me, I left the scene of my childhood for ever.

You, my diary, do not think that my political consciousness arose from my bitter resentment at a family's insensitive actions. No, it is the normal development of my secret aspirations. My ideas were fashioned by a proud, free and passionate father's work-worn hands. I must take in my own empty hands the only riches I possess: my youth and my hopes, to carve out a path for myself, however dangerous, difficult and painful, but necessary for the man I am determined to become.

7

Ali woke with a start at the sound of Khéïra moving about. The old woman's presence was reassuring, bringing him a momentary feeling of well-being and peace. He recalled his visit to the police station the previous day to legalize his new job. He remembered how nervous he had been, Monsieur Kimper's kind words and the feeling of security this kindly, sensitive old man inspired. Now he had to dig the garden, pick flowers for the drawing-room, get wood in for the fires and run errands.

Khéïra had immediately taken him to her heart. She was a jolly, lively woman, despite being bent with age. And what a chatterbox! She immediately undertook to tell the young man how the house used to ring with laughter in the old days, when Madame Kimper was still alive. Although they had no children of their own, their garden was crowded with those of their friends when they organized parties for birthdays or simply for fun.

Khéïra sighed as Ali did not reply, then exclaimed in a mixture of Arabic and French, 'Ya oueldi! Ladies like that, who love and respect their maids, you don't find them any more! . . . You, you're young and you're always so serious, you mustn't be like that! . . . If Madame was here, you know what she'd have done? She'd have sent you to a centre to learn a trade, she wouldn't have kept you as a gardener! The "p'fissor"'(that's what she insisted on calling Monsieur Kimper, thinking the title was flattering to him and to her when she spoke of him to her neighbours), 'it's not that he isn't nice, but men, they don't notice these things . . .' Then, wagging her finger at Ali, she added, 'You had better behave yourself and not mess about like some I could mention, where I live . . . It's a sin, ya Rabbi, to see these healthy lads hanging around in the street, counting the flies . . . You're a good lad, you are, you must work hard, that's all!'

So she chattered on like a magpie, until Ali reminded her she had work to do in the house. Then she went back in, shouting, 'Ya choumi! How time flies! And the p'fissor will be back any moment now!'

Ali did not see Monsieur Kimper until evening. Sometimes they had dinner together. Ali's room was on the ground floor. He had Thursdays off when the professor had a few pupils for private piano lessons. Then Ali went to the Béni-Ramassés district, to visit Tahar who gave him various jobs to do, for the most part leaflets to be typed.

While Tahar left, saying he had to drop in at the abattoir, Ali settled down at the typewriter. At half-past one, having finished part of the work, he sat down to have some lunch, glancing through a magazine as he ate. The house was quiet. The soft hum from the street reached him like a familiar, reassuring murmur. Suddenly he heard rapid steps on the pavement and Tahar rushed in.

'Has Mounir been here?' he asked.

'No, why?'

'Ramdane's done something stupid. I've just heard about it in town. Mounir was supposed to come here today!' he muttered wearily.

His features were drawn, as if he were consumed with worry. He dropped down on the mattress and asked Ali to make him some coffee.

'Perhaps he's on his way,' the young man said, as he filled the kettle.

'I hope so! Anyway, you haven't wasted your time, I see!' Tahar remarked, pointing to the pile of typed pages on the table.

They heard a knock at the door. It was Mounir. His normally pale face was now ashen. He flopped down on the only chair and sighed, 'Ramdane's done for this time!'

'What!' Tahar and Ali shouted simultaneously.

Mounir nodded fatalistically and told what he knew.

'He's had it! He swore at a policeman who'd upset an old

hawker's barrow at the entrance to the market. That cop's well known for the vicious way he treats any poor bugger who tries to sell things in front of the market without a licence. He'd had it in for this man in particular, and set about him with his truncheon. As you know, Ramdane's always hanging round that area, it's his favourite haunt and he knows everybody . . . He tried to defend the poor wretch who lay unconscious and bleeding on the ground with his fruit and vegetables scattered around him. He appealed to the cop to lay off, but he got all the madder and yelled, "A terrorist! A terrorist!" The patrol came up to help, convinced they'd got hold of a rebel. Ramdane lost his head; he struggled and kicked up a real shindy, hurling insults, yelling, "Filthy racists! . . ." You know that's his favourite expression. . . More policemen came along and wanted to take him to the station, but the soldiers wouldn't let them, on the grounds that this was a "dangerous, armed *fellaga*" and he was their pigeon . . . They argued over it for a while, then the soldiers took him off. He's had it now. God knows what camp they'll send him to.'

'They'll torture him and he'll speak!' Ali exclaimed, his face betraying his fright.

Tahar and Mounir shrugged.

'No danger on that score!' Tahar retorted. 'Ramdane's tough. He'll hold his tongue. It'll never occur to them that a half-wit knows anything. They think he's nuts, a troublemaker, a drunkard. But this time it's serious!'

Mounir declared pompously, 'Tomorrow, we'll be in the headlines: "Dangerous terrorist caught red-handed! Whole cell wiped out!" '

Tahar told him to shut up. He wasn't in the mood for Mounir's jokes. He was upset, as was evident from the rare bitterness in his voice.

'It's the first time he's used a knife! . . . He seemed very worked up recently: I did insist a sharp eye must be kept on him,' he said glaring at Mounir, who protested, 'That's just it. The fellow I asked to keep an eye on him couldn't intervene . . . Besides,' he added slyly to Tahar, 'why couldn't you just keep him here with you. D'you think I'd nothing else to do!'

111

Tahar controlled his annoyance and replied calmly, 'You know he doesn't like to stay shut up. He needs to be with his friends, all the old campaigners in the old town; so don't be so unfair, please!'

'OK! But I must go now,' Mounir said, making his way to the door and adding, 'I'll try and find out what they've done with him.'

Ali poured the coffee. Tahar glanced at the young man and noticed his anxious expression. 'What's up, Ali?'

'Well . . . You told me we were soon going to do a "job" . . . so I want to know . . . I think about it all the time!'

'So, you're suspicious now?'

'No!' Ali retorted sharply, 'I just want to be in the picture . . . You see . . . well, it's like this, it's terrible to be taken unawares, without being prepared psychologically . . .'

Tahar raised his eyebrows and looked at the youngster as if he'd suddenly changed into a white mouse . . . He repeated each syllable, like a pupil learning to read, 'Psy-cho-lo-gi-ca-lly! Well! well! You didn't bloody waste your time at school! *Ya Rabbi!* * What a scholar I've got here . . . But, my friend, if we had to be "psych", etc. prepared, the revolution would still just be pie in the sky . . .'

Tahar threw his head back and roared with laughter, slapping his thigh and repeating 'psych, psych', as if he were calling to a cat.

He grew serious again, and said, 'Well, since it gives you sleepless nights, I'll put you in the picture. Not only because I know why the idea of working with me upsets you, but also because I'm keen to have a companion who's fresh and rested for our nocturnal expeditions.'

The youngster blushed to the roots of his hair; he regretted using such a complicated word when he simply wanted to ask Tahar for any information which he was prepared to give him. Tahar's kindly voice aroused him from his dark thoughts. 'We were supposed in theory to do this "job" the day after your arrival, and you were to accompany me as guide to your village.

* Heavens above!

112

Salah was to explain the aim of this mission in the course of our first meeting. But when I saw you, I felt that this was premature. You seemed to be so upset by all that had happened to your family . . .'

Tahar broke off and patted Ali's cheek, as if to smooth away the frown that came over the youngster as he spoke: 'Come now! Listen to me like a real tough guy! You see, I felt instinctively I had to take you in hand, so to speak . . . So the matter was postponed till later. You were accepted because you knew the area. The station is one of the vital points for the transport of ammunition and supplies . . . Tomorrow, during the meeting which will take place here, you'll know as much as I do . . . That's all!'

Ali reflected. Then, as was his wont, he bit his lips before blurting out. 'The other evening, Tahar . . . You were prepared to . . . Well, have you already killed many people like that?'

This time, Tahar did not flinch, He looked as if he'd long been expecting this question. Now that he knew the young man's inquiring mind , he was simply surprised that he had not asked it sooner. With the strange mixture of affection and irritation that he often felt for Ali, he struggled to reply in a natural, even impersonal voice. 'Yes. That is in fact my main job . . .'

'How? I don't understand!'

Ali seemed determined to have this explanation, although the scene he had witnessed filled his nights with bad dreams and sometimes, when he thought of Tahar, he felt sickened. He was not afraid of him, but afraid for him. He wondered if a man's reason could hold out for long against this type of activity.

It was as though Ali were seeking to exorcise his fantasies, to harden himself and bury in the depths of his soul his sentimental childish self, who still returned to haunt his adolescence. Tahar, for his part, understood what was tormenting his young companion. He had had the same feelings at first . . . But the murder of the girl he loved, his companion in the struggle, as well as the memory of all those whose deaths had been caused by informers, helped to stifle any sensitivity, any pity for the traitors. Today, in the presence of this youngster, seemingly so frail, so touching, confronted so young with death, Tahar became aware of his own humanity. He let this feeling of compassion sweep over him and he was all kindness and love, in the face of the young man's passionate trust.

'Naturally, it's a rotten job, but it's a lesson to all who undermine our efforts . . . You must simply be convinced that what you do is right. A struggle for freedom is not carried on with slogans or tub-thumping, but with actions like not hesitating to cut the throats of traitors, and unfortunately this is an irrefutable argument . . . In this way they knuckle under, and we slip back into the shadows, with the sense of having done our duty and with no remorse.'

Ali replied, 'At the present time, while the revolution must fight its way forward, I agree . . . But what about afterwards? When we've won our independence, there will be other problems: people won't always agree over them! Will the rulers govern by fear also? If today it's all right for you to kill for freedom, will you kill tomorrow if some people don't agree with you?'

Tahar clearly didn't understand what the youngster was getting at. He shrugged his shoulders.

'Afterwards? I'll no longer be on the scene. If I'm alive, I'll go back to my village to breed horses . . . Politics is not my line. There are plenty of brothers in the maquis who are at each other's throats. You don't realize this, but I know a thing or two . . . not very nice things; one day tongues will wag! . . . But we must think of the immediate future, young feller-me-lad! Meanwhile, you just have to get on with your job . . . When I've got an identity, I won't worry about dictators and all that blah.' He stood up, walked over to Ali and said solemnly, 'But you sure as hell will be a bloody trouble-shooter for the country, with your mania for asking questions . . . If you started spouting those ideas in the maquis, you'd soon put people's backs up, and someone would sort you out on the QT! But joking apart, I hope you're satisfied with my speechifying.'

Ali smiled and poured himself some more coffee.

'You're not very encouraging. So, acccording to you, a fellow like me is better off in town?'

114

'Oh, no, sonny! The town's more dangerous, it's filled with informers, so we have to be constantly on our guard!'

Tahar glanced at the copies that the youngster had typed and gave an admiring whistle. 'Congratulations! You've done a good job. And now you can put a sock in it! Run along. I need some sleep. Be off back to the prof's. Here, take him these good cuts of lamb . . .'

He patted Ali affectionately on the back and pushed him towards the door, with another roar of laughter.

'Psychologically! I'll never forget that word . . . Off you go and see that you psychologically mind your step.'

Ali took his teasing in good part. He'd like to see him always in this mood. And knowing his own tendency to take offence, he was surprised to find how pleased he was when Tahar pulled his leg.

8

Ramdane was beaten to within an inch of his life, then thrown into a sort of lumber room, where he now lay, his body an aching mass, his face swollen, his hands sticky with blood. He groaned under his breath, incapable of moving. About noon the next day, a soldier with his sub-machine-gun slung over his shoulder brought him some bread and water, first kicking the poor wretch in the ribs and shouting, 'You lousy bastard! Daring to attack a policeman! You'll pay for that, you bloody wog!'

Ramdane did not react to the kick, but he shuddered at the insult. He dragged himself painfully over to the bucket of water to wash his wounds, his face contorted with pain at every movement. He spent the rest of that day praying they would not come and beat him again.

He had shown superhuman endurance. He had been beaten, immersed in a bath, hung up by his feet, given electric shocks, had water poured into his stomach through a funnel. Now he knew he was at the end of his tether. He was afraid he'd weaken and have to speak. Of what? Of whom? The only members of the organization he knew were Salah, Mounir, Tahar, Monsieur Kimper and young Ali. The others were dead, in prison, or in the maquis. This was a minute part of the immense pyramid which was victoriously defying the enemy. But for a man like him this tiny group was everything!

Ramdane's fate was being enacted in an adjoining room, where a lieutenant was reporting to his superior: 'The nut-case hasn't talked, sir.'

'You've tried everything?'

'Yes, we've worked on him for three days. He's in a critical state now and it's too late to get anything interesting out of him.'

'Has the medic seen him?'

'Yes, he'll be reporting to you. He doesn't think he'll last long.'

'Well then, see that he's evacuated to the special camp. Let him kick the bucket somewhere else. I don't want another stiff leaving this place.'

There was a respite until the evening when he was taken to another cell. He was dragged along underground corridors to the dungeons which Muslims referred to, in terrified whispers, as '*Silun*', a distortion of cell . . . a word that was synonymous with death. Anyone imprisoned there had no hope of ever seeing the light again and his family would lose all trace of him. How many men had been left to rot in these dark corridors! Yet Ramdane was brought out, after spending part of the night there; at midnight he was transferred to Bhira, a special camp in the south of the country.

Rows of huts had been erected in a vast pit, surrounded by electrified barbed wire . . . Not far away, at the foot of the hills, was the military camp. Those who were sent to Bhira never returned; any rare survivors were human wrecks, so disturbed that they ended up in mental hospitals.

During the burning summer days, this pit gave off a foul effluvia, emanating from the men's excreta, their sores and diseases. Herded like beasts, they succumbed to the effects of tuberculosis or dysentery and torture inflicted by some of the guards recently returned from the Indo-Chinese War.

An infernal red sun beat down mercilessly on this accursed place. Yet the prisoners retained a desperate courage and dignity. They supported each other in their physical and mental sufferings. Some of them had lost their reason and lay on the damp ground for days on end, without speaking; then a terrible fury would suddenly sweep over them, transforming them into wild beasts. They would howl endlessly in the night, digging their finger-nails into their own bodies and biting themselves in murderous rage. Their fellow-prisoners tried to calm them, but most of them died

117

eventually, broken by these violent bouts of madness. The prisoners themselves buried their dead.

Yussef, Ali's cousin, was among the prisoners in the camp; he and Francis had run away from the remand home to which the two boys had been committed. When Francis finished his schooling, he had been kept on as a monitor. He had once dreamed of enlisting in the Foreign Legion, but changed his mind. He had accepted the strict discipline of the reform school and had a record of good behaviour so he'd decided to stay on to train to work with delinquents. He never abused his authority but tried rather to make life a little easier for the inmates of this establishment, subjected to its harsh rules. When Yussef arrived he recognized him and the two boys became friends. With the outbreak of war, they had only one thought: to run away and join the maquis. This they succeeded in doing, thanks to the collusion of the school janitor, who was an active member of the local resistance cell. Francis managed to join the maquis. Yussef was caught and thrown into the Bhira camp.

He had been there for two years now. Isolation, hunger, blows, not to mention the inevitable torture, had not broken his spirit. A brute of a guard had put out one of his eyes with a cigarette and it was now one mass of inflamed flesh; the remaining eye reflected all the strength of his bruised but unbowed heart. One of his legs, too, was half paralysed. Nevertheless an astonishing vitality persisted in his crippled body, making him active and full of brotherly concern for others. He had taken Ramdane under his wing, wiping his swollen face and feeding him from his own mess-tin, one mouthful at a time, like a child.

The prisoners were guarded by *goumiers*, Arab mercenaries who were even more brutal than the European soldiers. The latter, it must be said, kept away from this vast human cess-pit. The *goumiers* were commanded by bully-boys, veterans of the war in Indo-China. When anyone died, they ordered out the prisoners who could still stand and made them dig graves for their comrades. There were other camps for political prisoners near to towns. These were commanded by officers recently arrived from France and the regime was more or less tolerable; the inmates could play sports or teach their illiterate companions. But in the desert regions, far from the control of any over-sentimental zealous officer, the mercenaries could give free rein to their sadism and their hatred of mankind.

When Ramdane arrived in this foul camp, with his untreated wounds, he was more dead than alive. The guards threw him in with the other prisoners and then rushed out as the stench arising from this hell-hole was such that no officer ever came near. For meals, they were ordered out, a few at a time, carrying their mess-tins.

Yussef and three of the more able-bodied prisoners took charge of Ramdane. They made room for him in a corner of the cell.

'Water!' Ramdane groaned.

One man went to fetch him some water in a rusty tin. He opened his eyes which shone with an unnatural brightness. He stared at these pale, thin, unshaven faces bending over him and forced a smile. Then, in the heavy silence, he broke into the original hymn of the resistance movement . . . *'Min djibalina . . .* from our mountains the voices of free men have arisen, calling us to independence . . .'

Ramdane struggled to raise up his quavering voice. Only a painful gargling sound emerged from his wrinkled throat, with its swollen veins. The other men immediately joined in, their strong voices drowning Ramdane's whisper. He fell silent, closing his eyes with a peaceful smile.

In the neighbouring cells, the hymn rose up like a roll of thunder. And soon it was a heart-rending chorus, uniting in one voice the message of hope for the foreseeable end to the nightmare.

The guards rushed up, aiming their guns at the huts. The *goumiers* came with reinforcements. But the voices grew more and more powerful, defying the threats. From outside you'd have thought these were the voices of strong young men. The guards began to lose patience; they pulled five prisoners at random out of each hut, and threatened to shoot them if the singing didn't stop immediately.

'No!' Ramdane groaned. 'Sing! Just go on singing!'

The old man was lying near the door, hidden by his comrades, but a guard who heard his cry seized him and dragged him outside to join the others. Ramdane could not stand but crawling on all fours he yelled, '*Min djibalina!. . .*'

The prisoners hesitated, seeing their comrades surrounded by the execution squad. Their voices died down. Yussef heard Ramdane's lone voice still singing through his tears, and he chided them, 'Sing, for God's sake! Our hymn musn't die on our lips!'

A strange magnetism arose from this lame, disfigured man, urging on the other prisoners who raised their heads and chanted the words of victory.

It was a massacre! The guards hurled themselves like vultures on their prey, lashing out at them with chains and the butts of their rifles. The men covered their heads with their arms and went on singing. They no longer felt the blows. Blood trickled from their trembling lips and their eyes shone with a mystic, aching resignation, not hatred for their tormentors.

In the cells, all hell was suddenly let loose among the prisoners. Yussef hurled himself on one of the guards and tried to grab his gun. A shot rang out and Yussef fell, his one good eye staring at the sky; there was a strange burning sensation in his breast . . . It seemed as if thousands of stars transformed the camp into an enchanted paradise.

'You thought you could act tough, hey!'

The soldier's sneer was mixed up in his mind with that of Monsieur Durand: 'You won't be acting the tough guy in the village any more!. . .' Dachra, his parents weeping the day he left. The clearing behind the Roumières' field. And Rachid playing his flute . . . When was all that? Yussef was crouching down with his cowboy magazines . . . He'd dreamed of going West one day to look for the Grand Canyon . . . he'd ride across the prairies of the Far West in pursuit of Palefaces . . . For he knew that the Redskins were his brothers . . . But what? Where is he? He was running away from the other noisy, laughing boys, he was climbing higher and higher into the hills to read at peace. The trees, the sky, the reform school . . . All were submerged in a new world. He did not utter a single cry. It was all over. He rolled on his side, uttered one sigh and his body went slack.

The door of the cells were promptly shut. Inside bedlam broke loose. The prisoners hammered on the walls and doors, shouting revolutionary slogans.

An officer, who seemed to be the commandant, drove up in a jeep. 'What's going on?' he shouted to the *goumiers* who were attacking some prisoners who had broken out of their cell.

'It's a mutiny, sir. The prisoners have revolted, they tried to disarm us . . .'

The officer pointed to the prisoners in the yard who were still alive and barked, 'Shoot all those bastards on the spot!'

They dragged the prisoners to their feet, facing the firing squad. Their trembling voices took up the song. Shots rang out. The voices were drowned in the final death rattle . . .

Days passed . . . Ali dug the garden, dressed in his blue overalls. He looked proud of his gardener's outfit. Every day he went by bike to buy bread, milk and vegetables. During the day he scarcely saw Monsieur Kimper. It was Khéïra who gave him the orders, hauled him over the coals when he sometimes dawdled at the market or took too long pruning the rose-bushes. She poked her owl-like head out of the window and shouted in a tone of affectionate reprimand, '*Ya Oueldi*, you hear me? That boy is always wool-gathering! Hurry up here and mend the iron for me!'

His experience as an electrician helped Ali come to the rescue of the old woman. She always had something needing repair: the boiler, the stove, even the pressure-cooker, which 'came apart in her hands' as she said. Then she raved over his skill, declaring, 'You're strong, son! What a fine thing education is . . .'

Sometimes it amused him to annoy her on purpose by putting the flowers down anywhere in her clean kitchen. She got angry and threatened to throw him out of the window if he didn't clean up the mess he'd made. At these moments, Ali was happy, he felt he was once more the naughty child who loved to tease his mother . . . Sometimes it even seemed to him that she resembled Mà Chérifa, when she lost her temper or laughed at his nonsense. The professor was a quiet man. Except when his pupils or friends came to the house, he didn't have much to say. Sometimes he paid

121

courtesy calls on colleagues who lived close by. He spent hours at the piano, causing Khéïra to grumble in her kitchen, 'He's very nice, but with the noise he makes with that what-d'ye-call-it I've often felt like leaving this job! When I get home, my head's simply splitting . . . Ah! Madame understood me! When he began banging out his music, she hurried to shut the drawing-room door, smiling at me, as if to beg my pardon . . .'

Khéïra had been very fond of the professor's dead wife and she never tired of talking about her. Sometimes she got mixed up and spoke as if she were still alive and had just gone away for a time. She acted in the house as if she had Madame Kimper's absolute confidence, and one had the impression that the dead wife was still present in the person of Khéïra. When she arrived for work, she could be heard talking to herself, 'Madame doesn't like pumpkin in the couscous . . . She wouldn't be pleased to see the ashtrays lying about everywhere . . .' Ali thought that Madame Kimper must have been an extraordinary woman to have left such an impression on her servant. Especially when you knew that certain Europeans treated their native employees like inferior beings created for the benefit of the white master-race. When Khéïra spoke, she freely mixed up Arabic and French, giving rise to amusing sounds and images. She punctuated her sentences with vigorous slaps on her thigh, and Ali imagined the old woman must be covered with bruises; one day, he thought, she'll end up breaking a bone . . . But he never tired of listening to her chatter. Naturally, she had to regale him with the story of her life in Madame's time.

'Before coming to work here,' she began, 'I was with a "dentiss", whose wife treated me worse than a dog . . . It was "Khéïra! Come here . . . Khéïra are you deaf! Khéïra, why haven't you cleaned there?" She drove me quite mad. Besides which they had two nasty spoilt children . . . *Ya Rabbi!* I swear, son. I've never seen such little devils! When I was doing the housework, you know what they used to say? They'd poke their heads through the window and rub one fist in the palm of the other hand, like this' (imitating the action for Ali), 'and singing "*Trabaja, la moukhère!*

Trabaja, la, la, la . . .* We'll catch a wog and put her in a jug!"
And I'd burst into tears and chase after them, but they were too
fast for me. And their mother! What a stuck-up piece, acting the
fine lady! You see, I knew her before. She was our local baker's
daughter. I remembered her: a skinny little shrimp. Then she
married this dentiss. The baker's family all went wild, they were
in their seventh heaven! As for the poor wretch, a *Francaoui*
who'd come to do a locum here, he went to get his bread one day
at the baker's and goes crazy over Cécile . . . And that's it . . .
Naturally Cécile's mother comes over all genteel and tells all her
customers her daughter's engaged to an important dentiss . . .'
Khéïra roared with laughter at her own humour and wham!
slapped her thigh hard! Ali waited calmly for her to get her breath
back and to wipe her eyes with her skirt. She opened her mouth to
resume her story, but shook again with uncontrollable mirth. The
young man grew impatient and to get her to compose herself he
made as if to go.

'Where are you off to?' she protested. 'I haven't finished my
story yet!'

'Well, get on with it then!'

She cleared her throat, took a breath and resumed her gossip.
'So there was the poor dentiss well and truly caught! The swan he
married soon turned into a goose . . . After the first baby Cécile
began to fill out, and with the second she got as fat as a pig!
Inevitably, she began to look like her mother and, what's more,
with a nasty temper, always quarrelling with everybody! The
husband didn't know the Arabic proverb which says, "When you
see a beautiful, virtuous woman, marry her daughter!" He'd no
idea what he was letting himself in for, poor devil! So he started
coming home later and later, saying he'd got a lot of work . . . But
I know what men are like, son! When a husband starts finding
excuses for not coming home, it means there's something wrong
at home, that's all! Anyway, you can see I couldn't stay in a place
like that, so eventually I left! A neighbour found me this job with
the p'fissor . . . And coming to work for Madame made up for all

---

* Slog away, Arab woman.

123

my troubles . . . You see, I've worked in so many homes, and ever since I was twelve I've spent my life in other people's muck . . .'

Khéïra sighed, her wrinkled eyes grew misty and she drew in her toothless mouth in silent distress which expressed all the weariness of dreary battles with broom and floorcloth.

'Only the person who has hit out and the one who has wept, knows the truth . . . Yes, Madame was someone really nice. I remember how surprised I was at her way of talking to me, not like the other Europeans when they speak to their maids. She used funny words . . . For example, she used to say *vous* to me all the time, "Khéïra, will *vous* do this, if *vous* please!" It didn't sound right for her to talk to me like that. You'd think there were two Khéïras! It worried me, 'cos, you know, I've got something up here, don't just think I'm a stupid old donkey . . . So, one day, I asked her just like I'm talking to you now, son. I said, "Madame, explain to me why you say *vous* when you speak to me; there's only one of me, not two! 'Cos I know that when there's a lot of people, you must say *vous* . . . I understand that, as people always say *tu* to me. Excuse me, you're very nice and I'm not complaining, but I want to understand . . ." Believe me, son! She didn't laugh at me but she discussed the whole thing with me. Things I can't remember now. But it sounded so fine, what she told me, it brought tears to my eyes, my heart was so moved by her words . . . But I still didn't understand. So then I asked one of my neighbours' sons, an educated boy. He used almost the same words as Madame. But he also told me that in our language there's a word like *vous* to show respect for someone, you say "*Entoum*".

'Can you imagine, Ali! That exists in Arabic, and I'd no idea! So, if I want to show a person respect I must talk to him as if he were two persons! . . . I know that really there are three of everybody: the good angel on the right, the bad one on the left and the actual person . . . But, all the same . . . education's very complicated!'

Naturally, after this story, Ali found another way of annoying her. He said to her in Arabic, 'Come here, *ya* Khéïra!' and then he asked, 'And where are the two others? She chased him with the broom, shouting, 'Satan! Devil! God help us!'

One morning, as Ali was weeding the garden, a grim official-looking person rang the bell at the gate. Ali recognized the local police superintendent. He let him in with his heart in his mouth, wondering what on earth the man wanted.

'The job OK? Is your boss in?'

Ali thought this a stupid question as the professor could be heard playing. He asked the visitor to follow him.

The policeman sized him up like some strange animal, in a way Ali found offensive. However he remained impassive and showed him into the drawing-room.

'What a surprise, my dear fellow! To what do I owe the honour of this visit?'

'I was just passing and felt like a chat to find out how my boy's getting on with his piano lessons. You know how keen we are on music!'

Monsieur Kimper was not taken in and guessed the reason for this visit. He smiled amiably and asked the superintendent to take a seat. Ali shut the door quietly behind him and left; the quizzical glance the man gave him did not escape the professor.

'Tell me, my dear fellow, are you quite satisfied with that lad?'

'Yes, he's a hard worker, he's discreet and has taken the load of the housekeeping off my shoulders . . . Why do you ask?'

His visitor looked worried, as if he wanted to warn the professor of some terrible danger. He moved over to him and mumured in his ear, 'These days terrorist attacks in the town are on the increase . . .'

He told him a European lawyer had been shot point-blank by a terrorist who had managed to get away. This was the first event of its kind to occur in the residential district. If the killers could infiltrate this peaceful area, things were getting serious! Another native had been found with his throat cut that morning. The people were beginning to panic as the victim was a mainstay of the business community. Among other things, he owned one of the biggest brasseries in Baladia. A wealthy man who despised and

125

hated the nationalists, he did not hesitate to pass on useful information to the police when necessary . . .

The professor knew the man in question. He'd often had a drink with his friends in that brasserie. He recalled the person: one of those newly rich, hail-fellow-well-met types, always ready for a chat with his customers. But he kept his ears open, too . . .

His waiters were mostly youngsters between eighteen and twenty. He liked to joke about how he adored having young people around him. But everyone knew his weakness for young boys. His vice was tolerated and even considered to be one more eccentricity on the part of a rich man with powerful connections. He was fair in his dealings and always ready to offer a drink on the house to new customers. He paid his waiters well, and gave them presents on religious holidays.

Because of his perversion, he tended to be jittery and obsequious with people. His body had been found behind the counter of his bar. One of his employees was suspected, the latest 'favourite', who possibly had a score to settle. The affair had seemed rather unclear at first, but there was no doubt in the superintendent's mind that it was a political execution.

He expressed increasing pessimism. The professor listened to him sympathetically, while methodically stuffing his pipe.

'We must be prudent, my dear fellow! Nowadays, having an Arab in the house is inviting death! I'll be frank with you, I've dismissed my maid, my wife has to manage the housework herself, but our minds are more at rest.'

He wagged a finger sententiously at his host as he concluded, 'Don't say I've not warned you! . . . I don't like the look of that boy.'

'He's surely not going to cut my throat just for fun!' the professor protested. 'I'm an old hermit, with no interest for anyone! This lad is quiet, as soon as he's finished his work he buries himself in a detective story . . . Sometimes he goes to the cinema or to town to see his aunt. Believe me, I'm a good judge of human nature.'

The policeman looked even more suspicious. 'You say he likes detective stories? All the more reason to be on your guard! Boys

126

like that have nothing in their heads; they kill gratuitously these days, to get an excuse to join the guerrillas . . .'

Monsieur Kimper protested with an air of mock terror. 'Stop, I beg you! You're really going to put the wind up me! I assure you this boy realizes he's found a good billet, he's well fed, I leave him alone, he knows this and does everything to deserve my trust!'

The superintendent had nothing more to add. Moreover, he was rather overawed by everything around him. The bookcase filled with books, the impressive piano, not an ordinary upright, but an enormous Steinway grand, standing proudly on its three legs. Everything gave off an air of refinement. He had begun his career as a constable on point duty, and thanks to the war had been promoted to the rank of superintendent. He was aware of his intellectual inferiority compared with Monsieur Kimper's extensive culture. He took his leave of the professor, assuring him he could rely on his protection in case of trouble. On his way out through the garden, he glanced sharply at Ali again, and in his eyes there was a trace of fear.

The night was unusually cool for the end of summer. The two men shivered. Ali leaned further out of the car to make out the path that was only intermittently lit by a capricious moon which seemed to be playing hide-and-seek, now lighting their way round a bush, now hiding behind the clouds. But the two men were in no mood for play this evening; they cursed the darkness rather. Eventually Ali recognized the path which climbed steeply upwards. He drove on to it then switched off the engine. Tahar jumped out. He pulled the toolbag out from beneath the back seat.

'You'd better keep quiet!' Ali whispered. 'I'm pretty sure of the area, but you never know!'

They started up the rough track. The darkness thickened, the moon having now abandoned them altogether. Ali had difficulty in making out the trees. Tahar cursed as he stumbled over low branches. Everything was perfectly calm. From time to time stones rolled down, a bird flew away with a loud rustling of leaves.

'I'd be surprised if there were only goods and weapons. There must be some workmen too . . .' Ali whispered.

'Don't question your orders!' Tahar reminded him curtly.

Ali nodded and stopped to get his breath. He thought the only thing that mattered after all was for him to make a success of the operation . . . This wasn't the place for sentiment, and if he started quibbling he'd put Tahar's back up. And who knows how he was likely to react . . .

'The trucks will be veritable powder-kegs,' he predicted. 'They'll wake up with a shock!'

After half an hour's climb they reached the approaches to the extension of the railway. Six miles further on lay the village of Dachra. Usually two watchmen remained on duty there after the last train passed down into the valley. But since the outbreak of the armed revolution, half a dozen men were left on guard, although they often preferred to sit playing cards in the station-master's office.

Ali knew this region well and could find his way about blindfold. They reached the isolator box. They could dimly make out the pylons. A sprinkling of grass muffled their footsteps. Tahar handed Ali the rubber gloves and wire-cutters and guided him with an electric torch. Ali was the first up the mast. He stopped to examine the section of wires between two insulators. He could hear a slight hissing. He whistled and almost immediately there was a bluish flash below him. At his signal Tahar had raised the circuitbreaker, so cutting off the current. Ali now easily cut through the wire. The weight of the cable dragged the insulator down and this fell with a crash, breaking against a girder, setting up what seemed a terrifying din. Ali waited anxiously. Tahar immediately switched off his torch.

He listened, holding his breath, clutching the pistol which he had slipped into his belt. It would be terrible if they were caught in the act. He did not know if the patrols came so far. There was a paratroop barracks in Dachra as in every hamlet in the country. The place was riddled with every type of uniform: members of the Foreign Legion, *goumiers*, paratroopers, riot police, gendarmes. But at night any troops who ventured into the maquis warned of their presence by the noise of their helicopters and the rattle of weaponry.

For the moment there were no suspicious sounds. Ali closed his eyes, his hands were moist, he panted slightly. He remembered he had climbed up a pylon once before, to mend a cable, many months previously. He had come with workmen and a military escort fearful of ambushes in the area. And he recalled his wonderment at the sensational view of the Dachra valley, with the *douars* all around in the distance, like an amphitheatre . At present, these scenes from his childhood only seemed like a cyclone threatening to engulf him . . . Ali was afraid. He slid back to the ground. He went off, followed by Tahar, to climb another pylon. Ten minutes later several yards of steel cable fell heavily to the ground. Tahar and Ali set about cutting them into small pieces to prevent any possible re-use after a temporary repair.

'That's your job finished, Ali . . . Hold the torch for me while I loosen the bolts on the rails . . . Pass me the bag! Then, I'll put the bombs in place. With the four that we have, one on each side, about a hundred yards apart . . . that should do.'

Thinking aloud, Tahar set rapidly to work. He loosened the bolts with precise gestures. He picked up a black box, set it and buried it swiftly in the earth under the rails. He worked silently with mechanical efficiency. The time seemed terribly long to Ali. He kept looking at his watch. That was the most difficult part of the job. Tahar was expressionless. He moved easily as if he did not know the meaning of fatigue. He brought an almost religious concentration to his actions. Now all the explosives were in place and the sabotage was completed.

'Done! You're the guide, get us out of here!'

They returned the way they had come, but this time at the double. When they got back to the car, they drove flat out back to town.

Tahar's rugged face showed no sign of fatigue. Ali noted the strange gleam in his dark eyes. The same as on that other terrible night. Ruthless, cold, and distant. The youngster lit a cigarette to help him regain his composure; he did not care for Tahar's

129

expression which made him feel that same panic that paralysed him in the first nightmare of his childhood.

Everything had been calculated exactly. A quarter of an hour before the curfew, they stopped the car in front of a garage near the entrance to Baladia. The steel door rose as if by magic; the man who opened it must have been watching out for them through an invisible hole, Ali thought. They alighted and followed their host up a little spiral staircase leading to what was probably his flat.

They were shown into a room strewn with brightly covered mattresses. A woollen carpet and the traditional low table completed the furnishing. They sat down with a sigh of satisfaction. They listened for a moment to the sounds of the household, women's voices, a child crying, probably not wanting to go to bed. Their host seemed to know Tahar well.

The two men were served a tasty tomato soup, flavoured with mint, which they ate with relish; this was followed by a *chakhchoukha*: galette sliced up very finely and cooked with meat and chick-peas in a deliciously hot, chilli sauce. This dish is said to be hot enough to revive the dead. The feast was rounded off by coffee, slightly flavoured with orange-flower water, which made the two companions pleasantly drowsy. They had not spoken a word as they ate. The setting and the meal reminded Ali of his home and his mother's cooking. He shut his eyes and fell asleep with his dream, like a kid exhausted by a long walk . . .

The next morning, they left the car at their host's and took the bus into the centre of the town.

'See you in a few days at the prof's,' Tahar said. 'Don't budge from there and don't come to Béni-Ramassés. You'd better lie low. If there's any news I'll get word to you through Mounir or Salah.'

'What about the rest of the work I've still got to do at your place?'

'You did the most important part the other day. That'll do for now! And don't forget you've a job at Monsieur Kimper's, my lad! The garden needs your attention!' Tahar laughed as Ali looked mortified.

'OK! Just as you say.'

Ali followed Tahar's lanky figure a short distance, unhappy at the thought of not seeing him for several days. He was as attached to him as a puppy to his master. Then he slowly went his own way. 'Curious man!' he thought. 'Not a word about our mission last night . . . no sign of satisfaction with the way I behaved. I didn't let him down this time . . . A bit nervous at first, but I don't think he noticed anything . . .'

These thoughts filled his head as he approached the professor's house. 'Tonight I'll re-read my diary and write it up . . . But I must be careful to hide it safely in the garden.'

9

Baladia . . . 30 June 1958

Two days after the 'operation' – my life has resumed its monotonous routine with the various jobs about the house. But this evening, I have important news to record. Yesterday, when I was out shopping for Khéïra, I bumped into Alain . . . I hadn't seen him since my mother's death, when he came with his parents to express their condolences. How he's grown! His hair was as bushy as ever and his big green eyes expressed pleasant surprise at seeing me. I felt a bit awkward at meeting him now, but he was so delighted to see me again that he didn't notice anything.

'Ali, good heavens! The last person I was expecting to meet, you old bastard! Where the devil have you been hiding? I wrote to you in the village several times . . .'

He grabbed my arm, thumped me on the back and in his excitement took hold of my face, waggled my chin and patted my cheeks. The people on the steps of the post office began to stare at us curiously. Eventually I managed to get him away from the crowds and tried to calm him down.

'Hey! Stop shaking me like a plum tree! You haven't changed a bit. I didn't answer your letters for the good reason that I'd left the village.'

'And the technical college? Did you give it up? What are you doing now?'

So there we were. I couldn't shake him off. I had to invent some story.

'I left the college some time ago! I didn't have time to tell you all about it when you came to my mother's funeral. But I started working on the railways when my father died . . . And now I've got a job as a professor's secretary.'

I didn't dare tell him about my clash with the foreman, my brief spell in prison and my present job as gardener-watchman . . . He would have smelled a rat as that sort of work didn't fit the picture he had of me. And he knew me better than anyone else! Besides which, I felt so old beside him and I didn't know how to escape his genuinely friendly advances.

'Secretary! That's right up your street, with your love of paperwork . . . For my part, I've got problems, old chap! What luck I met you. Come!'

He tried to take me off to a café to chat about everything, but I was in a hurry. I realized I was cornered and didn't know how to get away.

'Listen, Alain . . . I can't stay today, my boss is expecting me, I just came out to post some letters . . . But if you like, we can meet later . . .'

'Steady on! I'm not going to let you go just like that!'

He saw I was worried and said more calmly, 'I'll come and call for you and take you back to lunch with us . . . OK? Mother will be delighted to see you . . . Give me your address.'

'No, it's too far out of your way. I'll come to your place . . . where are you living?'

And so I found myself sitting down once more between Alain and his parents. Juliette was overcome with emotion and wept copiously as she thought of the village, my mother . . . And she was shattered to hear of all my misfortunes. Marcel, her husband, muttered 'Hum! hum!' all the time. At first I had no idea why. I understood when Juliette sighed, as she poured the coffee, 'Everything's changed, my boy! Life's lost its meaning for me now; you see Marcel wants to leave and go back to France! Just imagine! At my age, going to a country I don't know . . . This is where I was born!'

She got up to fetch a handkerchief, her eyes dimmed with tears. Marcel seemed exasperated and I sensed that similar scenes must take place daily.

'She doesn't understand that life isn't possible for us here any more,' he exclaimed, 'or for the business! In the bar, I've more customers than ever I had back there in the village. I've made far more money since we came to live in town, and even more since this damned war! But the atmosphere isn't the same any more . . . The place is filled with soldiers and the few Muslims who do come – I don't know if they're informers for one side or the other and I'm sick of it now, especially since they shot a paratrooper in my bar! I have to act the cop and that's not my cup of tea! You can't trust anyone any more. I've had it now! But just try and make women understand, by God!'

'Don't swear, Marcel!' Juliette cried, 'It's bad luck!'

'What! "Don't swear"?' Marcel repeated mincingly, mimicking his wife's expression. 'These Jewesses, talk about superstitious! They're worse than the Arabs!'

'What've you got against Jewesses? You married one, didn't you? Since you came to town and that fat old cow of a sister came to see you, you're not the same person . . . you're even spiteful to me now!'

Marcel got up with a shrug and left, slamming the door behind him and grunting, 'If that's how you feel, I'll be off.' To me he said, 'See you one of these days, my lad!'

Alain watched this scene ironically, apparently used to these noisy exchanges between his parents. Juliette was now weeping in earnest and lamenting, 'You saw that, children? He's changed. Every day he gets more and more disagreeable. He wants us to pack up immediately, and I can't resign myself to going to live over there! . . . I've all my family and friends here . . . I don't care a damn about the war. I've never been bothered. I still see most of my Arab women friends, I go to the Turkish bath just as I used to in the village, I'm invited to weddings, nothing's changed for me. It's the Europeans who don't like the Jews. The Arabs have never discriminated against us!'

Alain consoled her, 'Yes, of course, you're right, but Papa is too, you know that! He can't go on working in this atmosphere of fear . . . Besides, in France I'll be able to finish my *baccalauréat* in peace. You want your son to pass his exams, don't you? . . .'

134

I was sad to think what was happening to Juliette. I'd always been fond of her. I understood her despair; I couldn't imagine her deprived of the women's gatherings, her weekly outing to the *hammam*, joining in all the gossip and laughter, enjoying the ritual of massage by expert hands, then going for coffee at the house of the woman whose turn it was to entertain the others . . . No one who had breathed the air of Algeria, heavy with the aroma of mint, jasmin and aniseed, and the smell of fritters hot from the frying pan, could ever leave it without feeling a sense of death . . .

Juliette suddenly burst out, showing she knew all about the history of the suffering of the Jews. 'In the first place, it was the Europeans who ill-treated us Jews! The Arabs here never persecuted us or robbed us or branded us like animals . . . "ghetto", "inquisition", "gas chambers", "crematoria" . . . all those are things we learned from Europe! . . . Now the fashion's changed and they want us to side with them against the Arabs . . . But I won't play their game!'

Alain smiled at his mother's fiery outburst, but she wagged a finger at him. 'It's important for you to realize that, my boy, so that you never stray from the path of justice! We're all brothers, we've been looked down on in the same way, we've been the victims of the same irrational suspicion of our race . . . Except that in our case, we were forewarned and eventually assimilated, we became integrated by our hard work, and also due to our shrewdness . . . And for them, the Arabs, the nightmare is only just beginning! Our only salvation is in unity; the history of the majority of Jews in the world has been closely associated with that of the Arabs, so we mustn't now fall into the trap laid by politicians for their own ends.'

I remarked that life in the city had changed her, as I'd never known her show such flights of oratory. She agreed sadly. 'Yes, it's the lies I hear on the radio and read in the papers that have made me aware of the tricks politicians play . . . I only hate one thing: war . . . I know some people want you to believe the Arabs have never got on with the Jews; there are even some Jews who pretend to think that way and to approve that kind of heresy . . .

135

They are the results of the system, of racist ideas. They're trying to suck up to people for their own self-interest; they can't take us in, the mass of Oriental Jews . . . we despise them! You, Ali and Alain, must always stay united; you represent the true fraternity which ought to exist among men, irrespective of the colour of their skin or their religion, or even if they have no religion . . . What d'you call those people?'

'Atheists,' Alain murmured.

'Yes, that's right! Atheists!'

'But you're a revolutionary, Juliette!' I exclaimed.

We all burst out laughing. Alain applauded his mother, pretending to sound the trumpet for the hoisting of the national flag. Then he said, 'In that case let's go to Tunisia, like Aunt Sarah, then you won't feel so lost outside your cocoon. That won't be too much of a change from here . . .'

Juliette looked at her son sharply to see if he was joking. Then her face lit up with hope and happiness, like a child receiving a wonderful, unexpected present. She rushed at her son and hugged him, then turned to me, 'You see how clever he is, *ya Rabbi!* But that's a wonderful idea! They say it's just like here! Except that the accent is a bit different . . . You'll help me, won't you Alain, to talk your father out of his idea of going to France? Ali, why don't you come with us? There's nothing to keep you here, is there? Besides, you know you're like another son to me . . . You can continue your studies, if you like, there are colleges there, or Marcel would give you a job, why not?'

She got more and more excited and, as she took herself off to the kitchen, she shouted to me to hurry up and agree, continuing, 'I'm going to make some fritters now, children. You'll see, Ali, I can make them as well as Chérifa. *Allah yarhamha.* May her soul rest in peace.'

Alain looked at me and I could read a silent prayer in his eyes. He frowned anxiously. For a moment our eyes met, expressing everything we felt: our indestructible friendship, the bonds of affection woven in our childhood, our fraternity born from growing and breathing the same village air. He read also my refusal to leave . . .

136

To relieve the tension he got up and threw the window wide open. And with his hands in his pockets he murmured, 'I knew you'd never leave the country! And I suspect I know why; you're lucky to know for certain that everything here is yours . . .'

We did not need words to understand each other, but I needed to know one thing: his sincere opinion on what is happening now. 'This struggle can be yours as well!' I said. 'It concerns all people who love justice.'

He did not turn round but his voice grew serious, charged with a deep sadness. 'I'm too young and too dependent on many things. I don't rightly know what I am: an Algerian? I feel I am with all my heart, but will they let me call myself one later? Am I French? I've never really lived as a Frenchman, but in future I shall have to be one . . . A Jew? I'm proud to have a mother like Juliette; but as far as religious belief is concerned, I've never had any . . . But I know one thing: this is my country . . . I must tell you, often, when I hear the muezzin call to prayer, I have a terrible longing to be a Muslim, and I'm eaten up with fury at not having been born like you, then everything would have been simpler . . . But whatever the outcome, I shall come back to live here . . .'

I asked him suddenly, 'What about Israel? Would you go and fight there if you were asked? You know what happened in 1956?'

This time he turned round, moved over to me and retorted in a voice shaking with anger, 'Have you never understood me then? Where was I born? Where did I grow up? My mother, her parents, her grandparents? All their memories are here, linked to yours. Why should I go and die for a country I don't know? Because our ancestors travelled through it long ago? In that case, you ought to go and fight with the Moroccans and Tunisians to seize Spain back from the Spanish because it was Muslim for eight centuries! All that is an aberration, madness on the part of senile, intriguing Western governments . . . You take me for a bloody fool? You think I'm not aware of this masquerade? You think I have to follow them like a sheep?'

'No! You are the worthy offspring of the superb Juliette!'

'I know I upset people when I talk like this. The other day I had a set-to with a prof who's completely nuts; we were discussing geography and I said, "But, sir, Israel is in an Arab region, in the Middle East, so as far as geography's concerned it's an Arab country! Jews are not the only people there! There are plenty of Muslims and Christians . . . The Muslims are in the majority, so how come that minority has appropriated the country? It's neither logical nor just!" He turned ashen, as if I was Frankenstein in person. I thought he was going to conk out . . . However he put it down to my ignorance and took it upon himself to give me an incredible loony explanation, as if we were all half-wits . . .'

He continued emphatically, 'France is my country! If I were asked to choose between France and Israel, I'd choose the former; it's my legitimate country, the country of my father. And Algeria would remain the great love of my life . . . You believe me now?'

Yes, I believed him; he was not the neurotic or temperamental sort. I knew his convictions were solid. And age had nothing to do with it. In Algeria we mature very quickly, we don't go through the crises of spoilt adolescents . . . The troubles saw to it that we were precipitated from carefree youth into responsible maturity. And in his innermost heart, Alain was like a nomad, seeking a place to pitch his tent – whether in the land of his mother, or in that of his father, or of his birth.

Juliette burst in, bringing back noise and laughter. 'Why so quiet? I was getting anxious, you young perishers! It's just like when you were small: when I couldn't hear you, you were sure to be getting up to some mischief. So what's up now? You both look a couple of Jonahs!'

She put down the dish of fritters and resumed, 'Oh! I see, it's because Ali won't come and live with us? Why's that? Is your job interesting? You like being a secretary? Tell me about it.'

She brought the coffee cups and little white napkins and sat down to watch us eat.

'Well, it's like this . . .' I began. 'I type the correspondence; at first I didn't know how, but I soon learned, and I like working with the typewriter . . .'

'Oh, yes!' she interrupted. 'The neighbour's daughter is learning to type and she makes as much fuss about it as if she was learning to fly a plane! She talks about it all the time, and that's been going on for a year! And you've taught yourself? Though I say it myself, our country boys can beat all these stuck-up townies . . . Just look at Alain, he's top of his class, and he's sure to pass his *bac*!'

'By the way, Alain,' I said, 'have you made up your mind what you'll do after the *bac*?'

He'd not been one to worry all the time about his future career like the rest of us. So I'd never known what his vocation was, so to speak. He replied with an ironic glance in my direction, 'I shall take a leaf out of your book, old chap! I shall become a journalist just like you said to our teacher – I've never forgotten what you told me during the holidays: "I shall report on my country, pursuing the truth, tracking down injustice and lies" . . .'

Juliette exclaimed in surprise, 'Well now! That's news! Your father wants you to be a doctor! You'll get it from him, I promise you! . . . Tell me, boys, can you make money in that job?'

We both burst out laughing, once more the little monkeys who used to tease her in the past. 'Oh! loads of money, Mother! I shall have my by-line with all the main newspapers! . . .'

'He'll buy you a mink coat just like the film stars,' I added. 'You'll have a big house and pearl necklaces . . . He'll write books and get interviewed on all the radio programmes.'

'*Ya Rabbi!* As much as that! But what'll I do with a fur coat? You're pulling my leg . . . Anyway, the main thing is for heaven to keep you in good health!'

Then we moved on to gossip about the village. I learned that Monsieur Lavigne and his wife had left for France, Madame Roumière practically lived in Cannes where she owned a house, while her husband had stayed to manage their property but often went over to join his family. The Tagliotas had settled in the town, in another shop, selling household appliances now. Angèle was still boozing, and old Tagliota had gone a bit soft in the head since Francis went underground. He didn't know if he'd been killed or had managed to join the rebels. As for the others, the headmaster and all the teachers had been transferred to a city, as the school had become the headquarters for the SAS . . . Most of the Muslims were still there. Juliette had been back recently to

139

fetch some furniture that the Lavignes had sold her when they left
and she'd heard that Abbas had left only a few months ago to join
the underground. Slimane had disappeared from his college, to
join the resistance as well. Abdi, the 'big booby', had married one
of Meriem's sisters (so that dolt had become my cousin, so to
speak!). He was now managing Si Hafid's café. So most of the
young people had deserted Dachra; only women and old men
remained, guarded by the military . . .

Juliette concluded sadly, 'The past will never return! When I
think of all those kids I knew who are now revolutionaries! What
are we coming to? It's a good thing you've got a job that keeps you
out of trouble, Ali!'

Baladia . . . 1 July 1958

There are more and more frequent incidents of partisan attacks in
the towns. Europeans and collaborators grow daily more uneasy
as the mass of Muslims, who no longer smoke or drink in public,
desert the Moorish cafés, foregoing their noisy games of cards and
dominoes which give rise to animated gatherings. Thus, a law, a
hidden but effectual force, has undermined the settlers' power.
Those who oppose the resistance movement, and more especially
the resident Europeans, are seriously shaken.

One can sense in the eyes of passers-by an impenetrable barrier
of distrust and I recall the artificially created euphoria of a few
months ago . . . The farce of fraternization, launched by the
committees for public safety set up in May this year . . . The
political meetings which wretched Algerian family-men were
forced to attend . . . There was also the stupid dramatic gesture of
women tearing up their veils, when everyone knows that the
women in question worked in houses of ill-repute.

According to the triumphant *pieds-noirs,* tearing up veils
represented burying the hatchet, for the Algerians! In any case,
something has changed on both sides of the Mediterranean, and in
the world at large! The *fellagas,* having brought about the fall of
several cabinets, have finally overturned the regime and last

140

September appointed an official body to represent them, namely the GPRA.

Our growing successes, both in the cities and within the maquis, have had international repercussions. Neither regroupings, nor the policy of scorched earth, nor arbitrary internments over the last four years have succeeded in crushing the determination of a people set on reaching its goal.

Conscious of the effectiveness of the mass media, General de Gaulle continues to scale greater heights of oratory. He gets rid of the political manoeuvrers and surrounds himself with unknown faces. That is, if the truth be known, the way most wily heads of state go about achieving their aims . . .

In the course of our discussions in his house, Monsieur Kimper reminds Si Salah and myself that the old General was the first in 1940 to refuse to submit. 'Today,' he went on, 'after his long retirement, he's given it a lot of thought; he'll accept free Algeria. He's trying to decolonize Africa. He doesn't want a repetition of the hornets' nest that Indo-China turned out to be. And you must realize,' he added, 'that this war costs more than a billion francs a day.'

'All in all,' Si Salah interrupted, 'it's really France that he wants to save!'

'That's certain! De Gaulle has this arrogant dream of making France the third world power, so he can't continue to be burdened with this mill-stone round his neck!'

These discussions aroused me to a fever of enthusiasm in my corner! I was burning to get a word in, but I was inhibited by my respect for Si Salah and Monsieur Kimper and their vast knowledge . . .

An extraordinary future took shape in my dreams: one day we would make this country into a paradise, in which all children would be happy . . . where all people who love freedom would come to share our happiness. We would no longer be condemned to oblivion.

Already the young people are leaving home to make their contribution to the struggle.

Where is Slimane now, my muddle-headed, generous comrade?

What maquis is he with? Where is he crouching on the look-out for the enemy?

Abbas? It's strange, I can't imagine him struggling through rough undergrowth in the hills and obeying a leader . . . He's more . . . how can I put it? . . . more a man of ideas than action, and his courage is all concentrated in his calculating mind; he's most likely to be some resistance leader's adviser.

Rachid? I haven't heard what has become of him. I know his parents are still in the village, his father still works in the Roumières' fields. When anyone asks the old man about his son, he clams up, as if he had something to hide. But I can imagine Rachid, philosophizing on one verse or the other of the Quran, and perhaps listening with silent irony to his fellow students discussing the political events in the country.

Abdi, the 'big booby', has the village practically to himself now. It wouldn't surprise me to see him eventually take possession of the Moorish café from under his boss's nose . . .

Well, enough of that! My mind is on my inactivity which is getting on my nerves. It's not as though I haven't got enough to do here, but the garden and its monotonous tranquillity is beginning to bore me. There are also the newspapers and the professor who discusses things with me from time to time, so subconsciously completing my education. Tahar and the others are making a fuss about nothing! I'd thought the life of a militant was daily action, being constantly faced with danger, and here am I for the last few days living like a good, obedient little boy. Troubled by these thoughts, I have only my diary to help me see clearly in this labyrinth.

I've just re-read, like I do every evening, what I wrote about my childhood in my beloved village. My meeting with Alain and Juliette . . . All that has upset me and I feel as if Tahar has abandoned me . . I can't bear this idea. Well, tomorrow, whatever happens, I shall go to Béni-Ramassés, although he made it clear I was to stay here and not leave the house . . . Will he be angry with me?

10

Ali was getting ready to go out. He had warned the professor he
would be away all day, as it was not his day off. He was a bit
apprehensive about the way Tahar would receive him . . . He was
aware of disobeying orders but he was fed up with being kept in
the background, like a child who had to be protected. This
morning Ali was angry.

When he got to Tahar's place, he hesitated for a moment, his
courage failing him. Then, shaking off his misgivings, he gave two
sharp knocks. Suppose Tahar was not at home! . . . No, at this
early hour, he'd probably still be asleep . . . The door opened as he
was still wondering. Tahar was taken by surprise. His face
contracted, 'What's up?'

'I wanted to see you! Can I come in?'

'I told you to stay put! Mounir warned you, didn't he?'

'No, I haven't seen him. Can I come in?' Ali repeated, irritated
by this conversation in the doorway.

'I came to see you yesterday, but I was told you were out
visiting,' he heard Mounir saying, behind Tahar. Ali flushed with
anger and confusion at the scarcely veiled sarcasm in the other's
voice.

Tahar went back in and Ali followed him, closing the door
behind him. Faced with Mounir's irony and Tahar's ominous
silence, he felt like a child caught out telling lies. And as always in
like cases, he felt his anger rising; he shouted at Mounir, 'Couldn't
you come back later? And, what's more, my "visits" are no
business of yours!'

It was clear from his voice that he was in the mood for a
quarrel. But Mounir kept his composure.

143

'You're quite right. I wanted to let you know how the authorities reacted to the sabotage of the train, and I wanted to tell you there were more than thirty dead, including a dozen Muslim workmen, in addition to the material damage. Besides which,' he added in the same calm detached voice, as if he were reciting a lesson learnt by heart, 'the controls in town are very strict and you must on no account leave the house! That's the whole message I came to give you!'

Ali was overwhelmed to hear in the same breath of the success of their mission and the death of these innocent workmen. He felt his stomach heave, as if he were going to vomit. No! Not in front of them! . . . Especially Mounir. Why did he have to be the one to announce this news? Why not Tahar? . . . He'd have preferred to hear it from his mouth. He wouldn't have felt this nausea which came with distress and fear. There would surely have been in Tahar's eyes his usual gleam of pride in his young companion, probably hidden under banter such as, 'You did "psychologically" well that night, my boy, quite terrific . . . Didn't I say I'd make something of you, eh!' But Tahar was smoking without a word, his slit eyes half-shut, quite unmoved by the threatening confrontation between the two men.

'And you tell me now, after all this time? Are you trying to make a fool of me?'

'With the newspapers reporting so much poppycock, I didn't know what was going on!'

Ali clenched his fists and glared at Mounir. He felt an irresistible urge to smash his handsome, well-fed, complacent dandy's jaw . . . Mounir met this rising anger with a contemptuous silence, as if he considered it childish and unworthy of a militant. Curiously, Ali relaxed in the face of the latent antipathy in Mounir's expression which made him realize for the first time how much the other disliked him. Ali was, as always, disarmed by people's animosity towards him. When he discovered hostility or envy, he felt temporarily thrown off his balance, as if he had been roughly jostled . . . He was surprised to see Mounir turn away and take a cigarette out of a packet on the table. He puffed at it with an almost painful concentration. Tahar clapped his hands and declared, 'All right! If you've finished your little act Mounir, it's time for you to get back to your class. Your pupils will be waiting for you . . .'

Mounir knew when diplomacy was required; as he left he held out his hand to Ali with a smile, saying, 'No hard feelings, old chap! It was my fault and I promise you next time I've a message for you, I'll wait as long as necessary, OK?'

As soon as Mounir had gone, Tahar started in on Ali. 'You know perfectly well you were not supposed to come here! You've got a safe hide-out and you want to ruin everything! How d'you know you're not being followed by informers? Kimper's known and respected, but people know about his interest in us, and he may well be under discreet surveillance! Especially now, with so many committees for public safety and all that jazz! The grasses are everywhere . . . You're one of the rare ones to have a solid cover and you want to blow it with your fits of the fidgets!'

'Yes, I know, but all this waiting about ever since our "operation" got on my nerves . . . I was completely in the dark – I didn't know if it had succeeded, or if you were satisfied with me! I was fed up with just digging the garden, running errands, reading the newspapers and never leaving the house . . .! Tahar! Help me!' Ali pleaded. 'You talked of a "test". Well I've shown my mettle now! . . . I want to go to the maquis!'

'The maquis!' Tahar sneered. 'That's all you can talk about! Good heavens! You think you go to the maquis like you go to a brothel? You think any fellow who feels the urge in his belly can go and satisfy it like that! . . . They need us here! The city is our maquis! And, anyway, what they need there in the hills is weapons, they're not short of men! . . .'

He looked at Ali, shaking his head in discouragement, then he added, in a calmer, more ominous tone, emphasizing every word, 'You disobeyed orders, Ali! You know you can be penalized? Mounir, with his casual manner, is as wary as a cat and as obedient as a trained watchdog . . . And so are all the others . . . You, with your impatience, risk bringing the whole pyramid crashing down, by revealing one of the tiny but important stones in the structure. You are a part of the shadow-army, your

145

admission to the organization makes you a member of the resistance. You must abide by orders, even if you are only asked to pick roses every day . . . You are recruited for that, too. Every action is important.'

Tahar fell silent, seeming to reflect, then suddenly went to the back of the room. He bent down, unscrewed a plank and pulled out a revolver hidden underneath. Ali shuddered. 'That's it!' he thought. 'He's going to kill me! I'll be executed without trial, just as Si Salah said . . .'

Rooted to the spot in alarm, Ali waited for the outcome. Tahar noticed his pallor but, misinterpreting the cause, remarked jokingly, 'You've never seen a gun? You've already forgotten how quick off the mark you were with the dancer? . . . You want action? Well, here you are! Go and show us how brave you are! There are only two bullets: one for the victim and the other for you if you're caught . . . Only see that you don't shoot an innocent person! You'll pay for it with your life.'

Ali looked at the weapon with respect. He was gradually filled with great joy. At last he felt he could be relied on. He was going to carry out an operation all by himself! Organizing and acting alone! He was going to deserve Tahar's trust, even if he died in the attempt. He simply said, 'Show me how to use it.'

'Not necessary! You demonstrated with Dalila . . . Go now!'

The market was swarming with gossiping housewives, hurrying to finish their shopping by midday. Near the entrance, the street-traders selling spices, poultry, fruit and vegetables had drawn up their barrows and were shouting their wares at the tops of their voices.

'Come along, lady, fresh eggs and olives! All bright and shining like your gazelle's eyes, lady!'

They tossed off their patter in a series of well-chosen flourishes. Every now and again an urchin rushed up to interrupt their flow of oratory, warning of a policeman's approach. Then all the hawkers beat a swift retreat.

Ragged youngsters kept a look-out for women laden with baskets, offering to carry them to earn a few coppers. At the corner of the next street a policeman stood on guard, twirling his white truncheon. He shot fierce glances at the crowd, composed mostly of Muslims, who converged on the market from all sides. One of his colleagues directed the heavy traffic, a stream of jeeps and trucks loaded with soldiers, in additon to cars, bicycles and scooters.

All this created a bustle and a deafening din.

Ali had disguised himself with a false moustache and wore a beret, considered rather smart in this part of Algeria. He looked more like a Maltese or an Italian than an Arab. He approached an old man selling melons and pretended to examine them, weighing them in his hands with the air of an expert.

'They're quite fresh, son! And their flavour is like the kiss of a young girl in the midst of spring flowers! . . .'

Ali asked him casually whether he'd seen Ramdane lately. The old man's weather-beaten face contracted and he shook his head sadly.

'What! *Ya oueldi*, you must be a stranger hereabouts! Who knows where old Ramdane's buried? . . . He was defending a poor wretch like me, who was being beaten up by a policeman . . . Look, that's the one, over there! The man twirling his truncheon, the dog!'

The old man spat on the ground and continued, 'He's a fanatic, that fellow! There are plenty of cops after us, but that one's a devil! If he catches us, we're done for! The cut on his face is almost healed, you can scarcely see it! But it's made him wilder than ever! . . . Go away! Leave me alone! I don't want to think about these things! Your Ramdane's certainly dead by now! . . . So, are you taking that melon or not?'

Ali paid for several melons and told the man to sell them to other people. The hawker was quite overcome. Nevertheless, he took the money without a word, thinking this fellow must be mad. Nowadays, you shouldn't be surprised at anything, he thought philosophically.

Now Ali knew what he had to do. He walked confidently over to the policeman who continued to swing his truncheon, as if to keep the populace around him at a distance. Ali's hand closed over the revolver in the pocket of his jacket. Very politely he asked the way to the station. The man burst out laughing, telling him he was nowhere near it.

His laughter was instantly silenced as the blast reduced his head to a mass of splintered bone and bleeding flesh.

It all happened so rapidly that the policeman who was directing the traffic, deafened by the noise of all the vehicles and the roar of the crowds, heard nothing. His attention was finally caught when the line of cars which should have moved at his signal remained stationary and screams of terror arose on all sides.

People lost their heads, running in all directions, rushing to hide in cafés and shops. Steel shutters were lowered with a crash. Everybody fled to avoid the inevitable controls, the arbitrary arrests of anyone looking like an Arab. They fled from more possible attacks . . . They fled desperately, no matter where.

This was the way the crowd behaved after every partisan attack. People were so conditioned by events that even the slightest backfiring from a car caused them to take to their heels, and everybody followed without thinking.

Ali had stuffed his still smoking revolver in his pocket and mingled with the fleeing crowd. Eventually he came to a halt in a narrow street where there was no one about. Looking around, he saw the entrance to a block of expensive-looking flats. He rushed in with no thought but that he must hide . . . Where could he go, in any case? All the streets would be cordoned off by now. Suddenly he heard the creaking of a lift descending. He quickly took off his beret and shoved it under his shirt; then he pulled off the moustache and hid it in his pocket. He smoothed his hair, adjusted his tie, and tried to look casual. He noticed the bulge in his pocket made by the revolver; he removed it quickly and slipped it behind his back. He reckoned he now looked quite respectable.

A lady of about fifty stepped cautiously out of the lift. She looked about her carefully as the hall was dark and her thick spectacles showed she was very short-sighted. Eventually she noticed the young man. She walked over slowly, sizing him up suspiciously.

'I've never seen you before, young man! Who are you waiting for?'

'No one, ma'am, I was passing and I heard shots . . .'

The lady trembled, her curls a-quiver; she put her hand to her mouth and exclaimed, 'Shots, did you say? Where? Tell me! . . .'

She seemed so overcome that without realizing it she didn't give the young man a chance to answer.

'I think it was at the market . . . Someone was killed . . . Police or soldiers, or perhaps a passer-by, I don't know . . . Everyone was running, so I got scared too . . .'

He wrung his hands, not even pretending to be upset as he was genuinely worried, wondering how he was going to get away with this woman keeping him stuck in the doorway with her questions. And soon, he thought with horror, someone, the janitor or one of the neighbours, would come out and notice his peculiar appearance with the revolver biting into his back and reminding him every moment of the danger he was in.

Ali was half dead with fright. In the beginning, he had been all courage and heroism; now that he had made his gesture, his previous euphoria was followed by a sort of lassitude. His one thought was to get out of this area. The terror that overwhelmed him resembled his feelings at the prospect of the headmaster's finger-nails biting into his ears. He controlled his desire to throw up and proclaimed pitifully, 'My parents will be anxious! I must phone them immediately. I live a long way away, in Orchards . . .'

'How annoying! Just when I was going to do my shopping at the market! And I'm out of meat for Mimiche, my pussy! And the little rascal won't eat anything else!'

She shrugged her shoulders, muttering, 'People have gone quite mad!'

Then a sudden idea struck her and she looked more closely at the young man. 'You say you live in Orchards? That's a very smart area! But it certainly is a long way, and you risk having a long wait!'

Ali was growing impatient, he felt like falling on his knees and begging her to stop chattering and hide him. He felt he was at the end of his tether!

She turned round and walked instinctively back to the lift to return to her flat, resigned to abandoning her shopping for the day. It was as if she had forgotten the boy's presence. Then she seemed to change her mind and more or less ordered him, 'Follow me! What are you waiting for? . . . You can telephone your parents from my place and you'll be company for me meanwhile.'

She took his arm and pushed him into the lift. She continued her chatter during the slow ascent; the machinery had clearly seen better days.

'I've been living alone for ten years! I'm a widow, you understand. I was a teacher before that, and then time never hung on my hands. Since I retired, if it weren't for Mimiche, I'd be pretty miserable . . . But she's as fussy as a spoilt child . . . She'll refuse milk, you'll see, though milk's good for pussy-cats, isn't it?'

Ali understood now where her bossy manner came from, and her habit of talking non-stop. His heart was filled with infinite gratitude to the old lady.

She made him welcome quite naturally, with a sort of rough kindliness that reminded him of Monsieur Kimper. As she went on with her discussion, her monologue rather, Ali felt the urge to kiss her, just like that, on her wrinkled cheeks . . . But he controlled any such show of gratitude, just opening the door respectfully for his providential benefactress to allow her to pass. She was secretly flattered by his polite gesture and began to find him quite likeable . . . Such a well-brought up lad! And with that air of distinction, and such a sparkle in his eyes! . . . All this youthfulness suddenly erupting into her life was pleasantly exciting.

He followed her into a spacious flat crowded with old furniture, making it appear smaller than it actually was. Here a huge bulging chest of drawers with a vase of flowers on top. There, a large carved-oak sideboard with rows of painted plates. An enormous bookcase filled with books covered one wall. And a lamp, its shade adorned with silk ribbons, had pride of place on a table round which three worn leather armchairs bore witness to former cheerful gatherings of family or friends. Everything here was pleasantly restful. Ali felt more at ease. Something warm rubbed itself against his leg; he jumped and saw it was a cat. He recognized the Mimiche, cause of the lady's regrets. He bent down to stroke the animal.

'What a nice little cat.'

'Well I never! She lets you stroke her! She doesn't like strangers, usually. I've got a cleaning woman who's rather nasty to her. Mimiche gets her own back by scratching her whenever she comes near. Animals know if you don't like them, just like children . . .'

She took off her hat, put her shopping bag down on a chair and went on chattering as she bustled around.

'It'll soon be time for lunch, I'll see what I've got to eat!'

While she was in the kitchen Ali quickly removed the revolver which was sticking into his back and shoved it into one of the pockets of his jacket. The kitchen opened out of the dining-room and turning round he saw the lady watching him. For a moment he remained horror-struck. Had she seen him? . . . As in a dream he heard her saying. 'I've got no meat, we'll have to have sandwiches, is that all right?'

Relieved, he quickly replied, 'That'll be fine! But please let me help you. I'm used to helping my mother.'

He asked permission to take off his jacket as he was sweating profusely in spite of the open windows. He was still worried. 'She couldn't have seen me! She's very short-sighted – and besides, the room's so dark that I didn't notice the cat a moment ago . . .'

He took a quick glance at himself in the mirror in the corner of the dining-room. His neat appearance – white shirt and blue tie – put his mind at rest. He straightened up and said jokingly, 'I'm an only child, so I've had to learn to be a help in the kitchen, as you can imagine! For example, I can make hors d'oeuvres. Have you any tomatoes, an onion, olives, and possibly anchovies? And what about eggs? Just you wait!'

He set to work with enthusiasm, forgetting he was on the run, his youth blotting out all sense of danger and its consequences.

'A boy who helps his mother!' sighed the lady. 'There aren't many of those about . . . I've got a daughter who's married and lives in France! She's a good girl, but she's so far away.'

When the hors d'oeuvres were ready and had elicited the lady's warm congratulations, Ali insisted on laying the table. He bustled about, pleased to bring a smile of admiration and delight to the old lady's lips. She asked his name and he replied with the first Christian name that came into his head.

'Since we're going to eat together, we must get acquainted. My name's Colin. Come and sit down, you've done enough work . . .'

When they were seated, Ali sensed the change that had come over her; she was not so gruff, so curt. She seemed now to be lost in some mysterious dream of the past. She gazed at him with an expression of sorrowful concern.

'Why are you looking at me like that?' he asked. 'You haven't eaten anything either.'

She sighed. 'It's nothing. You bring back memories . . . Of times when this table echoed with the laughter and chatter of my daughter, her father and friends. It's a long time since I've had a young person to share a meal with me. That's what makes me sad.'

Ali glanced at the clock. Half-past twelve. He'd been here for three quarters of an hour. He ought to telephone. It'd be better to wait a little, as Monsieur Kimper wouldn't have finished his lunch yet. He knew the professor's habits and decided to phone in half an hour.

'You see,' he heard his hostess saying, 'our family have always been schoolteachers – it's a tradition like in the army – from my great-grandfather down to my daughter. My parents and my husband are all buried in the town cemetery. We are, so to speak, genuine Algerians,' she added with a laugh, 'and now "they" want to drive us out of our country. "They" say our country is France. I've only been there three times in my whole life, just imagine, the first time was for my honeymoon . . .'

She lost herself momentarily in a memory which lit up her face, then resumed, 'The second time was with my daughter, when she was thirteen, to show her the historic buildings, the Palace of Versailles, etc. And the last time was when my daughter was having her baby . . . But now, it's decided! I'm finally going to listen to my daughter . . . She's been urging me to join her ever since the outbreak of this war. I'll sell all this,' she said, indicating the furniture. 'I'll just take Mimiche with me . Its terrible at my age to start a new life! Everything I love is here . . . My father predicted this; he always used to say, "We are only in transit on this earth, from birth to death – and a day will come when we'll have to let them have their country back." He was right, life here isn't possible any more!'

Ali got up to clear the table and wash up. She protested mildly but he was insistent. Afterwards he asked if he could phone. She nodded and pointed to the apparatus. He rang the professor and spoke in a loud voice. 'Hallo! I couldn't get home for lunch as there was an attack . . . Yes, that's right. I'm in the sector that's cordoned off. No, no one can move for the time being . . . I'm telephoning from the flat of a lady who's been kind enough to let me stay with her . . .'

He could tell Monsieur Kimper was surprised; he realized from the way Ali spoke that something serious had happened, forcing him to put on this act. Ali continued, 'Are you there, Dad? You say you'll come and fetch me? No, just send the driver! You don't have to bother . . . Yes, that's right, about five o'clock, when the traffic's started up normally again. You want to speak to the lady? Yes, hang on, she's right here . . . Yes, see you at five then.'

At the other end of the line, the professor was dumbfounded; Ali had gone on asking questions and giving the answers without letting him get a word in. Before he could get over his stupefaction he heard an amiable voice saying, 'Hallo! Hallo! . . . I can't hear a word . . . that's better, I can hear you now . . . Don't mention it. It's quite natural. We must help each other these days . . . Your son's a delightful lad! Don't mention it, it's been no trouble at all, on the contrary . . . Goodbye!'

Madame Colin gave her address and hung up with a delighted smile, 'Your father sounds quite charming and he was obviously worried about you. Well, now you'll have to wait patiently. Tell me, son, what does he do?'

'He's a businessman, in real estate . . .'

She nodded, probably thinking of the mention of a driver.

'That's a paying business!'

Outside, the streets started to come to life. The 'suspects' had been picked up, identity cards had been checked amid the usual shouting and jostling.

In the course of the afternoon cars began to circulate normally. Ali played a game of rummy with his hostess. She loved cards and he'd learned when he was a boarder. So he filled in the time, commenting from time to time on the game. He saw to it that she won and she was so delighted with her victories that she gave little chuckles of satisfaction every time she was out before he could lay down his cards. She commiserated with him on his bad luck. ' "Unlucky at cards! . . ." as they say, but I hope the rest of the saying doesn't apply to you!' she commented, with a pretence of severity. 'I hope you're taking your studies seriously now. You say you'll be taking your *bac* this year; I wish you every success with that.'

From time to time, as she was shuffling the cards, he got up and went to look out of the window. She watched him silently through her thick glasses, while giving the impression she was absorbed in the game. He was glad when he finally caught sight of the little Citroën slowing down to check the number of the building. Not that the time had hung heavily on his hands; on the contrary, he'd really enjoyed spending the afternoon with Madame Colin, but he was anxious to get back to his room. In his heart he felt enormously grateful to her and now knew that 'the others' were not all selfish or cruel . . . Naturally, he thought, if she'd suspected that he, the nice young man, was really the one who'd shot the policeman and was the source of all the military activity, she'd probably have screamed and handed him over to the soldiers . . . On the other hand, he couldn't be so sure, now that he knew her a bit . . . He didn't know for certain how she would have reacted . . .

'The driver's here! I'll go down straight away!'

He was in a hurry, not wanting her to see the professor who was well known in the town. He grabbed his jacket and was just about to slip it on, when she said vaguely, 'No! Leave that jacket, it's really too loud and in such bad taste. I've never liked these American fashions.' She went to the cupboard and took out a navy-blue jacket which seemed too big for him.

154

'And here!' she handed him a handkerchief. 'Wipe that gum off your lip.'

Her face clouded over again, as when she was evoking her memories a little time ago. Ali did not say a word; his expression was inscrutable as he acted on her advice. He felt a sense of shame under Madame Colin's penetrating gaze. He turned round to empty his pockets, surreptitiously removing the revolver from his own jacket to hide it in the one that had belonged to the deceased Monsieur Colin.

Their eyes met briefly. Madame Colin's lips trembled slightly and the lenses of her glasses misted over, hiding her gaze completely . . . Perhaps she had shut her eyes. Or was she crying?

Ali impetuously took hold of her hands and kissed her fondly on the cheek; there was a taste of salt on his lips; she was crying. He ran out of the flat like a thief.

Down in the street Monsieur Kimper was horrified at the sight of the boy's ashen face. He noticed the jacket which was too big for him, and Ali's tense expression as if he were trying to contain his feelings . . . Without a word he started the car and drove back to the peaceful environment of his suburb.

The next day the newspapers reported in detail on the partisan attack at the market, stating that witnesses had described the assassin as having a moustache and wearing a beret and a brightly-coloured jacket. Naturally every man with a moustache in the neighbourhood was arrested.

Ali had buried the revolver in the garden. This time he waited quietly at the professor's for a signal from Tahar. Monsieur Kimper was in no doubt as to what had happened; he didn't need to ask any questions; the newspapers told him everthing he needed to know. He noticed a change come over the young man: he'd become more assured, less agitated.

Ali thought with gratitude of Madame Colin. A new truth began to dawn on him. He realized that Monsieur Kimper was not the only European who didn't think all Arabs were lawless assassins . . . There were others who kept silent and protected them. The professor was not lying when he said, 'Why won't you understand that the Europeans, as you call them, are not all racists? I'm not an exception, Ali . . . There are people among us who help you, who understand the meaning of your struggle .' But Ali had refused to be convinced by these words. For him, every European was a potential enemy, a threat to his safety, someone who thought him a wild animal not a human being. Except for the ones he'd known in his village and the professor, all were out to destroy him. When he met one in uniform, or even a civilian he didn't know, he was instinctively on the defensive, on edge, ready to attack; this was a form of defence mechanism on the part of someone who had long been the underdog. Paradoxically, the struggle had gradually changed him, with the knowledge that he would soon be free. The war was forging a new personality, gradually stripped of all the delusions of a colonized psyche. Monsieur Kimper had understood what was happening to Ali; he proceeded very slowly, gently and sympathetically, so as not to put the boy's back up or hurt his pride and susceptibilities.

Ali was not stupid enough to think Madame Colin a militant, like the professor! She had certainly been influenced by his youth. And yet he was convinced that she would have protected any other person, in his place, by her silence.

The next morning he went out as usual to do the errands for the household. He decided to make some purchases with the pocket money the professor gave him every month. Ali suspected it came in fact from Tahar. He bought four pounds of meat, a bottle of perfume and a bunch of flowers. He went to Madame Colin's building, rang at the porter's lodge and asked him to deliver these gifts to the lady. He went away with a lighter heart when he imagined her surprise.

But now his sleep began to be disturbed by unfamiliar longings. During the day he managed to ignore this burning sensation in the pit of his stomach. There was Khéïra bustling noisily around in her familiar fashion, and the garden to keep in order . . . But at night the beast was roused. He realized it was nearly a year since he'd been to the Black Bird . . . Was Rosy still there? . . . He wondered how he could manage to get to that part of the town. His papers were in order. On the other hand, Khéïra and his

156

former guardian from his college days lived in the area. But, after all, he was probably worrying for nothing! Anyone had the right to visit a cathouse!

He was pondering this problem when Tahar caught him by surprise. He had entered without being heard, as usual. He had a basket of meat for the professor. He gazed at the youngster almost admiringly. Then he patted him on the back. 'Well done! You and your bloody moustache!'

Then quickly becoming serious, he asked, 'Where's the revolver?'

'Under your feet!'

'OK. Understood! . . . Ramdane can rest in peace! You knew what was expected of you.'

They went into the house. Ali asked if there was work for him at Béni-Ramassés. Tahar realized the young man needed to get out and to be with him. He told him he could come that evening or tomorrow, whichever he preferred. Ali was surprised to be given the choice. Previously Tahar had set a day, an exact time when he was allowed to come. As if he hadn't trusted him. Today he left it to him, this evening or tomorrow . . . There were leaflets to type but he could do them when it suited him . . .

11

Baladia . . . 1 January 1959

Over the last few months I've had to undertake various missions. Irrespective of the leaflets, I've been responsible for the sabotage of several trains because of my knowledge of electricity . . . I've become quite a specialist! Always accompanied by Tahar who the rest of the time disappears about his own business. But I am more and more isolated. I rarely see any of the others. I still get in a most terrible funk before every mission. And this horrible nausea always stuck in my throat, in my guts, dormant most of the time, then roused like a monster in the face of danger. Nevertheless, I have learned more and more self-control. As for the beast that makes me think of Rosy, that also joins in the attack, so to speak . . . But I have that well in hand as well.

A little while ago, after dinner, the professor called me. He felt like a chat. He probably feels a bit miserable after spending New Year's Eve alone yesterday. I saw the light under his door up till two in the morning. He was playing all night – wonderful music, but so sad. I don't know what kind as I've no musical education, unfortunately . . . But I loved it. Fortunately Khéïra wasn't there as he played without stopping from ten o'clock till the stroke of midnight! He reminded me of Rachid and his flute. I'd have liked to see his expression at that moment. I was forced out into the garden, although it was awfully cold. But I had such a feeling of well-being as I leaned against a tree, smoking a cigarette, with Monsieur Kimper's nostalgic, disturbing music penetrating my every pore. I became once more the green fish with the golden fins of my dreams. Then the music stopped short. It was midnight.

The new year was beginning. I went back to my room from where I could see the light from the professor's window still streaming into the garden. And so I saw the first day of 1959 dawning. All day I have been in the grip of an inexplicable sadness and anxiety. No doubt I infected the professor with it unconsciously, as I noticed the same bitter expression in his eyes. Then I went up to him. We shared a delicious chocolate log and he even offered me a glass of champagne, which I refused at first with a shudder. He insisted kindly, assuring me that one glass wouldn't kill me . .

I took the first sip and waited with curiosity to see what effect it would have. The professor smiled and drank slowly. He watched me. Then I took a good gulp. And a curious sensation came over me: as if a light, invisible weight was pressing on the back of my head. I didn't move. I drank a bit more of the stuff which seemed at first to taste like cider. Monsieur Kimper told me to make a wish before I drank. And I made the silent wish, 'Allah! Grant that I may be alive on the day my country becomes independent!' I was aware of my impertinence in associating Allah with the drink reviled by our religion, but I burnt with too much curiosity to linger long over these spiritual considerations. Gradually, the weight lifted and made way for a nice warm sensation running happily through my veins, giving me a renewed lease of life. My anxiety vanished and I became curiously light-hearted. I was no longer tense, but rested, even the drawing-room furniture, the piano, the carpet seemed more substantial, so to speak . . . I really saw them, whereas before I was just looking at them . . . It was as if I really existed at that moment. I could feel my muscles moving under my skin, smells and sounds reached me with greater intensity than before. I'm sure the professor was aware of my transformation although I thought I was alone in my discovery. He said, 'I see you appreciate it, my boy, but don't develop a taste for it, all the same!'

He added with a laugh, as he put his empty glass on the table, 'Remember my boy, you can have too much of a good thing . . . You feel you've discovered paradise this evening, but it can change into hell if you abuse it too long . . . One glass has soothed you, several will make you sick.'

I know he's right, but in my case, the single glass was as delicious as my first experience of sex.

After that he began to talk to me about his friends in France; in listening to him I soon forgot my own problems. Referring to the superintendent's famous visit of a few months back, he said, 'You see, this worthy gentleman who was so worried about my safety, at the slightest false move on my part, he'd arrest me without more ado. The people who think it an honour to invite me to their homes, would reject me. I've learned to be a fatalist. I've acquired this philosophy in your country. It's when you're young, you're at your most vulnerable; faced with injustice, you rebel.'

I didn't know what the professor was getting at; all that seemed to be the rambling of old man crushed by his loneliness. Nevertheless, I replied, 'No! when you've an ideal, youth is the trump card, the one that will decide the game . . . And all the more so, when our fathers' ideal is at stake!'

The professor smilingly observed, 'I see you're a card player. But you must realize that someone can have an ideal that isn't necessarily that of our fathers, as you put it; all the children of one family don't necessarily have the same character. You loved your father, didn't you? Those soldiers, that system which humiliated him, you hated them with all your might! This has left its mark on you so that you associate your country's freedom with the father you adored. You avenge him by fighting against them. It's . . .'

I interrupted him, as I was angry. 'Oh, no! It's not out of vengeance. Why do you attribute such vulgar sentiments to me? It's quite simply because I'm convinced of the justice of this struggle . . .'

My anger caused me to stammer and I felt incapable of expressing myself, as happened whenever I was afraid of not being understood. Monsieur Kimper smiled in amusement at my outburst. And at this moment I thought of Si Salah's composure, Mounir's self-control, Tahar's irony, and I secretly envied the way they kept anger at bay. I always show my feelings, and when I think about it, it's too late. When I noticed the fatherly spark of amusement in the professor's eye, I was ashamed of getting worked up and stopped short.

160

'Don't be annoyed, Ali,' he said kindly, 'and don't be upset at getting carried away by your zeal . . . That's the wonderful thing about you . . . But suppose your father had been killed by the patriots? . . . By mistake. That has sometimes happened, you know.'

Then I knew what he was referring to. I am well aware that Muslims have been killed by mistake. People calling themselves the Front's executioners, have acted out of self-interest or jealousy. The Organization has punished these murderers. There have been cases of killings because of blunders and *fidaïs* acting too hastily. I know all that. There are always cock-ups! But I shudder at the thought. 'Suppose that had happened to my father? . . .' I tremble inwardly with revulsion: 'I'd have tracked down the murderer . . . I'd have tried to avenge my father . . . I'd have . . .' I finally regain my composure by thinking calmly, 'No! I'd have put the case to the Brothers; I'd have left it to the justice of the Organization . . . Yes, that's it, I'd have relied on those in charge . . .'

Then I looked Monsieur Kimper straight in the face and replied, 'I'd have left it to those in charge to find out the truth, and I would not have wavered in my commitment to the struggle.'

He clearly expected this reply. He sighed and there was sadness in his voice as he resumed, 'You are a man and such action is normal for you! But listen hard to what I have to say. I'm going to tell you the pitiful story of what happened to one of my best Algerian friends. Then you'll understand my remarks that first evening when I met you . . . Do you remember how furious you got when I referred to your youth and I said, "I'm afraid for the children of the future." I was thinking about the children who will be adults when the final victory is won . . . Who will have only known a sky filled with the storm clouds of war . . . These men will have been cut off from the carefree atmosphere natural to childhood and adolescence and they will find themselves with enormous tasks to carry out in a ravaged country . . . Will they know how to forgive? Will they be able to reach out a hand to each other and fight together for a new freedom? The freedom to live with laughter . . . I'm afraid that this generation which has sacrificed its adolescence will also lose its ability to live as adults. Or am I simply in my dotage? But later on, think of my words, Ali! . . . For the moment you all set out with the same enthusiasm; when you've reached your goal some will be forgotten, others will crumble under the popular acclaim, and the ones in best shape will watch each other suspiciously to see who'll be first past the post.'

I pondered on his words for a moment, to try to puzzle out his message. When I got it, I wanted to laugh at the grotesque idea which occurred to me . . . and containing my smiles I replied, 'If I'm one of those in good shape, I'll stand on the side-lines with a stop-watch and wait!'

He burst into a delighted peal of youthful laughter, which shook the glasses on the table. 'I sincerely hope that you'll arrive in good shape, my boy! But I'm sure of one thing now, those of your friends who remain loyal to you will be in luck, as you've got a pretty sharp tongue.'

But I was waiting for the story that he was eager to tell me. Knowing the professor's habit of skipping from one subject to another, and realizing that he'd gone off at a tangent to dissect my character, I reminded him of the subject he'd started with.

'So, what happened to your friend?'

'Oh! I nearly forgot . . . Yes, it was right at the start of these events . . . My friend was married to a Frenchwoman, whom he'd met while studying medicine. He settled in our town. He lived quite near us and had his consulting room in a poor district. His family had fallen out with him. His parents were dead but his uncle and cousins couldn't forgive him for marrying a foreigner. He was considered a renegade . . . As you know, certain prominent families, headed by a learned and respected patriarch, are intolerant of such marriages. And my friend's family was quite distinguished, consisting of *imams* and *cadis*. Of course, it often happened in such cases that the son would be rejected at first and with time he'd be forgiven and his wife accepted by the family. On the other hand, a girl who chose to marry a European would be cursed, or in extreme cases some member of the clan would take justice into his own hands and simply kill her . . . I know that these traditions are justified by the belief that when a man merges

162

with a woman and impregnates her it is like a wave eternally breaking and moistening the sands . . . And my friend's family was one of those which were most particular where the honour of their name was concerned.'

I marvelled at his knowledge of the profound character of our traditions. It's true that he has been interested in our country for thirty years. What he says about mixed marriages is perfectly correct. Blokes who leave to find jobs in Europe jump at any chance of shacking up with a woman there, often leaving wives and children behind in their villages. Then there are students, dashing and rather trusting young fellows, who let themselves be lured by the charm of long friendships. But it must be admitted that these mixed unions have helped to make up Algeria's unique character by creating a richer, more enterprising society, more receptive to today's world. For my part, I don't consider them scandalous or harmful.

I only deplore the way the children are brought up. They are kept carefully in ignorance of the language and traditions of their fathers, and then, when they are confronted with the realities of their country, they are disorientated and are suddenly like strangers in their own land . . . That holds good in both directions. But this dichotomy depends on the character of the couple and the quality of their love for each other . . .

I turned these thoughts over in my mind while the professor went on philosophizing about the energy which the future generation could contribute to a free country, etc. He noticed my expression of amusement and realized he'd lost the thread of what he was telling me.

'I'm getting old . . . I can't follow up an idea! Laura, my friend's wife, was extremely beautiful. I still remember her air of delicate refinement, but under her apparent listlessness she hid a strong will. She stood out among the ladies of her circle for her breeding. Her husband's colleagues secretly envied him such a distinguished wife . . . Whereas the women, guessing their husbands' admiration, disapproved of her for having married an Arab. My wife used to come home from their tea-parties, furious with what she called "these society ladies' hypocrisy"; they'd smile fondly at Laura and run her down behind her back. Laura was a music-lover and we used to have musical evenings here. She was very much in love with Amar. But I sensed her reservations about everything indigenous here . . . She didn't feel her cultured, sensitive husband had anything in common with the wretched, illiterate folk she came in contact with in the street or at the market. The truth was, she was secretly pleased her husband was estranged from his family. So she didn't have to put up with the intrusion of a lot of ill-bred folk. She'd been told that Arabs have a particularly large number of cousins, etc., and that they were a hospitable and over-generous race, so what belonged to one belonged to all . . .

'She kept to herself and did nothing to help reconcile her husband and his family. Incidentally, my friend Amar was a dreamer and rather weak. He was quite content to let things slide and enjoy his peaceful home life. They had a daughter who unfortunately didn't conform to Western standards of beauty. The mother was a bit disappointed with this dark-skinned child with deep-set eyes. Although her hair was smooth as silk, Laura sighed for a daughter as fair as herself, to avoid unkind comments from her family in France, so she said. At twelve the child was like most of the little girls here. She was wiry and fine-boned with a mat complexion and hazel eyes. She took after her father in the main. Everything about her contrasted with her mother's fair beauty and languid frailty.'

Monsieur Kimper paused for a moment. He scrutinized me as if he'd just made an important discovery and exclaimed, 'I know what it is! You've got the same eyes as Amalia! The same colour, that light brown which darkens when you're angry, the same long lashes and that expression . . . In life there are some disconcerting resemblances . . .'

I thought the old man was really losing the thread of his reminiscences.

'What eyes? Who's Amalia?' I interjected.

'Why! My friend Amar's daughter!'

I nodded. I was now getting greatly interested in his story. I must say the professor knows how to tell a tale and he handles words like the notes of his piano, lovingly, with precision and sensitivity.

'They called her Amalia, because in Arabic *amal* means "hope". But as a Latin name it also has a universality. Amar was delighted with his daughter. As she grew up he could see her mother's distingushed bearing and the same distant manner and way of holding herself very upright. But physically she took after her father.'

Monsieur Kimper poured himself a drink. Reliving his past seemed to rejuvenate him.

'And Amalia?' I asked impatiently.

He smiled, flattered at my interest.

'She grew up, pampered by her parents, like a little princess. She often came to our house for piano lessons, which she disliked, be it said. She used to say, "Learning to play bores me . . . I like music to come to me all by itself the same as cakes; I like them ready-made, not to have to make them myself!" She was already strong-minded and knew what she wanted. She hated anything that kept her in one place; she loved running about, being on the move. She never stopped asking questions. My wife and I were very fond of her. We called her "the little sprite" because she was never still, flitting about the house and her tongue ceaselessly wagging. She brought such life to our home! She wanted us to tell her everything as her mother intimidated her and her father was like a god to her. One day she arrived very upset. When I asked her what was the matter, she burst into tears and said that at school some girls made fun of her, calling her names, *"Papa Arbi, mama Roumia"* (Arab father, European mother). She understood what they were getting at with their jeering. They were ridiculing her first name and her ignorance of Arabic. She told me how she'd fought with the girl who'd made fun of her, and that she'd been punished for it by the teacher. She declared furiously, "And I'll do it again! I'll fight anyone who makes fun of me, even if they kill me!" I was overwhelmed by the child's despair, which gave me a foretaste of future suffering. I consoled her and told her not to tell this story to her father, as it would upset him too much.

'She calmed down and told me in confidence, "It's all Mother's

165

fault, she doesn't want me to learn Arabic. When I try, she laughs at me and asks me why I want to bother my head with it, and says I should rather learn to speak French properly! She says I've got a terrible accent and I talk pidgin like them." She could scarcely control her anger as she added, "She forbids me to invite my Muslim friends, not even Fella, my best friend . . . But I go to visit Fella without telling her. Her parents are very kind and always offer me nice things to eat there . . ."

'I scolded her for lying to her parents, but she was so unhappy that she unburdened herself in me, straight off. She told me she didn't want to go on holiday with her parents to her cousins in France, as they were spiteful and called her "Black Olive". She'd like to go to a holiday camp like Fella.

'I promised to talk to her father about it just before the summer but alas, that summer brought tears instead of joy. Amalia was fourteen when the tragedy occurred. This kindly, peaceful man was killed. I remember our discussions when the news of the armed revolution in the maquis reached us. He said to me, "This is it, my friend, the trouble's beginning! The fight will be long and bitter, but the victory is certain . . ." And he was shot in his consulting room by a young man not much older than you, Ali . . . His body was brought home while his wife was away at the hairdresser's . . . I'll never forget Laura's grief. She suddenly lost all her vivacity and assurance. She didn't shed a single tear. She just became hard and unforgiving. She sent everyone away, couldn't bear to see anyone except my wife and myself. Then she settled all her husband's affairs and left the country. When I asked her where she was going to have her husband buried she replied coldly, "In their cemetery; I leave them to get on with their ceremonials! And I shall do everything in my power to prevent my daughter returning to this country!" I could not reason with her. As for Amalia, she was strangely like her mother in these dramatic moments: the same hard expression, the same icy immobility in her features. She also turned from me, although I'd been her old mentor and confidant.'

A lump rose to my throat. I felt as though this tragedy touched me personally.

'What became of them both?'

'First I got a letter from Laura about their villa, asking me to see to the sale. She also let me know that Amalia was at high school and they were living with her elder sister who owned a picture gallery in Paris. A year later, two tragedies occurred, one after the other: my wife was killed in a car accident, and a few months later I heard the sad news of Laura's death. I went to France for her funeral. This proud woman had buried her grief in her heart; for a long time she suffered from deep depression and one night she took an overdose of sleeping pills and never woke up . . . Amalia was then like a stranger to me. She'd shot up like a young sapling and had grown very thin. Her face already bore all the marks of suffering. She scarcely paid any attention to me, as if I'd killed her parents with my own hands . . . She was left entirely to herself, living with an aunt who was kind and generous, to be sure, but rather scatterbrained and very much the society lady. What could I, a stranger, do? Her aunt, who is an old friend of mine, wrote to me from time to time. I didn't manage to sell their house. It's remained shut up ever since they went but just today I received a letter from Monique, the aunt, telling me she's arriving soon with Amalia for a short visit. I'm somewhat intrigued, as you may imagine. After four years' absence, why does she decide to return? Is it to try to find a possible buyer herself? I don't know and I await their arrival with curiosity. She said she'd let me know in good time.'

'So that's why I found you rather worried, today,' I said. 'This letter has woken sad memories for you. But why was he killed? If, as you say, he was a peaceful man, whose only fault was to have married a European . . . That's never been a motive for the Front to condemn a man to death!'

'You're right, it wasn't because of his wife. It came out eventually that the attack was the work of a fanatic, incited by the doctor's personal enemies who were jealous of his success . . . The murderer was executed by members of the Organization. They insisted on my conveying their apologies to the family. That's how I got to know Salah and his militant activities. But the harm was done in Laura's mind. That's how mistakes can destroy a whole life . . . Ruin a person and create a packet of hatred as dangerous as dynamite!'

It occurred to me that such accidents were bound to happen in the course of any revolution, and would form inevitable landmarks in the history of our country. Doctor Amar was for me one more victim, another unknown hero in the list of martyrs to the revolution. Then the professor's kindly voice broke into my thoughts, wishing me goodnight.

Baladia. . . 5 January 1959

How many pages have I blackened since I started this diary at the age of thirteen? I don't even write every day! If I had done so for nearly five years I'd have needed 1825 pages, at the rate of one page a day, and I've only got 300 pages altogether. I've still got some left, however, awaiting my confidences.

I don't know what's come over me suddenly . . . I'm no longer haunted by my dream. I'm no longer the little green fish with golden fins . . . I am a black dragon, no longer capable of spitting fire or water. There is a fire burning inside me that nothing can extinguish, not even my dear, silent diary . . .

I went up there again . . . to Rosy's, but she was no longer there and no one could tell me where she'd gone. She was the one I was keen to see, not any of the other girls. Madame Nini's still there and she greets me jovially, 'So you're back at last, Casanova! What's happened to your pals?' She shows me the girls sitting around the lounge; there were a lot of soldiers present. I suddenly felt so wretched and once again felt I was going to be sick. I looked at Madame Nini, shook my head and ran out of the place, bumping into a drunken sailor. I raced through the maze of narrow alleyways and finally came to a halt when I was calmer. I hailed a taxi and went to Béni-Ramassés. I so badly needed to embrace a woman to assuage my thirst for contact with soft, warm flesh. I was eager to hear a woman's soothing voice. To talk of anything, to see a female face and draw a little warmth from it.

Why seek out Tahar? Will he rescue me from my fiery furnace?

No matter, I'll just sit and talk to him, I need a friendly presence.

A glimmer of light is visible under his door. I knock.

'Oh, it's you! Come in. You're looking very smart! Did you put on that fine tie in my honour?'

Tahar fingers the material and jokingly pulls on it slightly. I feel rather foolish and shout, 'Stop! You're strangling me! . . . I've just come from the old town.'

'Well, well! . . . You've got family there?' he said.

'No! I wanted to visit the Black Bird . . .'

I blurted this out without looking him in the face. I have a great deal of respect for Tahar, but I think I have just the same rights as any other man. And after all! It doesn't show any lack of consideration for him . . . I worry my head over all these considerations, waiting to see how he'll react.

'So what? You ought to be more relaxed, happier, instead of looking as if you'd been to a funeral! Or did the ladies send you away with a flea in your ear, because you haven't got a beard?' he added casually.

Once more, I let myself be provoked, knowing full well that was exactly what he wanted. I growled through my teeth, 'They know me perfectly well, as it happens! I used to go there when I was at college . . . But this evening I couldn't, they repelled me . . .'

'Well, well! I didn't know you were such a young reprobate. Screwing at sixteen already! That's a nice how-d'you-do! And suddenly, you get all squeamish? It must be your "psychology" playing you up again!'

He burst out laughing in the funny way he has, thrusting his hands in his pockets and striding up and down the room with his head thrown back. Then he came to a standstill and jabbed a finger at me. 'Well now!' he resumed, still laughing, 'As I don't want to risk having a sex maniac on my hands, you'd better come with me!'

I don't know what he wants to do. Where does he want to take me now?

'I say! That's a bit thick! I'm not a sex maniac! I don't feel like going out. I'd rather stay and discuss things with you.'

169

'I've got nothing to discuss! I need an early night tonight . . .
And you'll get on my nerves with your tommy rot . . . Especially as
I can see you're as jumpy as a flea! So, get a move on!'

That's how we found ourselves outside a house not far from his
shack. An old woman opened the door. Her face lit up as she
recognized Tahar. He put his arm round her neck affectionately
and whispered something in her ear, to which she nodded. Then
he turned to me with his kindly, teasing smile. 'In you go, my boy!
And don't budge from here till tomorrow morning. Don't worry
about your boss, I'll phone him . . .'

And he vanished like a magician, while I thought I must be
dreaming. I examine the room. A simple bedroom, scarcely better
furnished than Tahar's. A door on my right opens and a young
woman comes in. She is wearing blue trousers; she is fairly tall and
there is something sensual in her gait. Her face has a charm which
makes one forget her features . . . As if some magic prevented one
paying attention to details . . . Her face is perfect. She is beautiful.
She screws up her lovely eyes to examine me. I notice she is
short-sighted. She says to the woman who is sitting by the brazier
watching the coffee. 'Go, leave us!'

Then she says to me, 'I'll pour you some coffee.'

I remain leaning against the door, wondering vaguely what I'm
going to do. Tahar has got a gall, really! Packing me off like this
to a woman I don't know. Besides, she intimidates me with her
remoteness; I respect her already without having spoken one
word . . . Yes, it's stupid what I'm saying! But I'm paralysed by
her reserved, natural manner. At Nini's establishment it was
much easier!

I shamble over to the basin and turn on the tap. Neither of us
speaks. I spend several minutes washing my face and neck. My
heart thumps and my head seems to be caught in a vice. I drop
instinctively down on to the bed. She hands me a cup of coffee. I
close my eyes and sip it. I ask softly, 'What's your name?'

'Houria . . .'

This time I open my eyes and look at her more closely. What a
strange name! Houria . . . *Hourie* . . . Liberty . . . Angel . . . Yes, to
be sure, in this period of hatred, fear and death, a woman like her

is a symbol in herself . . . She does not move; she is not screwing up her eyes now, but seems to be gazing into space. I grow impatient with her remoteness. What is she waiting for? For me to hurl myself at her? I tear off my shoes and fling them on the floor. I undress, suddenly fuming, determined to go to sleep as she doesn't even glance at me. Tahar and his female acquaintances, really, what a puzzling bunch! . . .

She stands up and calmly takes off her clothes. She walks about the room looking for something or other. She persists in ignoring me. It's true that her short-sightedness is convenient, as she doesn't see my expression of stupefaction at her complete lack of inhibition.

She is even more beautiful naked than dressed as her clothes detract from the fragile, touching grace of her body; white, with slender thighs, and a boyish build. She has nothing in common with the women from the other place, who are mostly fat and vulgar. Everything about Houria is slight, graceful, elegant. Her hair is piled up on her head, prolonging the line of her back. I gaze at her with a feeling of ineffable happiness. I have always been curiously susceptible to people and things. A word . . . A poem, a rose, a way of walking . . . A gesture . . . A look . . . A melody . . . A pair of lips, and I am melted almost to tears.

I would so like her to continue moving about so naturally, even if she does seem to ignore me; her self-confidence, her lack of modesty combined with her air of refinement, brings me nearer to her than any words. It is as though we have known each other for ages. She lies down next to me. I feel her soft cool skin against mine and have the impression of being draped in silk.

She closes her eyes, still keeping silent. I am curious about this woman's response; why this sad expression on her face? I watch her closely. As she caresses me, she utters hoarse sighs like a wounded animal. Lying close to this beautiful body, I feel the vice in my temples slowly loosen its grip. I float once more in an azure sea, a green fish with golden fins; the sky is no longer wine-dark, it is a thousand waves edged with foam breaking over me. And in the final wave, her eyes close in a kind of profound, wordless

171

sorrow. I too close my eyes to let myself drift on the ocean; it is all mine now and there is no more horizon.

It is a strange experience to spend the whole night sleeping beside a woman for the first time! I discover the sweetness of a woman's presence, like a favourite melody, sharing in sleep our repose and surrender. What of this unknown woman's past? Her actions? Her possible depravity or fickleness? All that is abolished, does not exist any more, she is there in my arms, in the same bed and what do her dreams matter? At this moment, by my side, she is mine alone. I am not falling in love with her, no, but I am discovering another person's tolerance and understanding.

The next morning we get dressed and have breakfast still in silence, for Houria is not the talkative type! She is permanently lost in a world that I do not know. Suddenly I am worried by the thought: 'How am I going to pay her?' I am embarrassed by her silence and her pride. At Nini's it was simpler! But with Houria, I really don't know what to do. So I decide to slip the money discreetly under her pillow while she is clearing the table. She surprises me in the act.

'What are you doing?' she says curtly.

'I . . . It's for you to buy something for yourself,' I reply, troubled by her harsh expression.

'Thank you! Tahar settled everything.'

I don't insist in the face of her determination and, somewhat crestfallen, stuff my notes back in my pocket. So it's Tahar who's being the good Samaritan for me again. And I recall Slimane. I find the situation so funny that I'm overtaken with a fit of the giggles, which becomes a roar of uncontrollable laughter. She doesn't understand the reason for my gaiety.

'You think that funny? His "present" amuses you?'

I regain my composure . . . 'I beg your pardon . . . I was thinking of something else,' I said. 'Really, I wasn't laughing at you. If you like me, I'll come again and the next time you'll allow me the pleasure of spoiling you myself . . .'

She smiled and nodded in agreement. Before I left, I asked her, 'How old are you?'

'Three thousand,' she replied calmly.

'You're taking the mickey! . . . Tell me the truth.'

'Take off two noughts . . .'

'Thirty!' I exclaimed. 'You really don't look it!'

I'd have thought her twenty. Her face is as smooth and fresh as any adolescent's.

'Why haven't you got a job?'

She screwed up her eyes, possibly to examine me more closely, or else to reflect on my question.

'I prefer to give love and consolation . . . That's my job.'

'Oh, indeed?' I said, somewhat disarmed by her reply. So that's how she feels about her many chance embraces? 'And how long will you continue with these acts of . . . loving consolation, as you call them?'

Her eyes glazed over and she murmured, 'Until the day when this land is free . . . then, the time of shame will be over . . . Then perhaps I will marry.'

She does not speak the same language as the others. The wall of solitude and independence which she seems to have erected round herself is a protection against curious and sentimental folk like me.

I feel a wave of affection for her. She acted spontaneously with maternal tenderness, in the face of my sadness. Taking my face in her hands, she brought it close to her own; she gazed into my eyes and pressing her lips to mine, she murmured solemnly, 'And if my country is ever double-crossed again . . . Then I shall once more take to "loving consolation", that is how I shall mourn for our loss of dignity . . . meanwhile you may come back whenever you like.'

She pressed on my lips a firm, lingering kiss that was by turns sweet and savage, as if she wished to imprint on them her own despair.

A week later

I am sitting at the table in my room. The window is wide open in

173

front of me. From time to time I look up to admire the well-trimmed trees in the garden. It so seldom happens that I sit writing in the daytime. Yesterday one of the best-known men in this town, who has been preaching the 'new wave of fraternization' was found in his car, near the port, with his throat cut ... There is talk of nothing else in the newspapers and in the streets. Was it Tahar? ... he's not been seen for the last five days. I've been back twice to Béni-Ramassés to type leaflets and I've not seen him. He's left a note with my instructions on the table, that's all.

Khéïra has been to knock at my door, but I don't reply to give the impression I'm not here. She doesn't think to look through my window. Too bad! Her errands can go to the devil!

She arrives late these days, explaining that because of the partisan attacks it's better to leave home in daylight, while the streets are busy, rather than before seven in the morning. I can hear her muttering, 'Where's that rascal got to? What am I going to do about lunch, with people coming? That boy's never there when you need him!'

She often talks to herself. I think the professor has invited friends today. I decided not to stir from my lair until I've finished writing. I love these moments when we are alone, dear diary, and my secret thoughts emerge, not to be brushed aside like dust the next moment, but to be engraved on the blank pages of your memory ...

I hear footsteps. This morning, there's no doubt about it, everything conspires to disturb me. That's why I don't like the daytime! Hidden by my curtain I can see the garden gate open; the professor enters, followed by two women: an older one, smartly dressed in a green suit, and a younger one. I can't see the latter very clearly; she's wearing large sunglasses and a red scarf over her hair, but she seems slender and taller than the lady. My heart misses a beat: it's the daughter of the murdered doctor! Amalia! I move over to the window to get a better view, and in my haste I disturb the curtain. Monsieur Kimper calls to Khéïra and asks her to come down.

The two visitors admire the garden. The older one exclaims,

'It's a paradise here! Oh! All these flowers still! Your autumn is like spring in Paris!'

She happily explores every corner of the garden. Her companion says nothing. They go into the house, passing my window. The professor goes out again and comes back shortly with his visitors' luggage which he leaves at the bottom of the steps, near my door. 'Leave them,' he says aloud. 'We'll take them up later.'

He's guessed I'm there behind the curtains. Oh! the professor's quite sharp. This is his way of suggesting I come out of my room and carry the cases up. I just have to make the best of it . . .

So when I eventually come inside, Khéïra scolds me at first.

'So there you are at last! Where were you? We've got visitors from France,' she says solemnly.

When I'm coming down again I hear Monsieur Kimper calling me, 'Ali! Come and meet our guests!'

He must have been spying on me, otherwise how could he have caught me so quickly? He ignores my reluctance and taking me by the arm drags me into the drawing-room. The lady smiles graciously as I'm introduced.

'The professor's never stopped talking about you.'

The girl didn't even look up, but held out a cold, limp hand and turned to the piano. 'Oh! your piano brings back so many memories! And your drawing-room, still the same, it's wonderful to see you again.'

She had taken off her scarf. She seemed beautiful to me. She was tall with slim hips, small breasts and held her head stiffly and aloofly. She is like a gazelle, a mixture of shyness and daring. But at the time I noted all these details with irritation as her 'Parisian' airs and graces jarred on me. And her accent! What a stuck-up snob! She paid no attention to me. I left and went to see if Khéïra needed me for anything. Then I heard her say loudly, 'I didn't know you had another servant! Can't you manage with Khéïra, your daily?'

I was crimson with fury. These words were like a whiplash. I wanted to go back and slap her face; she had spoken loudly on purpose intending me to hear. But the professor raised his

175

normally calm voice in indignation. 'Aren't you ashamed, Amalia? I told you he's living with me, in exchange for a little help . . . he acts as my secretary.'

'Secretary?' exclaimed the aunt. 'I didn't know a piano teacher needed one.'

'I told you I'd been elected chairman of the cultural committee and I found I couldn't cope with the mass of papers, with all the actors' parts for our plays.'

That was indeed quick thinking, and I took off my hat to the professor for his ingenuity, forgetting the spiteful remark by that silly half-wit of a girl from Paris.

Baladia . . . 16 January 1959

I heard that the professor took them to a notary to settle the formalities relating to the sale of the house. She came back alone.

I was in the garden. Childishly, I'd left off the overalls I ususally wear for work and put on a light pair of trousers and turtle-neck pullover, to show her I wasn't a servant.

She looked me up and down. 'Pick me some mint!'

'Pick it yourself! I haven't got time.'

'What's the matter with you?' she exclaimed angrily. If looks could kill I'd have fallen down dead!

I mimicked her accent, rolling the 'r' affectedly like her, 'What's the matter-r-r with you, your-r-self? I'm not your garden-boy and now get lost!'

I went on with the watering. She stamped furiously and went off fulminating, 'I'll tell the professor, you stupid oaf!'

I burst out laughing. She was behaving like a child. But I'm delighted to have shut her up.

Then, in the afternoon I saw Si Salah arrive. At the moment, I was surprised to see him. But I got the explanation later, as he dropped in to my room before leaving.

'The professor told me Dr Amar's daughter was here. I came to express personally the Organization's deep regrets for her father's murder. We are anxious to wipe this shame from his daughter's memory. She is Algerian after all,'

He sighed and got up. 'All this is very difficult! But, you see, Monsieur Kimper was so insistent, he said she had only come back for that, to find out the truth . . .'

I was dumbfounded. She only came back to find out the truth. What a strange girl! She could not live with the doubt. The ambiguity about that execution. She had to hear from those who were reponsible. Everything changes in my mind. This girl whom I thought self-centred, hard, spoilt, self-assured, has not chosen the easy path of forgetting. Moreover Si Salah told me she insisted on a signed certificate from the FLN proving that her father was not a traitor. This ceremony was to take place in the presence of Mounir, Si Salah, the professor and Tahar.

She is adamant in demanding the utmost, at a time when no one knows if he will escape from the furnace.

17 January 1959

This morning Mounir came to take her to lunch with his parents. They passed me without a glance in my direction. I hate both of them at this moment . . . It's crazy to feel like this! I look such a nobody, so wretched compared to Mounir's dapper appearance. Why am I being unfair? They grew up together, so to speak, it's quite natural for him to invite her to his house, and it's natural for him to pretend not to know me. I mustn't forget that we are members of an underground organization . . . Oh, God! What confusion in my mind!

I prowled about the house all morning, like a caged animal. I went to Tahar's, I did some work and then dropped in to see Houria. She wasn't at home. I came back in the early afternoon. While I was wandering about the garden, inspecting the flower-beds, Fella arrived, followed by Amalia. They were both laughing loudly, like children. I'd not seen Fella for a long time and scarcely knew her, but she ran up to greet me with obvious pleasure. 'At last!' she exclaimed. 'I can see you're wide awake

177

this time! You remember the day we first met? No, you've forgotten! . . .'

I protested, embarrassed to be reminded of a time when I was so awkward and shy. That's a long time ago! I've changed now.

'Don't hold that against me; I'd only just arrived from the back of beyond. And what have you been doing with yourself?' I added, displaying all my charm, conscious of Amalia's eyes on us.

She stood on one side, looking at me in her odd, haughty, condescending manner. Irritated by her attitude, I kept Fella talking. Sensing that she was enjoying our conversation, I made myself even more gracious. 'Come, Fella,' I said, 'I'll pick some roses for you to take to your mother from me . . . Even though I don't know her.'

I took her arm affectionately and she blushed with pleasure. She had clearly forgotten her friend was there. Amalia reminded her suddenly of her presence with a sharp retort. 'I'm going in. You can join me when you've finished billing and cooing with the gardener!'

Fella started and looked at me in surprise. 'Billing and cooing? What's got into her? And to call you "the gardener"! Don't pay attention, Ali,' she said kindly. 'She's all right, but she's changed since she's been living in Paris . . . The girls are a bit freer in the way they talk there; you must forgive her.'

She asked me to keep the flowers for her till she left and went to join her friend. A little while afterwards I heard them laughing. But I didn't forget the word 'gardener' . . . Her aunt Monique is nicer; she never fails to say a kind word to me when she meets me.

19 January 1959

I've not been able to think of anything since she's been here. It's crazy what's happening to me; I scarcely leave the house, except to do the necessary errands. Even Tahar and the others haven't got in contact with me. You'd think they'd passed the word round that I must be left alone with my new emotions.

I feel I'm in a constant state of grace (that's exactly the

expression). I only live now for Amalia's comings and goings in the villa. I believe I'm in love with her. It's ridiculous. Everything separates me from a girl like her. Especially her aura of inordinate pride, her arrogant self-confidence and the bossy way she looks at me that makes me want to . . . to hit her or kiss her hard! I'm mad, I know, to write such things. Nevertheless, there must be a crack in her armour somewhere. Yes, I'm sure it's a sort of defence. She can't be as strong as all that! She is . . . how can I put it? Yes, that's it! She's a castrator! . . . I sometimes feel like saying something nice to her, I feel an urge to approach her and suddenly she looks at me and I stop short . . . it's my turn to be icy. But, all the better, as I think they'll soon be leaving.

I mustn't get these ideas into my head. I'll avoid her in future.

This evening, Monsieur Kimper and Monique have been invited to dinner in the neighbourhood. Khéïra has prepared a meal for Amalia, who decided to stay at home as she is not keen to meet her parents' former acquaintances. I was turning these thoughts over when my door shook with violent knocking.

'Hey, you there! Open the door!'

The 'Hey, you there' didn't exactly endear her to me, and I took no notice. She banged even louder.

'Open the door! I know you're there!'

I threw the door open in her scowling face, but I was as annoyed as her, if not more so. I shouted at her, 'Have you gone mad?'

She simply stared at me with her usual patronizing expression, without a word . . . We stood there in silence, exchanging angry looks, like two wolves ready to fly at each other's throats at the slightest movement. With her loose hair, her flaring nostrils and her gleaming eyes, she was so beautiful and so touching, that I could only see before me the angry little girl whose schoolmates called 'Papa-Arbi-mama-Roumia'. I can imagine she must have looked just like this when she fought with the girl who made fun of her . . . I relaxed and burst out laughing; I don't know how it happened, but she must have been infected with my own amusement, for I suddenly heard her laughing too. And we were both overcome with irresistible laughter which lasted for quite a

179

time. Every time she stopped to get her breath, we caught each other's eyes and set each other off again. Finally, she flopped down on the step and holding her stomach, gasped, 'Heavens! I'll die of laughing! Oh! I've got a stomach-ache now, and it's all your fault . . .'

I collapsed on the floor of the corridor in front of her, without noticing at first her more familiar tone. We sat there, looking at each other with amused curiosity. Then she said softly, 'I've got a stomach-ache from laughing so much for no reason. Go and pick me some mint, I want to make tea . . .'

I calmly shook my head.

'You really are pig-headed! I want some mint! Khéïra hasn't got any in the kitchen!'

'Not like that!' I retorted.

'Oh! All right!'

She hesitated for a moment, with the embarrassed expression of someone who is not in the habit of asking favours. Then she looked at me with her big eyes and said very softly, 'Please!'

That was when I became aware she was using the familiar, friendly *tu*. I was so astonished that for a moment I simply gazed at her as if the rest of the world did not exist. The sudden void, and nothing but this extraordinary face which I discovered like a weary swimmer overjoyed to reach the shore.

After this I made the tea myself. I was like a puppy-dog delighted to obey her every whim. For the moment, she only wanted mint tea. She was dying for some, she told me. Ever since she left here she hadn't found anyone who knew how to make it, and now she had rediscovered the taste of her childhood. I was flattered and happy to see her pleased. She closed her eyes and slowly sipped the aromatic beverage. We sat in the professor's drawing-room and chatted like old friends, forgetting all our hostility of the previous days.

'It was your snooty expression that got on my nerves,' she confessed. 'When I saw you come in, so stiff and starchy, I felt like picking a quarrel with you. And I thought "He thinks he's a prince fallen among savages!" '

'That's funny,' I said. 'I thought you were the one who was

stuck-up and high and mighty. I wanted to box your ears, especially when you insisted on taking me for a servant, as if you were a queen!'

She curled up in the easy-chair, hugging the cushions, in the strange and touching way she has of sitting. She doesn't sit down normally, how can I put it . . . it's as if she'd lived all her life in a tent. She curls her legs under her on the chair, hugging the cushion like a teddy-bear, or a baby. This attitude makes her looks like someone who feels the cold and is always trying to get warm. When I remark on this she looks at me and murmurs, 'You know me already! . . . I can't sit in a lady-like way. I can't stand chairs. My aunt never stops moaning that I behave like a nomad . . . I can't help it. It's probably a throw-back to my ancestors.'

She told me about her friends at high school in Paris, her daily life there and her longing to be back here. She told me of her obsession with her father's infamous death, her shame at the thought that he had been executed like a traitor. Feelings kept alive by her mother who persisted in believing she had been the cause of his death . . . Now everything has changed, she is happy to know the truth. She wants to know all about me, my parents, where I come from, my friends. And I described to her my village, my family, my pals, up to my arrival at the professor's, naturally omitting any reference to my underground activities. 'And that's how I became a secretary-gardener!' I concluded. 'I've learned a lot from the professor . . . Who knows, later I may go back to my studies.'

'Why don't you come back with us? My aunt knows a lot of people in Paris. She'll manage to find you a job and you could go on studying at the same time. I'll help you, you'll be able to live with us!'

She was delighted to have found a solution, but I told her it was impossible for the time being. She remained silent, appearing to be lost in thought, then she resumed, 'There's something that keeps you here? . . . Is it Fella? I noticed that you were not indifferent to her and she raves about you . . .'

I'm astonished. Fella? I'd never thought of her in that way. She's never been very real to me. But ever since the professor told

181

me Amalia's story, I've been passionately interested in her. I felt attracted to a girl whose character and fantastic love for her father are so akin to mine. She has suffered because of the difference between her parents, because of her father's race; I have been marked by my father's unknown past and have borne in silence the burden of not having a name . . . . In spite of my mother's affection, I always felt I was different from the other children. No one ever laughed at those initials, SNP, which replaced a surname, but I reject them as being only a pale imitation of a past to which every human being has a right . . . Perhaps my father was a foundling, after all, and brought up by the Public Welfare? That must be the truth . . . Everything that he told me was just an adult's invention to pacify the child that I was. From what fault was my father the result? Was his brother really his brother? They are so little alike . . .

But I don't want to think of all that now! All I fear is to lose Amalia. She is leaving tomorrow! My heart is heavy, it's terrible! And she talks to me about Fella, when she is the one who has entered my life, like the reward for all my vague anguish . . . When she is the one I love.

'You see, Ali, I was helpless as I watched my mother's physical and mental decline. She sank into a depression, wasted away, found consolation in drink. I could do nothing for her. I wasn't enough for her, she abandoned me . . . People say that children give parents a reason for living, but it's not true; with her I realized that one can die for love . . . Whatever rational people may say!'

These words echoed my own despair in the face of my mother's transformation after her husband's death. So many similarities in our lives troubled me. Amalia noticed my abstracted expression. 'Ali, are you listening to me?'

She moved over to me, stretched out and gently rested her head on my lap. I did not move. Frightened and happy at her action, I scarcely dared breathe for fear of seeing her take flight. I stretched my arm out along the back of the divan and stayed there as if crucified, not with pain, but with immense joy, praying that time would stand still. Amalia spoke softly, as if talking to herself.

'As I grew up, with the developments in Algeria, I considered these men who called themselves revolutionaries, to be savage, unscrupulous murderers, sowing terror and destroying everything and everyone in their path. And then, every time summer came round, I was homesick for my country . . . The sun reminded me painfully of my childhood, when I rolled in the grass, under its warm caresses . . . Also some of my schoolteachers made snide comments about my name . . . Not all, just a few. Although my mother was French, my name is Arabic, so that, in spite of myself, I was forced to defend those people I thought I hated. Gradually, as I read the newspapers, and talked to schoolfriends whose parents were liberals, I learned to be proud of them. As I reflected on the circumstances of my father's death, I decided to come and find out the truth on the spot; I was sure, even if he had been killed by the opposition, my love for him would be the same and my pride in the triumph of this revolution would not have been shaken . . . I had some marvellous comrades in Paris who taught me a lot; although they are French, they are ashamed of what's happening here . . . Come back with us, Ali,' she begged.

'No!'

I can't say anything. I am condemned to stand by my refusal without any possibility of explaining.

Monique and the professor found us in the drawing-room laughing like two conspirators. It was nine o'clock. They were astonished at our new friendship, as naturally everyone in the house had noticed our stormy hostility of the first few days. The professor said nothing. Monique cried out happily, 'I'm glad you've made friends, children, as we're leaving tomorrow afternoon! Amalia, darling, it's time to go to bed.'

I shivered at the thought of this departure so soon. I've barely got to know her! Amalia went off to her room, lost in thought.

I went down to mine like a robot. Since she must leave, let this be our parting now, as far as I was concerned.

20 January . . .

I was puzzled by a scratching on my door. I opened it to find

Amalia standing there, all white in her long nightdress.

'What's the matter?' I whispered, afraid of waking the others. She came in quickly. I didn't know what to make of this nocturnal visit. A young girl coming like this at night to a young man's room! With my good village upbringing, my first thought was how embarrassing it would be if the professor or her aunt caught us . . . I said angrily, 'Why have you come now? Suppose Monsieur Kimper or your aunt woke up, what would they think of you, and of me? . . . Go back immediately.'

I was especially frightened for her, wanting particularly to protect her in spite of herself, against herself. But she sat down on my narrow bed, clutched the pillow to her and settled down as if for a long vigil. I was in a daze. She lifted her chin and retorted, 'It's no use grumbling at me like a brute, I'm not stirring from here. I can't get to sleep, I feel all peculiar, so I've come to chat for a bit with you.' She pointed to the ceiling and added, 'My aunt is sleeping the sleep of the just up there, and the prof also. What are you afraid of? Are you afraid of me?'

I shrugged my shoulders and sat down at my writing table. I looked ridiculous in my pyjama trousers, bare-chested and my hair tousled from sleep.

'Come and sit by me, country bumpkin!'

The moonlight flooded into the room and we did not need to switch on the light. I went to sit next to her, as she instructed. We talked of our childhood again. I made her laugh at our exploits at the Mozabite's. And she never tired of listening to me. What joy to read all her feelings in her eyes! Every word she speaks is so expressive, so warm, that I cannot help falling completely under her spell, just as when I used to listen to Rachid's flute for hours on end. She told me about her flirtations at high school. At eighteen she was very popular with the boys. She seemed to enjoy that, to have them running after her. It doesn't cross my mind to be jealous. That's how she is, after all! The sort of a girl who can appear anywhere, among the most beautiful women, and all eyes are upon her. There can be a suggestion of 'come-hither' in her expression, then suddenly it becomes icy, remote. She has the knack of making you feel uncomfortable, exasperated if she likes.

She can shock deliberately. She can be hard as steel, too. I feel that she is passionately alive, and I am suddenly miserable. I interrupt her curtly: 'These boys you go out with . . . Isn't there one you fancy particularly?'

She looks at me mischievously. 'Not any one particularly! I like them all! But the tragedy is that the one who interests me at the moment is an idiot!'

'An idiot?' I exclaim.

'Yes, yes! Just like you!'

'I'll have you know, if you don't mind, that I'm not one of your Parisian nincompoops!' I retorted in annoyance.

She laughed and hurled herself at me impetuously, then suddenly fell silent. She remained pressed against me. She was crying softly. I rocked her in my arms like a child, covering her face with light kisses. I wiped away her tears with my lips; the mixture of their salt taste and the scent of her skin was so troubling that I pushed her away.

'Go back to your room, Amalia! We're playing a dangerous game. I love you too much to do something foolish which you'd regret later . . .'

'No! don't send me away . . . You are more important to me than you think; you aren't an amusing flirtation My feelings for you, Ali, are those of a real woman, and I want you entirely. And then, no matter what happens, you will never forget me.'

She grew sad and her lips trembled as if she was going to cry again. I can't bear her tears, I can't bear to see her sad! But I want her to leave me, I'm thinking of her! She doesn't understand.

'We must be objective. You are under the country's spell . . . You are so happy to have got what you wanted for your father's memory that you fall for the first man you meet!'

She was about to speak, but I gently put my hand over her mouth, and holding her tightly to me I whispered in her ear, 'Don't say anything! Listen to me please . . . Yes, I'm the first man you meet, a nobody, you don't know me. I'm an Algerian, and that's what counts for you at the moment. You are not in control of your feelings. You are so passionate that you identify me with your violent desire for everything associated with this country . . .

Wait till you're older, you will meet other boys, you will be more composed, less influenced by all the torment of our lives now . . . In Paris, you will find your own milieu again, your own friends, everything will seem clear, and you'll laugh at your infatuation with a certain crazy country bumpkin! . . . Or else, later, Amalia! If your love for me is still the same, nothing will be able to separate us . . . Wait for the end of this war . . . I don't want to be the cause of bitter regrets for you . . . You are so young.'

She slipped out of my arms.

'And you, how old are you? We're the same age! And you talk to me as if you were an old man with one foot in the grave. I want you now, and to hell with later on! Later on, you must be the one to come and get me if you love me . . . And you will love me, I'm certain! Why waste time? It's because we're young and we don't know what tomorrow will bring . . . I don't want to be objective! Objective means never mentioning the reasons for things and I love you . . .'

We stayed together till dawn. Love took on another guise for me, it spoke of life, of light, of revelations and death. The next day Amalia was gone, and I was left alone with my world on fire. I sometimes feel as though it had all been a dream, if it were not for her red scarf which she left behind in my room, and her lingering scent which I try to detect every night. Amalia, my 'little sprite', Amalia with her quick temper and happy laughter, who hurls herself at me to kiss me wildy and then suddenly hides in my arms like a frightened child. Amalia, at once bold and fearful. Illusive and ubiquitous as air.

Shall I see her again one day? We swore never to forget each other. But had I the right to swear such an oath? Knowing that my life depends on the flip of a coin. Time will do its work . . . She assured me before she left, 'This time, I came to you; it will now be your turn to prove you love me . . . I shall always be waiting for you, you must come and find me, I shall give you no sign, it will be your job to come to me. But Ali, rest assured that I shall always love you as long as I live . . .' Yes, I shall seek her out, I shall find her. If fate wills that we see each other again and grow old together, then God will protect the children that we are.

186

But I am happy she came to me, deliberately, consciously; that is how one should act.

Baladia . . . 23 January 1959

Monsieur Kimper looks at me quizzically, scrutinizing me anxiously like a wounded animal. Khéïra badgers me a bit more than usual, moaning that I'm in a perpetual daydream. The professor tells her quietly to leave me alone. For three days after their departure I don't put my nose out of the door. I don't feel like doing errands for Khéïra and I can understand the old woman's anger. Tahar hasn't shown up either.

This morning I forced myself to go and wander round the square in the centre of the town where all the children and old pensioners stroll around. I was just ambling past the main post office when I caught sight of Alain, appearing to be looking for someone. He saw me and ran towards me.

'Oh, hell!' I thought, 'Just when I wanted to be alone . . .'

'You rotten swine!' he shouted. 'Where the devil have you been? You were supposed to phone me, you unreliable bastard! I've been coming here every day after school for the past week, hanging about like a bloody fool for Mister High-and-Mighty to deign to show up . . . the post office was the only place I thought I might find you . . .'

I cut him short roughly. 'Well, you've seen me now. What do you want?'

'What's up with you? You've forgotten we'd arranged to meet again?'

'Well, we've met! Now bugger off!'

'Are you crazy, or what? What have I done to you?'

He was quite stunned by my reception. However he's used to my sudden changes of mood. When we were small, and he followed me to suggest we play with our tops or have a game of football, I would sometimes give him the brush-off and we'd end up quarrelling as he would give me as good as he got.

Today, we were just the same. Instinctively I made him the butt of my anger. I was obliged to control myself in front of the professor and Khéïra . . . I didn't know how to express my grief, and Alain, my only friend, eventually appeared on the scene and unknowingly allowed me to give vent to all my spleen. He walked beside me, hurling abuse at me.

'You filthy rotter! Are you going to tell me what's up, yes or no?'

'Shit! Can't you mind your own business, you louse!'

'Go and get buggered, you silly cunt! . . .' And then there followed more abuse in Arabic and in French, getting more and more smutty. The bastard hadn't forgotten a single one of our obscenities. Then he stopped short and flung at me, 'It's because of Juliette, all this! She keeps on nagging me she wants to see you . . . She's ill . . . Otherwise I don't need to see your ugly face, you swine.'

I came to a sudden halt.

'Juliette ill? What's the matter with her?'

I turned to him but he was already on his way. I ran after him. Quite out of breath, I caught him roughly by the sleeve.

'Juliette? What's the matter with her? Tell me, you donkey!'

Alain's eyes were glistening and his face was damp. Was he crying? He didn't give me time to find out. He ran off, shouting, 'If you want to know, go and see her yourself. I don't want to have anything more to do with you!'

I turned round and hurried towards his parents' house. My heart was sore at the thought of my mother's affectionate, jolly friend, Juliette, who is a force of nature, ill? I can't remember ever having seen her take to her bed. Perhaps it's the prospect of their departure which has upset her. I knock at the door.

Juliette comes to open it. She is rosy-cheeked and fresh as a spring morning. She exclaims happily, 'At last, you little perisher! I was worried sick about you!'

I understood that scoundrel Alain's trick . . . I answered her in the same tone. 'And I've been worried sick about your health, my dear Juliette!'

'My health? There's nothing wrong with me! What are you talking about? You know we're leaving tomorrow and I wanted to see you before we go for good.'

188

She took my arm and pulled me into the sitting-room which was almost empty; there were only a few chairs left. It was obvious that the preparations were well on the way. Juliette brought me coffee and sat down facing me while she went on chattering.

'*Ya oueldi!* If you knew what I've been through! That sly Marcel arranged everything without consulting me! He sold the bar and prepared to move to Nice without saying a word to me. As I was saying, he's bought a restaurant and a house and everything there! With that old maid of a sister of his, hand in glove with him. And Juliette left out in the cold.'

'How could he buy everything without going there himself?'

'Wait, I'm going to tell you! He went away for a week, saying his mother was ill and he had to go and see her! After nearly twenty years, he suddenly decides to go and see her! And his sister who never stops phoning with her "Dear Juliette, I really want to get to know you, and the boy too . . ." I'll say, the old hypocrite! When he came back, I heard everything. He found a little restaurant on the sea front, with a flat above; he brought me back photos of his paradise . . .'

Juliette got quite worked up at the memory of her quarrel with her husband.

'Just think! And all the time I was talking about Tunisia. He used to laugh and say, "But the Europeans are done for there, as well, my poor Juliette, you don't know anything about what's going on!" And stuffing me with a lot of false rubbish! He could vanish into thin air, and I'd not be any the wiser, poor me! Then he said it was all very nice, there's the sun there and all! But I couldn't care a damn about their sun! Oh! Ali, my boy, I'm all torn to bits, and my mother, you realize? She'll be all alone here . . .'

Just as this moment the person in question appeared – a tiny, wrinkled little old lady, wearing a purple *gandoura* with a pink floral design. Her hair was hennaed and covered with a scarf tied on her forehead, like the old women from hereabouts wear. I recognized her as I'd seen her when she visited Dachra. She can't speak a word of French, but she understands it quite well. She asks how I'm keeping, then begins to complain. 'Everything's changed, to be sure! The people are leaving one by one . . . Fortunately my son André isn't going, I'm staying with him. But a daughter-in-law isn't the same as one's own daughter. And mine are all far away now! Two in Morocco, one in Tunisia and the only one left is now off to France!'

She wipes her eyes with a deep sigh. I remember her son, the lawyer, whom the whole family's so proud of. He's done very well and owns a block of flats in the town, as well as his office. The people here appreciate him and respect him.

Whereupon Alain puts in an appearance. He makes straight for his room without deigning a glance at the three of us in the sitting-room. Juliette frowns. 'What's bitten him? Didn't he see you or what?'

I lean back in my chair, chuckling, as Alain's furious expression is a sight worth seeing. Juliette jumps up, grumbling, 'What sort of behaviour's this? He's been looking for you like mad for days and now you're here he has to throw his weight around!'

I can hear her reprimanding him loudly. The grandmother, not understanding a word of what's going on, shakes her head and calls on heaven to witness all this fuss.

'What are we coming to? Even Alain's beginning to lose his head; he's usually so gentle, and now he slams the door and doesn't speak to his friends . . .'

She taps my knee and murmurs, 'The main thing is not to lose your faith! You must pray, pray . . .'

I listen to her soliloquizing, while not losing a word of what's going on next door. Juliette shoves Alain back into the sitting-room, keeping up her scolding, 'You've gone clean off your rocker! Is it our departure that's sent you crackers? Kiss your brother!'

He catches my eye and we both burst out laughing. He's certainly thinking of the trick he played on me, making me believe Juliette was ill, and I'm delighted to have his mother think he's the one to blame. I put on an innocent expression and add, 'I don't know what's wrong with him. I've done nothing!' . . .

And upset by my downcast expression, she continues to haul

190

her son over the coals, while we laugh louder than ever. Suddenly she interrupts us, with tears in her eyes, unusually solemn for her.

'We are going to part, Ali. So I want to give you my blessing and then you'll never come to any harm.'

She looks at me and places her hands on my shoulders; I've never seen her like that, so solemn and serious. I try to make a joke of it. 'Steady on, Juliette! I'm not going to peg out when you're gone!'

'Sh! don't laugh! If Chérifa were alive, she'd do the same . . . *Allah yarrhamha,*' she adds in a voice breaking with emotion.

Juliette's really impressive now! With this new air of mysticism she is so imposing that Alain and I stop laughing and look at her respectfully. She gets up slowly and goes to fetch something from the kitchen. She comes back with some unleavened bread, a handful of coarse salt and a basin of water. I don't understand. I look at Alain for an explanation. He winks at me and whispers, 'She did that to me once when I turned seventeen . . .'

She placed the bread in my hands telling me to eat a piece. I didn't know how to get out of it. I'm very fond of Juliette, but I didn't know what to make of her now. I said stupidly, 'I say, Juliette! You're not going to turn me into a Jew, are you! . . .'

There was a glint of amusement in her eyes, but she bit her lips to stop herself laughing, and whispered, 'Keep still, you rascal!'

She resumed her serious expression, saying, 'What I'm going to do will protect you for ever against your enemies and all bad luck. You'll always get out of a tight corner, get over the worst obstacles and even the most desperate situations. You will triumph over those who lay traps for you . . . As for death, only God is responsible for it coming when He wishes . . .' I held the bread while she traced seven circles round my head with the salt and then told me to spit seven times into it while she repeated her mumbo jumbo. Then she sprinkled a little salt in each corner of the room, seeming to be hunting out something invisible with a grim expression. She harangued some demon or other under her breath. She threw the remaining salt into the water and told me to spit into it seven times again . . . Then she took it back to the kitchen. Afterwards she made me eat all the unleavened bread, declaring, 'I only do this for people I love . . . Go, son, don't be afraid, nothing will happen to you, neither men nor demons will harm you . . . The only thing to fear is God's judgement . . .'

Alain joked to break the spell of the emotion that I felt overcoming me.

'Have you finished casting your spells, Juliette? Can we talk now?'

His mother shook her fist at him with a smile and went off to get on with the packing. She came back into the room from time to time, ruffling my hair as she passed or thumping her son on the back, while continuing to put linen and crockery into cases. She told Alain to write down their new address in France for me, adding that I shall always have a room waiting for me with them.

So I spend a few hours with my friends. We promise that our friendship will not die with the distance or the political quarrels that separate us.

I returned to the villa with Juliette's blessing on my head, like a solid shield of love, fashioned with a woman's innocence to offer protection from the pitfalls of life, and Alain's friendship which I know to be genuine, surmounting all the differences which might emerge one day in our lives.

And you, Amalia? Where are you now? By the end of this January, I have lost all the ones who are dear to me. I prepare myself now to live with their memory.

And you, too, my diary, you are going to leave me. Tomorrow I shall leave early for the village, where I shall entrust you to my cousin Meriem. You must go into hiding. The battle is raging all round. Seventeen countries have recognized the GPRA, delegations have visited Arab countries, India, Pakistan, Yugoslavia and the Republic of China. Here the famous elections organized by the army of occupation have taken place, under the supervision of the government authorities and a 'French supervisory commission' . . . Raids have become more frequent and if you are discovered, the whole edifice of our underground organization will crumble . . .

And who knows? If one day I escape the blood bath and find

myself among the survivors, then I shall return to the village and bring you back, with my dreams. One never knows! If it happens that I do not return . . . To whomsoever finds you and reads you, I leave this message:

I have sown my laughter, my youthful unconcern, my anguish, my despair and my loves. – And you, who harvests them, take also – A sigh of affectionate understanding – My heart which has room for the whole of humanity – Take – Take – Like a treasure that is offered – My pages throbbing with love and hungry for life – Take also – The silence that surrounds the echo of a secret – You, who are a free man – Quench this eternal, painful thirst by your actions – After my uncertain steps of a wounded child – Take also – With great care my ruffled wings – And in the cup of your memory – The children of yesterday – Will live again . . .

12

In Dachra, everything had changed too. Ali went to his aunt's hoping to see Meriem. But at the mention of her daughter's name, she burst into tears. 'She's gone, my boy . . . We don't know if she's dead or alive . . .'

So Meriem had taken to the maquis! She had turned down all her suitors. One by one, the village lads left and every departure was a blow to her heart. She was confined to her father's house, shut away from contact with men. She paced the courtyard like a caged animal.

One evening, a shadowy figure stole out behind the cottage wall, braving the curfew to slip away to the nearby forest. Meriem left, just like that, wearing her floral dress, taking nothing but her youth and her dreams of a real life.

Before disappearing into the undergrowth she turned round for one last glimpse of the village lights which seemed to wink at her from afar; she took her leave in a half fierce, half tender whisper: 'Farewell, Dachra! . . . And you, Ali, you are no longer there . . . No matter! Algeria remains . . . It is time for us girls to die, not for love of men, but for love of our country . . . Under the falling autumn leaves, or under the snow, in wind and sun, surrounded by danger and death . . . I shall be a free woman!'

The next morning, no one was really surprised to find her gone.

Meriem wandered through the forest for many days. When she heard suspicious noises she lay hidden in a bush, hardly daring to breathe. She had taken one of her father's water bottles which she hung on her belt. She lived on grass and birds which she shot with a catapult. Once she managed to kill a hare. She was beginning to cut it up with her penknife, relishing the thought of the first real food she'd had for days. Suddenly she caught the sound of men's voices. She just had time to stuff the meat into her blouse and clamber up a tree. She remained hidden among the leaves for two days and nights, wedged between the branches watching the troops setting up camp. Fresh-faced young men in brand-new uniforms and steel helmets pitched the tents and unloaded the supplies of ammunition and food. She watched them eating in the evening round their campfire and she felt faint with hunger. Then she pulled bits of the hare out of her blouse and chewed the insipid-tasting meat.

Two days later, when she had become so weak that she was about to roll down from her perch, the preparations for striking camp began. Weapons were reloaded noisily into crates and the soldiers left the clearing to the accompaniment of back-firing jeeps. Meriem closed her eyes and let go; she was vaguely aware of her skirts catching on the branches, the wind stinging her bare legs, then the weight of her body tore the stuff free, she rolled through more branches and fell on to the grass. That was how a maquisard unit found her. They picked her up, shook her, shouted in her ear, but Meriem did not respond. They carried the unconscious girl to their hide-out, the forest closed over them and all was still. That is how Meriem realized her dream.

Eventually Ali entrusted his diary to Meriem's mother and returned to Baladia.

He thought no more about joining the maquis. He became a *fidaï*, one of the shadowy figures whose swift murderous actions were on the increase. His inventive genius and his skill with disguises made him elusive. He sowed terror and confusion wherever his missions led him . . .

While carrying on his underground activities he never neglected his care for Monsieur Kimper's garden.

In the town, suspicious streets in the poorer districts were blocked off by barbed-wire entanglements to facilitate the countless house-to-house searches. European and Muslims alike barricaded themselves in their homes. The two worlds lived side by side, separated by a wall of mistrust, no longer trying to understand each other. The town was split into two: Europeans moved out of their homes in Muslim sectors and in the common climate of fear there was a mutual exchange of flats.

A new organization was born, the army of the 'Red Hand', that dealt death by night and returned calmly to their normal activities by day. It was said that its members were policemen, young thugs and even respectable family men who were transformed by night into bloodthirsty vampires. This sinister gang, disguised as soldiers, savagely killed thousands of Arab civilians in their homes. The nights become more than ever a nightmare.

The CNRA held its first meeting in Tripoli. Elsewhere, intellectuals sifted through their leaders to see if they could come up with a legitimate head of government. For the moment, they found fault with them all. One was too Westernized ... Another too fanatical a champion of the East ... There were rumours that X had been responsible for the death of certain young men in the resistance movement, because he was jealous of their education and feared their future claims ... Some were suspected of being opportunists, happy to divide and rule ... The armchair experts sat comfortably in their haunts far from Algeria, waiting to see with what sauce the country would be dished up.

Ali continued his operations without worrying about plans for the future or the character of this or that political leader. As far as he was concerned, the first thing was to rid the country of the yoke of colonialism. He made his contribution as a militant, conscious of his task. The 'sauce' mattered little to him, as long as it was Algerian.

But he did wonder from time to time whether the future leaders were to be found in the prisons or the maquis.

That year was marked by violent clashes between the ALN and General Massu's troops. On 28 March, Colonel Amirouche and Colonel Haouès were killed.

*

The routine of many people's lives were upset. Khéïra had to stop working for Monsieur Kimper, as the sector became too dangerous for Arab daily women. Some were waylaid in deserted districts on their way to work, and murdered by activists of the 'Red Hand'. Mounir, with an eye to the future, departed for France. Fella left school and never went out of the house.

Pandemonium was let loose every night in both halves of the town: to the cry of 'Algeria for the French' came the reply, 'Algeria for the Algerians'.

The two sides confronted each other furiously, the one with cries of victory, the other yelling with the foreboding of imminent defeat.

The professor and Ali were alone in the villa. This Sunday morning, Monsieur Kimper, who was a devout Christian, got ready to go to church to play the organ for the hymns. 'Don't wait for me for lunch,' he said, 'I'm invited to eat with Father Germain . . .'

Then he commented with a note of concern, 'You've got very thin lately! . . . Just look at your hollow cheeks and sallow colouring! Come on, put your back into it, my boy! We still need you, don't forget!'

He pinched the youngster's cheeks with a smile, patted him affectionately on the back and made his way to the gate.

'See you this evening, Ali!'

The youngster watched him and could not help marvelling at the vitality of this sixty-year-old. In spite of his corpulence, he was as sprightly as a young man. With his laughing eyes and everlasting pipe in the corner of his mouth he was the personification of an unshakeable confidence in life. He often used to say to Ali, 'Time and life win every battle . . . You must never grow impatient or let yourself be downcast by set-backs . . .'

Ali was thinking about this when suddenly he heard the sound of a terrible explosion near the door. When he got there, only a tangled mass of smoking iron was to be seen. He lost his head and screamed, uttering one long interminable shriek like that of a wild creature howling at death . . . Until the police dragged him senseless into the house.

197

Monsieur Kimper's funeral took place on a stormy day. A few cars solemnly followed the hearse. His sister and nephews came from France to see to the winding up of the estate. Ali arrived just when they were closing the coffin. He could not yet believe that the professor was no longer there. He continued to think of him as if he were still alive. He could still hear his soft voice with its soothing intonations and the music which told of his presence in the house.

He noticed people's surprised expressions and heard them whispering, 'Who is that young man?'

'His protégé,' someone murmured.

'He always had Arabs in his house, he had these cranky ideas, that's why he was killed, poor man! . . .'

Ali couldn't get these words out of his mind: 'He always had Arabs in his house! . . . That's why he was killed . . .' This death left him by turns stunned and panic-stricken at suddenly finding himself alone. He went down to his room, refusing to follow the funeral procession. He sat at his table with a blanket round his shoulders, trembling with cold and despair, like a sparrow fallen from its nest. Monsieur Kimper's friend, the superintendent, dropped in to see him before leaving with the others for the funeral ceremony. He considered the young man with what seemed like a gleam of pity in his eyes.

'Come, my boy, pull yourself together! . . . He wouldn't like to see you so down, he was very fond of you . . .' He sighed and after a moment added, 'You have a week before you have to leave the house, my boy. The professor's cousins have many things to settle and they count on you to help them as you're familiar with his affairs . . . Meanwhile look for another job. If you don't find anything, come and see me, I'll help you . . .'

Ali nodded, thinking, 'One week! . . .' His mouth was filled with the taste of bitter despair.

With great daring he planned his attack on the most closely guarded sector inhabited solely by Europeans, the Orchards district itself . . . It was common knowledge that the murderers who had planted the plastic bomb came from the neighbourhood. The professor had received threatening letters which had not bothered him.

The Sunday after his death, Ali chose a smart cinema. The results were spectacular. The superintendent, who was far from stupid, realized who must have been the author of the attack. He turned up the following morning with several inspectors and arrested Ali just as he was putting his things together to go to join Tahar. He went quietly.

The superintendent arranged for the young man to be transferred to a prison in France. For he knew that in Algeria, in this atmosphere electric with hate, Ali would have faced summary execution, like so many before him.

Had Juliette's blessing started to play its part in his destiny?

Tahar could do nothing for him. He paced dementedly backwards and forwards in his hut in the shantytown . . . He recalled Ali's look of a youngster eager for justice, so vulnerable, in spite of his determination to harden himself. Ali flushing when he was teased. Ali controlling himself so as not to vomit when he was frightened and caught in the grip of his terrors. Ali transfigured, confronting risks with a sort of unthinking courage. And Ali, who killed and wept over his victims . . .

And that strange presentiment he had had on his return from Dachra . . . He had come back intensely moved and under a cloud of melancholy; he'd told him about his cousin Meriem's departure for the maquis. Tahar recalled their last conversation.

'I've stowed everything away at my aunt's . . . I'm really alone now, all I have left is my life . . .'

'Why? Weren't you alone before?' Tahar remarked ironically.

'No! I had a fetish which went everywhere with me. My aunt is keeping it safely; there's no risk of her leaving the village; if I come out of all this alive, I shall go back there and get it . . .'

Tahar sighed, 'You've got the knack of complicating existence with words and things . . . I've never felt the need to have any "fetishes", as you call them. Everything is in here!' he said, pointing to his head.

Ali looked at him with a fond and fierce intensity and said

199

softly, 'If one day we are separated, Tahar, wherever you are, my friendship will follow you like a faithful dog.'

Tahar was taken aback and disguised his embarrassment with a sudden cough. He put his hand to his mouth, hiding half his face. He, who normally was quick with his retorts, was at a loss for a reply.

Ali put both his hands on Tahar's shoulders, forcing him to look at him.

'If we come out of his hell alive, you know where we must meet? On 1 November, in Dachra, in the village café . . . 1 November of the first year of independence! No matter which year that is . . .'

Tahar had given him his word. Now, alone in his hide-out, the scene unrolled before his eyes blinded with tears, like a desperately silent film.

Ali was incarcerated in the Santé Prison in France. No one knew what had become of Mounir. Tahar eventually joined the maquis. Si Salah doggedly continued teaching Arabic at the high school and his underground activities in his local cell . . . He was the only one who knew where Mounir was. Not a day passed without Fella thinking of her friends. Her mother grieved as she went silently about her daily tasks; her father, a senior orderly at the local hospital, sometimes took her to help him in his work. Thus trapped between her parents, Fella could not join the other women who had left to fight beside the men in the maquis. She waited . . .

Events moved with incredible speed.

21 October 1960: General De Gaulle declares, 'Peace in Algeria is at our door.'

December 1960: The first popular demonstrations in Algeria.

9–12 August 1961: The CNRA meets in Tripoli and elects a new provisional government.

The OAS sets up barricades which are rapidly broken up.

Demonstrations by Algerians and French left-wing in Paris.

7 March 1962: Conference in Evian on the ceasefire.

15 March 1962: People working at social centres, including the writer Mouloud Féraoun and three Europeans, murdered by the OAS in el-Biar.

19 March 1962: Ceasefire in Algeria and sudden appearance of the 'Martians', last ditch militants and *moujahideen* . . .

20 April 1962: Salan arrested – general offensive against the OAS.

2 May 1962: OAS offensive in Algiers: 100 dead, 150 wounded, including victims of a car bomb.

7 June 1962: The OAS sets fire to the University library in Algiers.

12 June 1962: The GPRA guarantees Europeans, 'The Evian government is the charter for your future.'

27 June 1962: OAS resistance crumbles in Oran. General Gardy flees.

4 July 1962: First ALN detachments enter Algerian towns.

13

> *'Then We appointed you viceroys in the*
> *earth after them, that We might behold*
> *how you would do.'*
> Quran, sura X, Jonah, revealed at Mecca

Independence brought an end to the nightmare. People everywhere gave themselves over to rejoicing, flourishing flags stained with the blood of patriots who had died in the struggle. Prisoners came back to their families, maquisards returned to the warmth of their homes. Promises of happiness loomed large on the horizon.

In France, Algerians and foreign friends celebrated together. Algeria's future was more than ever the main topic of discussion among the young Algerians who forgathered in cafés on the Left Bank. Some hoped for a Russian-style socialism; others for that of Yugoslavia ('the land of happy socialism!'). The most extreme nationalists cried out for a purely Algerian road to socialism! Every model was passed in review: Cuban, Arab, Chinese . . . everybody advanced their own ideas based on the subject they had best assimilated.

Ali was among the released prisoners returning to Algeria. After their medical examination they were all invited to a 'couscous' given by the Federation of France, and so he found himself plunged into this atmosphere of passionate argument. These endless discussions left him speechless . . . As a man who had gone straight from his village to action in the city, then to France of which he had seen nothing but its prisons, he felt he had landed on an unknown planet.

He observed these people and listened to their speculation on

Algeria's future. One proclaimed that he was returning to put his experience and qualifications at the service of the country. Another, on the contrary, clearly annoyed at being left out of important political decisions, expressed his disillusionment with the turn of events, and preferred to live in exile . . . Wasn't the new government banning the communist party? . . . And demanding Arab socialism? . . . What sort of anachronism was that? some people lamented . . . The boldest sneered, 'Poor old Marx and Lenin must be turning in their graves!' The disillusioned ones drowned their bitterness in a flood of destructive criticisms of this or that political personality . . . Ali tried to intervene to make them clarify their own political differences . . . If at the dawn of independence, at the the time when the country was licking its wounds and trying to provide bread for its people, if it also had to tolerate several dozen political parties which began by mutual destruction and denunciation, it would be anarchy . . . Just like in this room . . . What more could be said about all this post-independence ballyhoo? Ali listened. Mounir was there, naturally. He was now one of the leaders of the FNL in France. He had matured. His features had firmed up in the course of the underground struggle. He greeted Ali warmly, calling him 'Brother'. That was, of course, no proof of his particular pleasure at meeting him, since they all called each other 'Brother So-and-So' or 'Sister-So-and-So', thus conferring a note of fraternity on the relationship between men and women. The man who accompanied Ali and his comrades was a lawyer celebrated for his energetic contribution to the Algerian cause, Maître Liegeman. He chatted with all and sundry.

Ali smiled bitterly at all this excitement which was turning these men into greedy children jostling for their share of the enormous cake. He remembered his discussion with Monsieur Kimper: 'I think,' he had said, 'I shall invest straightaway in a stop-watch.'

And then an even more distant memory, that of his father's words as he dressed his wounds, 'The dogs bark and the caravan moves on' . . .

Mounir came towards him with a smile. 'Ali, you look bored.

203

You haven't changed! Still looking so solemn and anxious... It's all over now, we're free!'

Ali protested, declaring that he was simply tired after so much excitement . . . Maître Liegeman, beside them, said, 'You know, Ali, one of your friends, Si Salah, never stopped asking for news of you. He'll be meeting you tomorrow at Algiers airport . . . He and I were continually in contact . . . He's very attached to you.'

'Lucky devil!' exclaimed Mounir. 'Everybody wants to fuss over you, like some precious object!'

Ali gradually noticed that everything in Mounir's attitude towards him was forced, he laughed too much and never stopped fidgeting around, provoking him to comment, 'You've got something on your mind, Mounir! What is it?'

'Someone you know well has been invited this evening and will be here soon . . .'

'Who? . . .'

Ali felt a hand on his shoulder. He jumped and turned round sharply.

It was Alain. For a moment they looked at each other without a word, with eyes only for the friend of their childhood. Then they hugged each other.

'So you've been trailing me, you wretch?' said Ali.

'I told you I'd find you wherever you were, you ruffian!'

They took each other by the arm and went to sit a little distance from the others. 'Juliette hasn't changed,' Alain told him. 'She's gradually got used to living in Nice. She still talks about Dachra. As for me, I had a blazing row with my father when I decided to study journalism instead of medicine and then I came to Paris. My pals and I all militated for Algeria's independence.'

He told how he had got to know Mounir, how he had been in the forefront of the demonstrations in Paris against the Algerian war. He'd heard that Ali had been killed in his cell in Baladia . . . Ali wondered who in Paris could have spread such a lie? Then he thought that everything at the time had been so confused that it was not surprising people believed anything!

'Mounir's a decent sort, you know!' Alain concluded. 'What's more he's got a marvellous wife.'

204

'What!' Ali exclaimed. 'Mounir's married? He didn't say a word to me, the secretive bastard! Whenever did he find time for wedding bells?'

'I think it was about a year ago. I've only seen her twice, but she's really stunning!'

'A Frenchwoman?' Ali inquired.

'Frankly, I don't know . . .' Alain stopped and pointed out a woman who had just come in.

'There she is!'

Ali looked where his friend was pointing and fell silent, completely stunned. Was he dreaming? Amalia was greeting people. Mounir was holding her arm. He seemed nervous and kept glancing anxiously towards the table where the two young men were sitting. Amalia seemed to be looking for someone. Then she let go of Mounir and slowly walked over to Ali. Mounir had gone white. He turned round and moved over to a group of friends who were calling him.

Ali stared at Amalia, he saw her lips move but no sound reached him. She was standing there in front of him, she was alive, the same person, with her expression, her mouth . . . But what was she saying? He would never hear her.

He felt Alain touch his arm and heard him murmur anxiously, 'Ali, what's come over you?'

Amalia held out her hand.

'Hallo, Ali,' she said softly.

Alain realized that something was happening or had happened between these two. He got up to give his seat to the young woman.

'I'll make myself scarce, Ali . . . See you later? I'll still be around . . .'

He said goodbye to Amalia and left them.

'I only heard a month ago that you were alive and in prison in France. Mounir didn't know either!'

Ali reacted suddenly at her naïvety.

'Mounir has always known! From the moment I was transferred to France, he knew . . .' He gestured wearily. 'In any case, what's the use now . . .'

Ali was overwhelmed with despair. Where had this long, long road he had travelled led him? He reeled, there was a hammering in his head, beating against the walls of his senses. Like a vaguely remembered light from the past, the young woman's voice rekindled in the depths of the mist of anguish, the sensation of her very real presence.

'Shortly after the professor's tragic death, we heard you'd been arrested and executed in a camp in Algeria . . . I searched . . . I contacted everyone here, no one knew anything, political events moved so fast, most people were caught off balance by the military putsch and the only reply I ever got was that nobody knew what had happened to the prisoners. Then I fell ill, I was all alone, a prey to anxiety. I couldn't take an interest in anything. I was rapidly going out of my mind. Then my aunt sent for Mounir, thinking he would help me regain my reason . . . I spent three months convalescing in the sun. Mounir was constantly at my side. Then I married him out of weariness. I scarcely knew what I was doing. I was sedated all the time. My aunt couldn't cope with me any more. Mounir took me under his wing. That's it! And now, you are here . . . Mounir told me a month ago, adding that I was free to choose . . .'

Her features were drawn, she seemed exhausted. Her complexion was dull, her eyes, formerly so bright, so lively, so mobile, were veiled, their light dimmed by impenetrable nightmares. Even her movements which used to be ample and luminous, had contracted within her emaciated body. She held herself stiffly, her hands slightly clenched on her knees. Her voice at times seemed strange, somewhat staccato, and she kept faltering as if her memory failed her . . . Then she resumed, like an accused before an implacable judge. But Ali had retreated far from her, into grief as solid and cold as a block of ice. Life had played one more nasty trick on him. And Mounir, whether he was at fault or not, had played his cards well also . . .

He heard Amalia saying softly, 'I have a five-month-old baby. I've called her Alia.'

He jumped up, overcome with an insidious choking nausea . . . He had to get out of there. All these people around him like thousand-headed dragons. He searched desperately for the exit. Someone near him said with a laugh, 'Here's a brother who's celebrated his release not wisely but too well!'

Yes, he was drunk, but with nausea; he was one mass of nausea. He lurched between the tables and the laughter, thunder was exploding in his head, where was he to go? Where could he flee? Alain ran up to him. 'I'm here, Ali . . . Lean on me.'

Alain's voice broke with emotion. He realized that his friend was in the grip of a nameless torment. Amalia followed like a sleepwalker. Mounir came up to her and whispered, 'Let Alain go with him . . .'

Amalia clutched her handbag and replied, in the same tone, 'It's no longer your business, Mounir . . . Go away!'

No one noticed the couple's brief exchange. Mounir, shrewd, capable, brave, but wary, was concerned about his reputation; he liked to surround himself with respect and composure. He took refuge in the classic cliché: 'Amalia, don't forget Alia needs you at home . . .'

She had gone already.

Ali leaned against the door outside, sweating profusely. Alain mopped his forehead with his handkerchief, speaking to him in Arabic, using the expressions of their childhood, 'Ali, pull yourself together. Be a man . . .'

Suddenly struck by this expression, he straightened up and seized Alain by the collar, roaring, 'Enough! I don't want to hear that word again! I'm not a man! I'm a human being . . . A human outcast! We're all scum . . . I spit on all men, and I'll spit on them till I die! Buggers! Silly buggers! All of them! . . .'

Alain was strangling under his friend's grip. He struggled, trying to calm Ali's fury as a policeman was approaching with a suspicious expression.

'What's up, gentlemen?'

Amalia answered, in a voice that she tried to make sound casual, 'He's had a drop too much, it's nothing, we're just leaving!'

She helped Alain drag Ali to her car which was parked close by.

'A man! Look what men have done to her!' Ali shouted,

pointing to Amalia. 'Deceived her, broken her, made her into an old woman . . . One of our heroes has lied to her. *Khaïn! Khaïn . . . Khawana!* Traitor! Traitor . . . Traitors! Man is a monster who devours the fortunes of women . . .'

He no longer shouted, his voice broke, he wished he could weep so that his tears could wash away the multitude of sharp pebbles that were rattling in his brain, but his eyes remained dry and burning.

Amalia got into the car and as Alain was about to follow her she said, 'No . . . Please, leave him to me! I want to be alone with him.'

'But . . . I can't abandon him like that . . . Where are you taking him?'

'I don't know . . . I want to be alone with him,' she repeated softly.

'All right, but you know all the former prisoners are leaving tomorrow for Algiers; he has to be at the airport at 5 p.m. Bring him back to my place, here's my address. I live quite near here . . .'

'Thank you, Alain . . . I promise to bring him back to you.'

Amalia moved very gently over to Ali, as if she were afraid of scaring him. She loosened his shirt collar and smoothed his forehead, whispering, 'Come Ali. We'll drive around Paris. Forget everything . . . Nothing has happened . . . There's been no war . . . No Mounir . . . We are free and young and . . . we've just met . . . Nothing else exists . . .'

He didn't say another word, as if he had thrown in the sponge. She was right, nothing had happened. They had scarcely begun their history.

Amalia drove, feeling once more serene and whole . . . Feeling the peace and security which she thought to have lost for ever, since . . . . but she thrust all her worries from her mind, concentrating on being an attentive guide to Ali.

Near Saint-Germain-des-Prés she slowed down to point out the Old Navy, the meeting-place for young intellectuals or others at a loose end. Further on she suggested they stop for a drink at the

Saint-Claude, a favoured stamping-ground of Algerian students, militants and businessmen. Ali refused, saying he wasn't keen to be exposed to the idle chatter of his 'gallant brethren'. Neither the Deux Magots nor the Royal, on the opposite pavement, found favour with him. He wanted to be far from any possible contact with the high spirits and grandiloquence of some exuberant compatriot. 'All right!' she announced, 'I'm going to take you to a place I know, one of Monique's favourite haunts, frequented by Anglo-Saxons.'

'You've got to know English people?' Ali asked, unable to prevent himself feeling jealous, cut off from everything that had occurred before . . .

'You're bound to get to know them if you live in a city like this! Don't forget my aunt owns a picture gallery and does business with them . . .'

He gazed at the girl's profile; the harmonious purity of her features was marked here and there by tiny wrinkles at the corners of her eyes and lips . . . He felt a surge of tenderness for her, and seizing her fingers he kissed the palm of her hand. She whispered, 'You do know that I love you?'

'Yes,' he replied with quiet certainty.

'Am I going to lose you again?'

He ignored this question and said, 'My return to Algeria is very important to me . . . I looked forward to it for so long! When I set foot on the soil of my free country, I shall be all alone . . . What will it smell like . . . sound like, now? . . . I have a long journey to share with her: Algeria.'

'With Algeria? . . .'

In her emotion Amalia let go of the wheel and the car skidded; other drivers stared hooting. Ali cried out to her to be careful. She pulled herself together, trembling, not from fear but from mute despair at the young man's admission . . . Did he mean to imply that he would never see her again?

Harry's Bar welcomed them with its babble of lively conversation in which exclamations in English were mixed with others in a peculiar French which made Ali laugh. He found the place picturesque, its laid-back clientele seeming to come straight out of an American film. It was very crowded so Amalia decided to go downstairs where the atmosphere was more intimate. There were a few small tables along the wall and a pianist playing as if to himself, ignoring the customers. The young couple sat down facing the pianist who raised his head from time to time and looked at them kindly. For a moment they let themselves be soothed by the music and the indifference of the anonymous strangers who formed a sort of invisible, protective rampart around them.

'It will be a disaster for me to be parted from you again, my life will become a wasteland . . .'

Amalia returned to the attack, eager to make Ali understand that her one desire was to follow him. But Ali still did not reply to her direct questions. He remained silent, trying to delude himself that at this moment there was no threat to their rediscovery of each other. And all around them the ripple of laughter and the clinking of glasses on the tables seemed to be one long toast to their love.

Then they set out again to drive round and round. Late Amalia parked the car on the Champs-Elysées and they walked down the broad brightly-lit pavements.

'I have always lost things just when I needed them most,' Ali said.

Amalia ran her hands through her hair, her eyes had a distant look.

'No,' she said, 'I am the one who loses everything. First I lost my father, leaving a great gap in my life, then my identity: I'm neither Arab nor European . . . All my feelings and perceptions have been warped . . . I have no roots anywhere! And all the independences in the world won't recreate me . . . They've turned up too late in my life, like you. So I shall always be condemned to a reality that I shall never recognize! And today, more than ever, as you don't want me.'

Ali halted and took her in his arms.

'At present, it is both too soon and too late to build our life together. What's more, you're not just anybody's wife . . .

Whatever Mounir has done to separate us, he is first and foremost a fellow-fighter. An Algerian who has given his youth to the country, like me. You have his child, he is your husband . . . That's the reality, and that makes you sacred to me. That is a code of honour which your European upbringing does not understand, I know . . .'

Amalia was choked with sudden rebellion. She stammered despairingly. 'It's . . . It's not fair! How can you sacrifice us? . . .'

She freed herself from his embrace, recoiling as if she were afraid of him, afraid of some danger from his contact. Her voice shook . . . she was once again the little girl subject to storms of anger as in the past.

'For some old, out-moded, cruel principle! Life is so short! Why lose still more time? Why do you want to cut short our history before it has even reached its fulfilment? . . . In the name of some dusty, inhuman morality . . . I don't want to suffer any more!' she sobbed. 'I've had enough of sacrificing myself!'

Unable to control herself, she recoiled, howling like a creature at bay. She seemed suddenly to have lost her reason, she was becoming hysterical. Ali ran to her. Taking her in his arms, he rocked her like a child, begging her gently to compose herself. As he spoke she became aware of something for the first time: Ali was no longer the sensitive, romantic boy she had discovered one day; she felt him to be cut off behind a solid, impenetrable wall.

'Be a woman, Amalia . . . A genuine, strong, responsible woman; you have a life marked out for you: your baby and all the rest . . . You think you won't survive if we are parted for ever? But you are mistaken . . . We are caught up in the daily routine of life and its demands . . . For my part, I don't feel I shall be losing you, as you will always be alive within me. Just remember that somewhere a man without a name has two stars: Algeria and Amalia . . . And I love you as I shall never love anyone in the world.'

Ali took her hand firmly and they continued walking through the city streets. Never had the sky been so bright and clear as this October. Thousands of stars as big and luminous as those of Dachra lit up their path. So many lost civilizations, so much past greatness, so many cries and deaths flowed through the blood of these two young creatures, frantic with love and so soon to be separated.

They walked like sweethearts, and Paris connived by enfolding them in her deep calm midnight blue. Even the moon lingered for them, as if eager to soothe and reassure the lovers.

At dawn, Amalia returned home.

She did not take the lift, as if she wanted to prolong her suffering or put off the moment when Ali's presence within her would weaken and disintegrate with the many humdrum commitments of her everyday existence.

She slowly climbed the five flights. Step by slow step, her mute cries kept time to the rhythm of her grief. She must learn once more to live with a new wound. For how long? Where? What would give her the strength to endure?

She felt exhausted and drained. Tomorrow she must think of her duties as wife and mother . . . she must mingle with the crowd again. She began to tremble. What are you afraid of, Amalia? Be patient, you are stronger than you think.

Her face was drenched with tears. Her lips formed a monotonous, heart-breaking litany: 'Ali . . . The first step: A . . . the second step: L . . . the third step: I . . .'

Three letters imprinted on every horizon.

The light on the stairs went out. Amalia groped in the dark. She found the switch, went on up, resuming her murmuring in which the intolerable and the absurd blended in a vertiginous whirl which sent her bumping, bounding then floating once more in the void. And the echo in her heart continued its doleful lament:

'Ali-youth-truth; Ali-mystery-history; Ali-sweetness-distress; Ali-madness-sadness; Ali-remembrance-endurance; Ali-laughing-suffering; Ali-defiance-reliance; Ali-dreamland-fatherland; Ali-panic-romantic; Ali-hand-tracing-curves-over-my-body . . .'

When she reached her door, she sank down on the step. She remained sitting there for a long time in the cold air of the silent building. The light had gone out and she did not bother to switch it on again. She wept. Through her tears flickered, 'Ali – A for – ALWAYS WAITING, from now on.'

Ali was amazed by the Algiers that he discovered, noisy, radiant, restless as a boisterous girl. Si Salah had not changed, his face had a few more wrinkles, his blue eyes had retained their gleam of intelligence and natural kindliness. He had an important post at the headquarters of the National Assembly.

Knowing the young man's taste for studying, he took him under his wing as if he were his son or his brother. He put the whole of the first floor of his house in el-Biar at his disposal; this consisted of a bedroom with a large balcony, a sitting-room-study and a bathroom. Ali was delighted with his new lodging. But when Si Salah suggested that he work with him, he refused.

'No! I've already told you I want to spend the next two years working for my *baccalauréat*, as an independent student.'

'Really! And what will you live on?'

'I intend to look for a part-time job.'

'Meanwhile, you are my guest. You will live with us. My old mother will be delighted to have one more son. I know you went on studying in prison, and I can coach you to help you catch up. Then I'll get you enrolled at a high school so that you can follow the classes normally, and I'll get you a bursary, which isn't difficult for a former *moujahid*.

Ali laughed. 'It's funny to hear oneself called "a former *moujahid*" or "a former prisoner"! . . .'

At twenty-two one thinks oneself finished, crumbling like an old building . . . Si Salah evidently knew all about Amalia's existence and her marriage to Mounir. So he was pleased to see his young friend laugh and think of his future.

During the ensuing months Ali threw himself whole-heartedly into his work, driven by a dogged will-power. He finally took the road to the *lycée* that he had dreamed of long ago. He was not much older than some of his schoolfellows. They adopted him with affectionate admiration for a former member of the resistance. His teachers appreciated his seriousness and the quiet influence he had over the noisier boys. He took advantage of the holidays to visit Baladia and Dachra.

213

'The martyr is the man who gives his life
For other than fortune.'
Hadith

14

A shady street, the finest in the Orchards district, bears the name of Professor Kimper . . . The main square of Baladia, with its fountain and flowerbeds is named after Tahar. Martyrs whom Algeria honours, like all those who gave their lives for a certain freedom.

Tahar whose wish it was to fight and die with his weapons in his hands, not to be assassinated in cowardly fashion, was yet caught unawares by death on the day of the sole and final truce.

Fella tells what happened.

Shortly after Mounir's departure, his family left their home and went to live in the Muslim quarter in the old town. Committees were set up to organize a neighbourhood watch at night. As the inhabitants had no weapons to defend themselves, they filled bottles with methylated spirits and lobbed these Molotov cocktails at any suspicious individual who ventured near their homes.

The curtain of fear was everywhere.

Midday on Monday 19 March 1962 was the time appointed for the ceasefire. That morning Fella's father, a senior medical orderly, was on duty at the hospital; before he left home he advised his daughter not to go out as there was a risk of the plastic bombers in the city choosing that day to go on the rampage in a final act of retaliation.

However, during the afternoon a veiled woman came to ask her

214

to go and attend a wounded maquisard. Fella had been trained in first aid by her father and there were medical supplies in the house. She had occasionally assisted her father in this kind of mission. The woman, who acted as a liaison for the maquisards, was known to her so she took a first-aid case and followed her. A man was waiting for them with a white Peugeot.

He drove off the main road and two hours later turned into a narrow, tree-lined track where he switched off the engine.

The chirping of the birds was the only sound to be heard. At three o'clock on this March afternoon, the countryside stretched out lazily in the early spring sunshine. They left the car and walked in silence for some hundred yards till they saw a young man draped in a peasant's cloak, guarding his flock of sheep. He calmly scutinized the trio and greeted them with, '*Allah!*'

The man accompanying the two women replied, '*Inawar essama' wa'l ard*' (May He light up the sky and the earth), thus completing the password. The young man who could not have been more than eighteen, turned and whistled. A man appeared, wearing a similar cloak, under which a sub-machine-gun could be guessed at.

'Follow me!'

They climbed in single file up goat-tracks and soon a *mechta* came into view on the crest of the hill. Fella was a bit out of breath. Children were playing here and there. Men in burnouses with guns slung over their shoulders watched them in silence. They passed among the shacks of the settlement where women were bustling about amid their clucking poultry.

A very tall bearded man in fatigues, with a pistol hanging down over his right hip, came towards them. Fella could not distinguish his features as his face was hidden behind dark glasses and the thick black beard with silvery flecks. But something in the way he trod stealthily, like some wild animal, reminded her of someone. Her heart beat faster. The man took off his glasses unhurriedly and said with a smile, 'You have changed your job, little sister?'

Fella was stunned. She cried out in surprise, 'Tahar!'

She trembled with emotion; her first impulse was to rush

215

towards him but all these silent, solemn people intimidated her. She stammered, 'Oh! God, I'd never have thought I would meet you here today!'

Tahar broke into a peal of laughter. His white teeth glittered against his black beard. He moved in the same calm, leisurely way and had the same loud, uninhibited mocking laugh. His face, tanned by the winds of the maquis, reflected the same serenity.

He seemed even bigger than she remembered him: a giant, sturdy as the forest trees, she thought affectionately. He awoke memories for her of the time with her brother Mounir and the others . . .

'Don't stand there like a statue, little sister! Come and see what you can do for our patient. We had a violent skirmish five days ago, in which we lost some men, including our medical orderly and all our medical supplies. We withdrew here with one brother in a very bad way . . .'

The girl noticed a wooden hut over which an Algerian flag hung. She stopped short, gazing in astonishment at the colours they had dreamed of for so long, now flapping casually in the breeze. It was the first time she had seen the flag for which so many men and women were dying. Tahar took her arm and whispered, 'You're wondering how we managed to hoist it here?'

'Yes, aren't you afraid of being discovered by the army?'

'The ceasefire has been proclaimed! We respect it, and so do they.'

Inside the post a young *djoundi* was sitting typing. He looked up as they entered, smiled and went on tapping away at the keyboard.

His youthfulness reminded her of Ali. She looked at Tahar who sighed sadly. 'Yes, Ali . . . He's in prison in France. But I'll soon be seeing him, don't worry.'

He remained silent, staring right through the young secretary-wireless-operator.

When she had done all she could for the wounded man, Fella and her friends sat down in a circle on the ground. A man brought tea and hot *galettes*. Fella asked, 'Are you really not afraid of being attacked, remaining in the open like this?'

216

'Not at all!' replied one of the *moujahideen*. 'The soldiers aren't attacking any more. We'll be going home soon.'

Fella said musingly, 'Mounir has given no sign of life! We've no idea what's happened to him. Let's pray he comes home safe and sound!'

Tahar patted her arm kindly. 'Don't worry about him, he'll be all right, he was born under a lucky star. Like me, you see! I've led every attack and got off scot free; I've got all the thorns of our mountains in my feet; I know every bush, every inch of our maquis. I've remained hidden for three days in a *wadi*, I've crossed the electrified fences twenty times, I've fought hand to hand with the enemy and never been wounded . . . Apart from a few bruises. They call me "The Serpent", the symbol of strength and life . . . Everything that this carcass of mine has endured, encountered, is nothing! According to the Brothers, it would seem that I have *baraka*, but I actually think that ill weeds never die, it's the good ones we lose.'

'No!' Fella's companion replied, 'God is protecting you!'

Fella looked at her watch and stood up. 'It's five o'clock already! We must go; the village check-point is closed at seven and we shan't be able to pass after that.'

'Then stay with us!' one of the men cried. 'Spend the night here! We've got some fine fat chickens to cook for dinner with a good couscous. Today's a day for rejoicing and there's nothing to fear any more.'

The woman and man who had brought her agreed, but Fella shook her head explaining, 'No, tonight it's not possible! My father doesn't know where I am; he was out when I left and he'll be anxious. I don't want to worry him. I'll come back tomorrow, I promise! I'll stay with you and I'll bring you cakes and cigarettes! . . .'

The men seemed a little disappointed, but Tahar accepted joyfully. 'Fine! So tomorrow you'll be our guests of honour!'

While they were all taking their leave they heard the throbbing of aeroplane engines overhead. They saw two planes flying over the *mechta*. The men quickly dived into the undergrowth. Tahar's face contracted but he said lightly, 'It's nothing. They're

217

watching us. It's been like that since yesterday, then they go away. It's the flag which attracts them no doubt.'

He appointed two armed men to accompany them back to the car.

As they scrambled down the slope Fella stopped and turned round; she caught sight of Tahar's huge figure and raised her arm to wave to him. He shouted, 'Don't forget, little sister, bring us a date *macroud*!'

As soon as she was in the car Fella nervously rubbed her neck. She felt she was suffocating. She was overcome by anxiety, a clear, undeniable sense of foreboding. Those planes . . . It wasn't normal, she thought.

Tahar's smile, the men's quiet assurance, the inhabitants of the *mechta*, the children . . .

And the monstrous thousand-legged beast gripped her temples in an icy vice, whispering, 'He is dead! they are going to die! No, No! It's the ceasefire! They are practically unarmed! . . .'

The reconnaissance plane continued flying low over the *mechta*. It was followed by two more, then three, and finally five, almost skimming the ground, so that the inhabitants had to bend double as they fled to cover under the branches.

Tahar gave the order to the *djounoud* to disperse in groups. There were only about fifteen of them left in fact as most of the unit had been wiped out in a serious engagement a week before.

The men clutched their machine-guns and aimed at the attackers, their bodies jerking as each bullet was fired. Now the bombers streaked across the sky, dropping their bombs and scattering napalm. The resisters countered doggedly, with all their fire power.

The strafing continued. They had the advantage not only of surprise but also of attacking from the air. They flew so low that the men could almost distinguish the pilots' faces. The under-carriages spat fire before the planes rose up again with a dull, terrifying roar.

Tahar was now practically alone in front of the post, with the flag waving above him. His machine-gun formed an intergral part

218

of him. He could hear the groans of his companions and of the villagers who fell like flies, mercilessly mown down.

The *mechta* was one blazing inferno.

Suddenly the young wireless-operator ran out screaming, 'Si Tahar! Come back inside!'

'Get back inside, quick!' shouted Tahar.

At that moment a rocket exploded at their feet. Tahar turned, grabbed the youngster by the waist and hurled him bodily into the hut. His face was distorted by a grimace as he shouted at the boy, 'Stay there, you understand?'

Flames were licking round his feet. Tahar aimed at the plane which had just dropped the bomb and fired, fired with all his might. He just had time to see the plane judder, go off course and disappear behind all this smoke and hellfire.

That was all he saw. He thought he had hit the plane. He clung frantically to his machine-gun, ignoring the blood which spurted from his belly and the flames licking around him. And suddenly an interminable peal of laughter emerged from his throat, growing louder in the sudden surrounding silence.

Tahar fell with the laugh on his lips, and was still.

The raid had ended. The ground was strewn with corpses. The ruined huts were still smouldering. The young radio-operator ran out of the shed which was miraculously undamaged with the flag still waving above it. He ran wild-faced through the *mechta* which smoked with death and desolation.

He was the sole survivor of this hecatomb. He crouched down beside Tahar, closed his eyes and began to cry softly.

The sun was rapidly falling below the horizon. On this 19 March a whole *mechta* had been wiped out in cold blood and Si Tahar had died laughing.

The narrow streets of Dachra were busier now after independence. The place wore once more the air of a prosperous little market town. Ali's father's shop now bore a clumsily written sign, 'Barber'. The relative who had bought it had transformed it into the village hairdresser's. Ali wandered about in search of his memories. Most of the faces were unfamiliar. Si Saïd, the Mozabite, was still there, shrunken with the years, but still bright-eyed. He was very moved to see the young man, and greeted him with sincere affection.

'You remember the day when you nicked all my sweets? Oh! What terrible little rascals you were! . . .'

At Meriem's parents' he was surrounded by aunts and uncles, amid resounding ululations! The children gazed curiously at this cousin with his city ways. His aunt returned his diary to him and told him all the changes that had taken place in the village since independence. Ali wanted to talk about Meriem, but his aunt didn't let him get a word in.

'This is yours; all these years I kept it hidden among the dresses of my daughter's trousseau . . . Oh! What joy we felt when Meriem came back to us with the *djounoud* on Independence Day! She's become really beautiful, *ya Allah!* But then time has changed everything, even our daughters! Do you know she doesn't wear a veil any more, my son?'

All this tumbled out; then seeing Ali smile, she added, 'How stupid of me! As if she could be bothered with a veil in the maquis! . . . But I can't get used to the idea of my daughter going about with her face uncovered, like a man . . .'

Ali stroked his diary with emotion. He opened his mouth to ask where Meriem was, but his aunt went on chattering away happily.

'Do you know that the café belongs to Abdi now. He's my son-in-law, of course, but I must confess I've never liked him . . . He's full of himself! The former owner, Si Hafid, was executed by the Front, because he'd never give a penny to the organization, although he was so rich . . . And Abdi bought the family business for a song. He's got his wits about him, when all's said and done. They say he helped the Brothers. Anyway he kept well in with both sides,' she concluded maliciously.

Ali had not yet seen Abdi, 'the big booby'.

He noticed that his aunt was getting ready to launch into more gossip so decided to interrupt her firmly. 'Where is Meriem? I haven't seen her yet!'

220

She smiled and answered complacently, 'She's at a meeting at the mayor's office with the men and women of the Party, as they call it.'

Ali was silent, he could not imagine his cousin as a grown woman, discussing politics. And what did his uncle think of all that? He was about to speak when the curtain stirred and Meriem appeared. She stopped short for a moment. She held herself erect, her lips slightly parted as she stared at Ali with a strange gleam in her eyes. He gazed in astonishment at this new woman . . . Tall, slender, long-legged, wearing black slacks and a white blouse.

She held herself proudly. Her hair was scraped back under a white scarf, giving her face a certain austerity. She looked at him as if seeing him for the first time.

His aunt broke the silence. 'Well! What are you both waiting for? Aren't you going to kiss? You've both brought honour and joy to our hearts.'

Meriem was the first to murmur solemnly, 'How are you, Ali?'

Ali smiled and replied in the same even tone, 'Well, thank you. I am pleased to see you again . . .'

His aunt went out to prepare the dinner. Meriem threw off her head-scarf. Her hair, which used to come down nearly to her knees, was now cut short. Freed from the scarf, it framed her face, giving her a softer, younger, more accessible look. If it were not for her snub nose and bright, mischievous eyes, he could have been in the presence of a stranger. Her years in the maquis had toughened her physically and her body gave the impression of being hard and muscular. She dropped down on a mattress, ran her hands through her hair and remarked, 'Everything has changed, but our home is the same . . . And what about you, Ali?'

'For me, everything is beginning . . .'

A silence, then she said softly, 'I've seen Slimane . . . He told me everything that's happened to you . . . It's true, everything is beginning for us.'

What exactly did she know about him? Why did he feel embarrassed in her presence? Why dare he not look at her and seemed to be absorbed in his thoughts?

He felt Meriem's hand on his head; she had moved close to him

221

and raising her face to him she whispered, 'You and I have escaped death, and we have not yet kissed . . .'

He kissed her. There was no violence in Meriem's kiss, on the contrary, a great gentleness, more poignant and more terrible than passion. Ali was filled with a feeling of sadness. He freed himself rather sharply from the girl's arms and she moved quietly away from him. She sat down again facing him, leaning against the floral velvet cushion; she gave off so much vitality, so much strength that he suddenly felt a prey to a similar intoxication as on the day when Tahar had put in his hands the weapon which he was to use for his first attack . . . And suddenly, he who had eliminated all physical fear, was terrified by the emotion which invaded him. Can the body be drawn violently to another, while the heart, the soul is filled by someone else?

'Why are you afraid?' she said.

She was right. She could see through him as in the past. He still felt the same *malaise* in her presence, especially when she looked at him appraising him with her strangely pensive gaze. Love had made of Amalia an open book for him; she had often irritated him, but never inspired this sort of anguish which resembled fear . . .

Amalia . . . The only one who could soothe him, whose touching frailty made him want to protect her. Amalia with all her faults, multi-faceted, fascinating and at the same time baffling. Amalia with her secret torments, her arrogant outbursts, Amalia with her doubts, her impulses, her remorse.

Ali's thoughts were suddenly of her, he had erected once and for all a high and impenetrable wall between himself and his childhood. And Meriem came brusquely to shatter his citadel.

Just as he was about to reply, his uncle entered, followed by his wife. Meriem got up to help her mother lay the table for dinner. This evening the women would eat with the men.

Later, when they were sitting round drinking tea (Meriem had changed into a long dress like her mother's) Ali's uncle asked him, 'What are you going to do now, son?

Ali told him about his studies and how he had settled definitely in Algiers. His uncle nodded. Ali turned to Meriem and repeated his uncle's question about her plans. She shrugged her shoulders and replied, 'Oh! Me . . . I don't know yet . . . Let's first see what Algeria wants to make of us . . .'

Her old mother muttered, 'We want to see her stay here, get married! Commander Si Achour has asked for her hand! But she refuses . . . This girl has never been able to say anything except "No" all her life!' She added angrily. 'You took up arms the same as the men during the war; now let everyone go back to their proper job . . . And the woman's place is in the home!'

Ali smiled knowingly at his cousin. Their eyes met in the affectionate understanding of young people in the presence of parents. Finally their awkwardness disappeared in this shared amusement. They burst out laughing simultaneously. Meriem retorted, 'Nothing is decided yet, little mother. I am still as committed as the men to the future of our country.'

Ali gazed at this delicate, sensitive face and thought that Amalia would have been Meriem's friend, accomplice. Yes, she would have loved his cousin, his family . . . Why still think of the past? Meriem added, 'I shall do everything to ensure that it is my actions and not my person that are important in people's eyes! I refuse to become a monument because I once bore arms like the men.'

The next day Ali went for a last walk around the village. He drank tea with the men of his family in Abdi's café. The latter welcomed him with sincere transports of joy. But Ali thought of his rendezvous with Tahar which would now never take place. He had died as he wanted – on his feet. Ali dreamed that perhaps his friend's tall figure would appear in the doorway at this moment. Tahar would screw up his slanting eyes and tease him, 'So, Mr Psychologist, you came out of the furnace alive! Will you come and help me breed horses now in Nememcha, my *douar?* . . .'

There was no more sadness in the air, everywhere children's merry shouts could be heard in the streets where there would be no more fear . . . Life was reclaiming its rights.

15

Ali was standing at his window, looking out over the twinkling lights of the city. By night Algiers decked herself in all her jewellery, a courtesan sure of her power over her lovers. The lights, the stars cloaked the city in an atmosphere of unreality in which every corner seemed created by a fairy's wand. Ali had fallen in love with this saucy city who never abandoned herself all at once, who was full of surprises. On every side, the sea played hide and seek with the visitor who would glimpse the tip of her nose from a hilltop, at a sudden bend in a winding street, from the upper storey of a building. In the kasbah he was caught up and swept along by the colourful, good-natured crowds, teeming with life and human warmth. During Ramadan everything took on an extraordinary relief. People thronged around the Ketchaoua mosque, some bustling about their business, some idly loafing. And the Martyrs' Square extended its arms in welcome to cocky little Algiers street urchins and all the youngsters attracted to the capital from up-country. They arrived with their bundles, having heard only of the Blacet el-Aoud (the Square of the Horse) as a meeting place and landmark.

Almost three years had elapsed since the day when Ali thought to have arrived at the fabulous land of his childhood dream, where everything vibrated with human vitality, freed from all constraint. He had believed in a better future in which men would start to pull themselves up by their shoe strings.

He gradually sang a different tune . . . People's joyful dedication and solidarity of the early days had weakened, giving way to a kind of disillusioned, bleak indifference, and they now seemed overwhelmed by the tasks they had undertaken at first

224

with enthusiasm . . . They no longer felt concerned. Ideals were veiled with words. Ali felt the terrible weight of this atmosphere which had descended on Algiers. This city had seemed born for joy and freedom . . . possessing everything needed for happiness: youth, culture, wealth and beauty; but blind and jealous men had draped her in a silken *haïk*.

On the slightest pretext, crowds were rounded up to listen to speeches. By these periodic infusions of instructions and demonstrations, individuals were boosted up with empty words. Here and there rough-and-ready improvisations and plays were performed, still further debasing history; here and there some scientific progress took place . . .

The death of President Kennedy, assassinated in Dallas as he drove to a luncheon in his honour, was the occasion for the people of Algeria to pay tribute to the American president and to name a square in el-Biar after him. Ali was present, moved and astonished by the crowd's meditative mood.

Then came Morocco's attack on Algeria and the denunciation of President Ould-Daddah. History wept silently. . .

National 'Tree Day' in Algeria. Proclamation of the fate of lands which had belonged to wealthy individuals. And Ali cannot get the following dates out of his head:

19 March 1963: France explodes an atomic bomb in the Sahara, Algeria protests.

26 April 1963: Creation of the CAD (Caisse algerienne de Développement – Algerian Development Fund).

29 May 1963: A cyclone destroys Dacca in Pakistan leaving 10,000 dead and 500,000 homeless.

3 June 1963: Death of the great Turkish poet Nazim Hikmet in Moscow. Death of Pope John XXIII.

June 1963: The Algerian politician Boudiaf declares to a French newspaper, 'The socialist measures are improvised and demagogic, it is more exact to speak of opponents than opposition.'

14 June 1963: The Soviet astronauts, Valery Bykovsky and Valentina Terechkova, on board the 'Vostok V', accomplish

eighty-two and forty-nine revolutions round the earth. Valentina is the first woman astronaut.

26 June 1963: Four people arrested in Algiers, including M. Boudiaf.

1 October 1963: All land in Algeria, previously owned by foreign settlers, is nationalized.

28 October 1963: Creation of the Union of Algerian Writers.

29 October 1963: A conference is held in Bamako, under the chairmanship of Emperor Haile Selassie of Ethiopia, on the suggestion of President Modibo Keïta of Mali, to draw up a treaty between Morocco and Algeria; the ceasefire on the western frontier to come into effect on Saturday 30 January 1964 at midnight.

September 1964: Popular militia units created by the Party . . . The country enters an era of collective suspicion .

Unrest in Aures, Blida, Borgj Menail, Rouiba, Larba, Constantine, etc. . . .

Meeting after meeting after meeting . . .

Space experiments arouse Ali's interest.

28 November 1964: USA launches 'Mariner IV' hoping to reach Mars.

30 November 1964: USSR launches 'Zond II' hoping to reach Mars.

1965: a year of unrest.

Buddhist monks burn themselves to death in Vietnam.

25 January 1965: Monseigneur Duval, Archbishop of Algeria, is made a cardinal. He declares, 'My promotion to the rank of cardinal is a demonstration of the Church's love for Algeria and all its inhabitants.'

18 February 1965: Gambia becomes the thirty-sixth independent African state after four centuries of foreign domination.

22 February 1965: The Muslim fundamentalist leader Malcolm X is murdered by cowardly racists.

18 March 1965: Fantastic achievement by Soviet scientists: an astronaut walks in space.

5 May 1965: In Algeria 20,000 candidates sit for the Primary School Certificate.

226

The sinister sound of death and tramp of boots on the frontier between Algeria and Morocco finally ceases.

Today the Brazilian footballer, Pelé, is invited to demonstrate his prowess to the Algerians. Ali thinks to himself that for once the crowd will gather to admire something authentic . . .

Ali is aware of the most terrible mixture of hypocrisy, suspicion and deceit, everyone obeying the instinct of self-preservation.

One day Si Salah invited Ali's former schoolfellows, Slimane and Abbas, now both Deputies, to meet him again. They were delighted to see him and reminisce over their past. And soon they were able to exchange news of the others. They heard that Francis had succeeded in joining the maquis. Slimane had happened on him in one of the combat *wilayas*. After independence he had left for South America where, he said, other struggles awaited him. He had acquired a taste for danger and revolutionary causes, and had gone to join other guerrilla units. Abdi, 'the big booby', had heard of Abbas's promotion and arrival in the village, and hurried to welcome his old friend with expressions of sincere friendship.

Immediately the two men felt convinced that they could form a natural partnership. Abdi found another object for his inherent servility. Abbas studied the person they used to call 'the big booby'. He was a man now, with something vaguely untrustworthy about him. His little deep-set black eyes made him doubtless seem harmless at first, but his greedy look soon aroused sneaking suspicion as to his true character. And Abbas had his wits about him! As devious as Abdi, but not so stupid, he saw he could use this slippery customer as his stooge.

Abbas considered him calmly, then observed solemnly, 'It's really a scandal that your abilities should be wasted in a miserable Moorish café!'

'Oh! It suits me all right,' Abdi answered humbly.

'As far as I'm concerned, I'm convinced you'd be just the right man for a more active job in the administration.'

'Nowadays, you need papers for everything! I did help the Brothers during the revolution, well, I did my duty, but I can't prove anything, you understand.'

Abbas shrugged off all Abdi's fears. 'You weren't a *harki*? Well that's all that matters. I'll see you get your testimonial!'

'You'll do that for me, Abbas? You're a real brother!'

Abbas chuckled inwardly at his friend's surprised gratitude.

'I'll be eternally grateful to you,' Abdi insisted, and in his eyes could be read all that he would be prepared to do for his new benefactor . . .

'Right! Then you'll come back to Algiers with me, I'll take care of your papers and get you taken on in the police force.'

'A policeman! . . .' Abdi murmured, transfigured by astonishment. 'The dream of my life . . . I've always loved the uniform.'

Rachid lectured in the Faculty of Arts. Ali met him at the house of one of his friends. At first he barely recognized him in his well-cut suit and short hair – a real professor! The flute belonged to the past! He still had the same attentive air of concentration. He could still cast the same spell over his comrades and enjoyed holding forth to them on some Arab philosopher or scientist or other. Fascinated, they became once more the silent little boys in the clearing in Dachra. But it was the magic of Rachid's words which captured their imagination.

As for Slimane, he was as generous and helpful as ever to his friends. He readily gave away anything he possessed and was delighted when his gifts were accepted. This curious detachment from worldly possessions was the result of having risked his life for many years in the maquis. But his youthful exuberance was now transformed into indifference and asperity. Slimane often invited Ali to his villa on the outskirt of Cheraga where he was only happy when surrounded by friends. Ali had the impression that Slimane was running desperately away from solitude. In spite of the presence of his parents who kept house for him, as soon as he was alone he would phone this friend and that to come and share a meal. He would leave these friends rabbiting away over every subject under the sun while he occasionally retreated into a distant daydream. Ali would chaff him good-humouredly, 'Are you asleep, Pasha?' He'd given Slimane this nickname because he kept open house to all and sundry. Slimane would laugh softly as he retorted, 'No, "I think, therefore I am" . . .'

He had been deprived for so long of the power of giving to others that he was now intoxicated with the pleasure of sharing everything he had, without it making him any the happier: he lacked the security essential for his equanimity. At times Ali wondered what could have been the cause of this inner instability in Slimane . . . What traumas had he experienced during his years in the maquis? What tragedies had he witnessed to have become so detached from people and things?

At bottom, Slimane was not sure he could take his position and his future for granted in a country where everything was gradually weakened by uncertainty. But bone-idle and apathetic into the bargain, he made no attempt to improve his situation, simply finding satisfaction in acting the good Samaritan, with his clumsy, touching generosity.

Ali tried to discover what made all these people tick, and waited with interest to see where this rat race would lead them .

Often a single conversation was sufficient. His extreme sensitivity, his passionate curiosity about other people and his gift for nosing things out allowed him instinctively to read a person's character much better than any detailed investigation. So he could not have explained the reason why he tended to avoid Abbas's company, in spite of the latter's repeated invitation.

Fella pottered along. She had abandoned her dreams of the theatre, giving up any attempt to impose new ideas on minds still sclerosed by taboos. She had begun to paint. She painted large Algerian frescoes, telling the history of the war, depicting scenes from the daily life of the people in the pre-independence period. There was always a rose to be found in her pictures, hidden in the midst of exploding bombs or anguished faces. This crimson flower, with a dewdrop caught on one of its petals, was an unexpected, strange and moving image. One of her pictures was strikingly realistic, expressing with poignant, desperate force the catastrophe of war. It represented a long procession of men, women and children in rags, their faces contorted with terror,

229

fleeing from their burning villages, fleeing from death. And the red rose like a blood-stain seemed to weep its drop of dew, cast there like a stranger on the rough path.

But when she gave her first exhibition an embittered artist, claiming to be one of the 'avant-garde revolutionaries', reproached her in pompous, obscure terms. 'Revolutionary artists,' he wrote, 'cannot paint our valiant people's struggle in such a futile manner; roses are incompatible with the socialist revolution, they are the manifestation of a latent neo-colonialism . . .'

Fella replied placidly and gently, 'My country is a rose to me . . . I shall always paint it in this way, no matter if my way does not comply with the codes set out by revolutionaries wielding a pen or a paint-brush! . . . I was thirteen when I first discovered fear, death and khaki-coloured landscapes, when the sound of bombs and cries echoed in my ears . . . Now, life with its tragedies or joys will shine out for me in the crimson rose . . .'

Shortly afterwards, Fella married Slimane. The ceremony took place in the presence of all Slimane's childhood friends and their respective families. Mounir came specially from Paris, where he now worked as an attaché in the Algerian Embassy. Amalia was not able to accompany him as she had just given birth to their second child. Ali and Mounir met without excessive warmth. It is true that the presence of many other people took the tension out of this meeting. Amalia was trapped once and for all in her role as a mother! . . .

Was everything for the best in the best of all possible worlds?

Ali had just begun his first year of political science at the university.

And suddenly the thunder-bolt strikes again in his vicinity . . .

One evening some men turned up at Si Salah's house, to take him away, no one knew where. Was the nightmare beginning again in the land? And what exactly was independence?

Ali was stunned; he stared vacant-eyed at Si Salah's sobbing parents. He did not understand, it was all beyond him! The old

230

people begged him to help them solve the mystery of their son's arrest. Had he militated all his life to be thrown into prison like a common bandit? . . . Ali listened to them horrified. Had he mistaken the period? Yet he was in Algiers, wasn't he, with his briefcase under his arm, leaving to go to study at the Institute? He wasn't dreaming. He was certainly living through the period of independence! Had the country simply changed one set of colonizers for another?

He hurried frantically to Slimane's who looked solemn but could tell him nothing. He rushed to see Abbas, who adopted a woebegone expression to deliver a sort of speech in which strange words occurred: plots, counter-revolution . . .

What? Si Salah with his passionate love of his country, the incorruptible, cautious militant, speaking little, for whom the Party was his whole life . . . and now he was being accused of plotting! Ali, who knew the irreproachable behaviour of his former chief, felt utterly at sea.

Where could he go? To Rachid . . . The only reply he received was a cryptic Arabic proverb:

'If you get mixed up with the bran you risk getting eaten by the hens! . . .'

What did he mean to convey? That Si Salah should have stuck to teaching instead of going in for politics? 'But he was working,' Ali yelled, 'building, organizing . . . He wasn't plotting!'

Fear kept all the friends away. Ali knocked in vain on every door until Abbas came to advise him to keep quiet, otherwise he would get into trouble too . . . Ali calmed down. He interrupted his studies and went to work for a private firm to be able to support his friend's elderly parents.

He avoided his old friends, realizing that he embarrassed them by his presence, which was like a silent reproach. In fact, he felt no resentment against them. He understood that they were powerless to help Si Salah, they themselves being caught in the struggle to survive . . . He didn't hold it against them. Slimane had a family to maintain, Abbas his political career, Rachid some distant,

mysterious aim, and all the others their day-to-day safety. They
had became adults . . . They were growing old . . .

Ali felt he had lost his greatest hope: for the dawn of truth for
his country.

He spent his evenings standing at his window, gazing out over
Algiers. And every time he felt the same tug at his heart strings. All
the houses seemed to come and prostrate themselves at the feet of
the sea, and let themselves be caressed by the cool waves.

'My God!' he growled. 'How beautiful our country is!'

He realized the quality of the soil, the age-old wealth, the
potential. He recognized them and felt their presence like the
muscles beneath his skin.

The crazy, tumultuous, extravagant city echoed with sounds of
all sorts. He thought that honour was still the power of life and
death. One day they would wake up! For the moment, in spite of
all the blood shed by her sons, the country remained undefined,
her freedom an impenetrable mystery. Innocence collapsed,
crumbling to dust in the intrigues of the new times. The best had
lost heart and the worst were still feathering their nests.
Everything fell apart, you couldn't rely on your memory, you
thought you were sure of something, you believed in truth, in
justice, you based your conduct on it, you thought that love,
dignity and security would be distributed equitably and suddenly
everything collapsed.

Authority was transformed into a power of contempt!

'What can be done to make all these people feel really
concerned, and see that their enthusiasm isn't stoked by envy and
peevish criticism? – Thus are all dreams made and unmade, a trifle
and everything vanishes! – What shall we find at the end of our
night, we the adolescents of 1954? – The awakening will be all the
more stormy and bitter the longer the sleep lasts. – If it is not us, it
will be the children of tomorrow! And what of the heroes of this
land and elsewhere? . . . They will be satisfied with a minute place
in men's memories; but they will endure through the eternal
breath of freedom.'

Such was the substance of Ali's meditations when his eye
alighted on an open book. It was a French translation of the

Quran which Si Salah had given him when he passed his *baccalauréat*. He flipped over the pages and stopped at this verse: 'Have patience, but patience is only possible with the help of God. – Do not be afflicted on their account, let not your heart be anguished – Because of their machinations, for God is with those who fear him and do good' (The Bee, sura XVI, delivered in Mecca).

Ali was a little troubled by these words, which in some mysterious fashion were a reply to his deep anxieties. He was irresistibly drawn to his old black-covered diary. He began to write . . .

How one became a man when one turned thirteen in 1953. – Muslims, Jews, Christians were only abstract notions. There was only one real truth: was one rich or poor? – To be rich meant wearing a three-piece suit or a dress and floral hat – the poor man was dressed in a grey burnous and grey turban; these are phantoms, obscure creatures, whose true faces can never be distinguished. – This difference was glaring, unmistakable then, but it was drowned in our child's mind by the magic of street games. – Barefoot, in short trousers, our clothes new or patched, what matter! – We leapt carefree over the bracken, brandishing our swords of love at the sunlit hills.

Suddenly the sun stopped in its golden course and we lived under a sky of porphyry.

To learn to live as free men and women! – An exciting, cruel infinite adventure. – Freedom? Where does it begin? First of all, freedom for whom? – When? By what means? For how long?

But the caravan moves on and the dogs sleep – and the partridge's young are all scattered.

Ali continued to write . . .

EPILOGUE

1965, 1966, 1968, 1970, 1974 . . .

What has become of all the partridge's young? . . .

Mounir is mouldering away, out of sight!

For he is still in the diplomatic service . . . in perpetuity. Attached to the Paris section, he is in a fair way to becoming the specialist in everything relating to Paris, not to mention France! At every recall, his name slips the memory of the decision-makers. He has lived abroad so long he is out of touch with the realities of the country so that when he does return one day to the fold he will genuinely be 'the stranger'.

Amalia, at his side, plays at being alive.

As for Slimane, he finds himself in a quandary!

Should he eat to live . . . or live to eat? As both require a certain amount of effort, he eventually chose to give up his government job (what he called his 'bureaucratic existence') and go into business. But as he is too lazy to make the effort to act, speculate, lick boots or grease palms where necessary, he's managed to let others do business for him. His wife, Fella, lives happily ever after with the husband whom she has all to herself and who never bores her. They now have four children! When all's said and done, Slimane was best suited for a life of love-making and procreation.

Rachid pontificates before his students!

He has his doctorate in Arabic literature and is now dean of the faculty. He regularly appears on television! At every 'round table' organized on various cultural themes, there he is, holding forth, never looking people in the eye, but gazing at some mysterious distant vision. There is something ossified in his features. A forced, cold expression about the mouth. Never giving his thoughts away. Everyone imagines him to be their friend, but in the long run they know nothing of his real opinions about people or events. New personalities, who have nothing in common with him, gravitate around him. But he is flattered by their company, for as he grows older Rachid has become somewhat egocentric and easily swayed. Whereas he used to give the impression of having a strong character, now even those fine human values acquired in the modest and authentic village cradle have become eroded by the comfort and intrigues of modern times. He is more self-satisfied and easily won over by good manners and flattery. He married a woman who bore a strange resemblance to Madame Roumière . . .

He lives at the top of The Tower, a block of flats in the capital that is well suited to his enigmatic character. No one knows his secret hobby – his flute! When he is tired of men's company, he loves to be alone on his large balcony overlooking the city.

And faithful to his childhood flute, Rachid plays for hours on end. And he is soothed and charmed by fantasies. Gazing down from the top of The Tower at the city sleeping at his feet, he is sure of one thing at least: if he is not the greatest Arabic philosopher of his time, he is certainly the best flautist in the country!

Abbas continues his machinations in the city!

Through all the ups and downs of the times he goes from strength to strength. But a subtle change has taken place in his character. He has married; but that is of secondary importance in his life. He is a different man. It is impossible to say in what mould Abbas has acquired this honeyed ease. He has lost all trace of the violent, over-sensitive child and become a devious, calculating creature. He avoids his former village friends, going his own way accompanied only by the 'big booby', Abdi, whose situation he ensured. But to tell the truth, the ability to decide on men's fates does not move him, as it might others, but rather fills him with pride. He feels a malicious sense of satisfaction, and his

235

vanity swells in proportion to his added responsibilities and power over others.

At first sight, he seems amiable and of unshakable integrity. However, his eyes in which a perpetually anxious light burns, betray his lack of assurance and his many complexes. Pride and an overweening ambition make him in turn suspicious, hard and ruthless to those who ignore or obstruct him. Abbas is never sure of himself, sure of nothing or anyone. Gloomy and pessimistic, he hides his true nature under a wary exterior. He can lavish good intentions, but one should look out for his underhand tricks. He seems placid, but he is a prey to inner tensions. He's a perfectionist, but finds fault with anything that's not the result of his own ideas. Sensitive at times, but self-centred and self-absorbed. Gregarious, but with a morbid fear of possible pitfalls. In a word, not having managed to make himself admired, he has eventually chosen to be feared.

Pot-bellied Abdi likes a punch-up as much as a knees-up.

Over the past years, in addition to his paunch he has acquired another stripe on his uniform and a second wife – a youngish townswoman (the first one not having been repudiated but simply sent back to her father's home with all the honours due to her rank!) for it is noted that Abdi has become very acquisitive; he has a mania for possessions – material, cultural or emotional.

And Si Salah still has his faith.

As soon as he was released from prison, he went back to work for the Party. He seems to have dedicated his life to politics. An honest-to-goodness militant, he is one of the most respected decision-makers in the country . . . A most uncommon phenomenon, as a matter of fact. Steadfast as a rock, he does not let himself be deflected from what is well-nigh a religious duty for him. He is married and Ali still lives on the first floor of his villa.

And the impetuous Meriem? She has never answered Ali's letters. She eventually married Commander Si Achour. They live somewhere in Algeria. What became of her dreams? She has ended up as a monument in spite of herself! Silently receiving men's

236

touching tribute. She has striven to break a certain law, but has not managed to find a law for herself . . . Engaged in her duties, the victim of her own conscience. For, after she tried to work, to be active, the pressure of the society around her became so great that she gave in and married the man chosen by her parents.

A man is busy packing. Suits . . . ties . . . socks . . . where is everything? He rummages frantically through his drawers, tossing things on to the floor. A young woman appears at this moment, protesting, 'Whatever are you doing, Si Ali? You should have called me, really!'

He turns round to reply irritably, 'Khéïra, I've told you not to touch my things, I want to put them away myself; you just mess everything up!'

He's the one who out of sheer cussedness continues to turn the room upside down. The woman calmly picks up the clothes after him, apparently used to her boss's outbursts. He grumbles, 'You're going to make me miss my plane!'

The woman is young. He engaged her a few years ago, on account of her accent which reminded him of Tahar's . . . and her name, Khéïra, reminiscent of Monsieur Kimper's daily help . . . These were the two deciding factors in choosing her from all the women sent by the employment agency. He is still a bachelor and she keeps house for him in a slapdash fashion, compensated for by her loving concern for his welfare. Ali is fond of her. He fusses over his files which he is trying to stuff into his briefcase, while Khéïra II closes the suitcase.

Ali stands for a moment in front of a large photograph in a silver frame on his desk. He regains his composure and smiles as he gazes at the laughing faces of Juliette, Marcel, Alain and his wife, all frolicking happily in the sea. That was last year . . . Juliette comes every year to spend the summer with Ali. Alain and his wife regularly join them. Alain has become a well-known journalist whose name is associated with all important investigations into the crucial political events of the world: Vietnam, Latin America, Asia and now the Middle East. Wherever hatred, injustice and killings are rife, Alain is on the scene ready to denounce every

237

atrocity, everything that is unacceptable, intolerable in the world.

The thought of his friends has relieved Ali's tension; he goes to the cupboard and as he slips his hand in to get some handkerchiefs he touches something on the bottom of the shelf. His black-covered diary . . . He feels gently comforted as if by the light touch of a kiss. As he opens it his heart misses a beat at the sight of a short length of red silk, carefully folded and pressed between the pages. He sniffs this scent of the past that he has never lost . . . Amalia . . .

Then he puts it all back at the bottom of the cupboard . . . At the bottom of his heart.

Ali has written nothing since he finished his studies; then his responsibilities gradually diverted him from his dreams. His work-table and his life are now swamped with figures, statistics. The light in his room burns late into the night. But Ali no longer writes of his feelings, his observations, his vague yearnings. He studies files and projects, checks and initials them, each one more ambitious than the last . . .

Ali no longer grows impatient. His words no longer outstrip his thoughts. Moreover he has mastered his former nausea. He is so immersed in his new concerns that he gives the impression of having been suddenly catapulted on to the brink of old age. It was as if, in some repects, Ali knew true loneliness when he stopped being afraid. He has become a new man.

And so he is getting ready to leave, a suitcase in one hand, a briefcase in the other. A car is waiting for him at the front door.

This is a different Ali, almost a stranger . . . He is of indeterminate age. His hair is receding but he hides his premature baldness by carefully combing the remaining strands across his pate. There are a few silver threads on his temples. His face is still surprisingly unlined, which helps to emphasize the tiny wrinkles at the corners of his eyes, from which the light seems to have faded. This somewhat unfathomable, glazed look gives him the appearance of someone who is lost in thought . . . or half-asleep . . . It is impossible to say!

Or has he deliberately adopted this veil to hide from curious people the flame which burns within him? Ali lives with one memory. His habit of finding fault with others, his frantic pursuit of ever greater achievements are the result of an inner fire, kept alive by the memory of a certain love, a certain face. . . Like the lingering smell of poverty, hunger or death once experienced or even glimpsed, so his lost love will ennoble all his actions, urging him on to greater heights . . . For the men of today, those who were the children of 1954, do not die of broken hearts, failure cannot destroy them; on the contrary, they march on and on, and construct. And their silence never fails to augur great changes.

Ali is but one executive amid many. One of the countless officials filling planes which fly to the four corners of the world. He is off today for some negotiations or other!

In his well-cut suit, looking solemn even slightly grim, he makes his way with the dignity commensurate to his responsibilities, towards the Dar el-Baïda Airport concourse. Suddenly his eye is caught by a beautiful woman in an elegant white costume with long gold chains round her neck, who emerges behind a porter. Everything about her indicates a woman of means. She takes off her dark glasses and cries, 'Ali!'

'No! It can't be! . . . Houria!'

They throw their arms around each other. The porter, clearly impatient, doesn't know what to do with the luggage. Houria breaks loose from her friend's embrace and says to the man, 'Can you drive? Perfect! Here are my keys, be a good man and go and get my car from the car-park . . . it's a white Peugeot.'

She tells him the registration number and turns delightedly back to Ali. He gazes at her in evident astonishment, but also with emotion as Houria reminds him of so much and especially of Tahar . . .

'You've grown old, my poor Ali,' she says half laughing, half serious.

He asks her what she is doing, if she got married. Houria answers solemnly, 'Yes . . . at independence; two years later we got divorced. He was nice . . . he was . . . Oh! What's the use of talking of all that?' For some time she says nothing, seeming to be lost in distant memories. Then she adds with a mischievous gleam

239

in her eyes, 'And now I've become a nomad again . . . *De luxe*. But I don't complain. I live neither in virtue nor in vice, neither in wisdom nor folly, I live by learning to survive in this concrete jungle that has been built for me . . .'

Ali does not think of what she is but of what has been done to her to prevent her from being.

He points out to her, with a sad little smile, that she has not changed; she still talks in riddles, forming a maze of words in which those who pry too deeply will get lost. The car drives up, the man gets out, loads the luggage into the boot, receives a generous tip and departs. Houria, at the wheel, leans out of the window, looks at Ali with her strange way of screwing up her eyes and murmurs, 'Then it's anybody's guess!'

Before she drove away Ali walked round the car to stop her and leaned over to ask, 'How old are you, Houria?'

'Forty-four thousand . . .' Then, as the engine purred into action, Houria waved goodbye and disappeared from view.